PRAISE FOR THE WORK OF

STEPHANIE LAURENS

"When it comes to dishing up lusciously sensual, relentlessly readable historical romances, Laurens is unrivalled." *Booklist*

"Laurens's writing shines." *Publishers Weekly*

"One of the most talented authors on the scene today...Laurens has a real talent for writing sensuous and compelling love scenes." *Romance Reviews*

"Stephanie Laurens never fails to entertain and charm her readers with vibrant plots, snappy dialogue, and unforgettable characters." *Historical Romance Reviews.*

"Stephanie Laurens plays into readers' fantasies like a master and claims their hearts time and again." *Romantic Times Magazine*

Other Titles from Stephanie Laurens

STEPHANIE LAURENS

The Curious Case

of

Lady Latimer's Shoes

SAVDEK MANAGEMENT PTY. LTD.

SAVDEK MANAGEMENT PTY. LTD.

P.O. Box 322, Macedon,

Victoria 3440, Australia.

THE CURIOUS CASE OF LADY LATIMER'S SHOES

Copyright © 2014 by Savdek Management Proprietary Limited

ISBN: 978-0-9922789-5-3

Cover design by Savdek Management Proprietary Limited

For information, address Savdek Management Proprietary Limited, Melbourne, Australia.

Website: www.stephanielaurens.com

Email: admin@stephanielaurens.com

First print publication: June 2014

The SL logo and the name Stephanie Laurens are registered trademarks of Savdek Management Proprietary Ltd.

58182023

The Curious Case
of
Lady Latimer's Shoes

CHAPTER 1

March 1838
Fairchild House, London

*L*ady Fairchild's ball was one of the premier entertainments of the Season; everyone who was anyone attended, and the event was widely regarded as the true opening of the Season for the haut ton. Standing to one side of her ladyship's ballroom, Penelope Adair looked about with genuine interest. Heavy with gilt and laden with crystal, with its walls a brilliant white and the parquet floor glowing with the warm tones of old oak, the room was a spectacular sight. It was nearly eleven o'clock, and a goodly crowd had gathered; the buzz of myriad conversations filled the air, the vivid hues of this Season's gowns scintillating under the light of the chandeliers, the men providing stark contrast in their regulation black and white.

Somewhat to her surprise, Penelope felt a certain smug pleasure on registering that her own gown of plum-colored silk, with its pleated organza ruffle at hem and neckline and its tightly fitting sleeves, placed her very much at the forefront in the fashionable-young-matron stakes.

The diamonds clasped about her throat were a stunning final touch.

It seemed odd to think of herself as a matron, yet her son, Oliver, was over a year old.

And while she also found it odd that she, who had never previously paid all that much attention to her appearance, should even register her fashionable standing, perhaps that was an outcome of her recently embarked-on personal quest to better balance the various aspects of her life.

Beside her stood her husband, the Honorable Barnaby Adair,

third son of the Earl of Cothelstone and occasional consultant to the Metropolitan Police; he was presently talking earnestly with his father, the earl, and Lord Carnegie, a senior peer. It was through an investigation Penelope had assisted with, late the previous year, that she had come to understand the need to actively manage the time she spent on her various endeavors in order to achieve the success her personality demanded in each sphere. Unless she met her own standards, satisfaction in life would elude her.

That realization had left her much more aware of the different roles she played and the degree of attention each role demanded.

For instance, tonight, she was Barnaby Adair's wife, but as she was also Viscount Calverton's sister, first cousin to the Earl of Dexter, and connected by marriage to a host of other noble families, her social standing had a very wide base. More, because of her excellent memory for details, she had been unanimously elected by her family and wider connections as the principal keeper of family information and all social stories—and also, as she mentally termed it, the chronicler of skeletons.

What exactly said social skeletons were, who they related to, and how and where they'd been buried.

Lady Osbaldestone had even dubbed Penelope as that august lady's successor in that role.

Consequently, Penelope was currently listening to her mother, Minerva, Dowager Viscountess Calverton, and Helena, Dowager Duchess of St. Ives, as they shared the information each had gleaned on the latest indiscretion of the highly placed son of one of their peers.

Another skeleton for Penelope's closet; one never knew when such knowledge might prove useful.

Minerva concluded her confidences with, "Mind you, I have no idea if his poor wife knows."

Penelope swiftly reviewed the pertinent facts. "Oh, she knows."

Her mother and Helena fixed avid gazes on her face.

"How can you be sure?" Helena asked. "She hasn't given any sign—has she?"

"Well," Penelope temporized, "she has had Lord Cranborne squiring her about, both in the Park and in Regent Street, and I know they're old friends, but she walked into the ballroom tonight on Cranborne's arm, while as far as I've seen, her husband has yet to show his face."

"And how do you read that, if I might ask?" Her dark eyes

twinkling, Honoria, Duchess of St. Ives, had come up in time to hear Penelope's last remark.

Touching cheeks with her mama-in-law, Helena, then with Minerva, who Honoria knew well, Honoria arched a questioning brow Penelope's way; although older than Penelope by some years, Honoria was one of Penelope's staunchest supporters and in some respects a mentor.

"I assume," Penelope said, rising to the challenge, "that her ladyship intends it as a statement, as a reminder to her husband of just who in their marriage wields the social clout. She does. And if he wants to continue to sail under her banner and reap the social rewards, so to speak, he needs to reassess his behavior."

Her lips curving, Honoria nodded. "I agree." She glanced at the milling crowd. "At the very least he needs to exercise significantly greater discretion. It will be interesting to see if he can read and interpret her message as clearly as you."

The two older ladies were eager to learn what other snippets of social news Honoria had to impart. The conversation broadened into a general recounting of observations, all of which Penelope dutifully absorbed, catalogued, and stored.

Devil Cynster, Duke of St. Ives, ambled up in his wife's wake. As dangerously charming as ever, he greeted the ladies, then moved on to join Barnaby, who was still talking with his father and two others about politics as they impacted the police. Knowing she would hear a summation later, Penelope remained focused on the ladies' discussions.

Various others joined their group, then Lady Fairchild swept up. Their hostess was in fine fettle, happy and delighted with the way her ball was progressing. "It's so gratifying to see everyone here." Touching cheeks and pressing fingers, Lady Fairchild accepted the ladies' compliments with becoming assurance.

Then she turned to Penelope, who was something of a favorite. "And it's lovely to see you, my dear, and looking so well. How is little Oliver?"

Penelope felt her face light, as it always did when her thoughts shifted to her son. "He's well and growing, and walking now, too."

"Excellent!" Lady Fairchild shot a glance at Barnaby. "He'll be following your dear husband around soon, wanting to get into everything."

Penelope grinned. "Actually, at present, Oliver's more interested in getting into my desk."

Honoria nodded. "He has good instincts—your desk is where all the really fascinating things are hidden."

All the ladies laughed.

Sensing the presence of a large body looming between her and Barnaby, Penelope glanced over her shoulder—and up, into the face of her cousin-in-law, Hugo, Barnaby's uncle's second son, and, until recently, something of a black sheep. Hugo had joined the cavalry at an early age and, by all accounts, had led a colorful life as a rakish, debonair, and reckless hellion. But he'd sold out last year and was, the family felt, quietening down and somewhat tentatively finding his way into more acceptable social circles.

So Hugo being there didn't surprise Penelope; what made her blink, then focus her considerable acuity on him, was the ashen pallor of his handsome face.

His dark brown hair looked as if he'd run his fingers through it. Briefly, he met her gaze; his dark blue eyes looked...stunned. Shocked. But his attention deflected to Barnaby. Hugo raised a hand, gripped Barnaby's sleeve at the elbow, and tugged.

Sliding out of the ongoing conversation, Barnaby turned to Penelope, brows arching—then he followed her gaze to Hugo's face.

Barnaby's features sharpened. "What is it?"

Hugo met Barnaby's eyes, then tipped his head toward the far end of the room. "I went out to smoke a cheroot. On the side terrace..." Hugo dragged in a tight breath. "There's a body—some lady—on the path. I think you'd better take a look."

* * *

*H*e'd been watching Lord Fairchild, waiting to see someone come and whisper in his lordship's ear, reasoning that, sooner or later, the body lying on the path below the terrace would be found. An hour had passed since he'd returned to the ballroom, and he'd started to fall prey to rising anxiety—but, at last, a fair-haired gentleman with a sober and serious Lady Fairchild on his arm approached his lordship.

The pair were followed by a short, dark-haired lady accompanied by another gentleman and two others he recognized as the Earl of Cothelstone and the Duke of St. Ives.

The group waited until Lord Fairchild, noting them, excused himself from those with whom he'd been conversing and joined them. A short conference ensued, and then, now distinctly sober himself,

Lord Fairchild turned and led the small group from the ballroom.

He tried to imagine the scene—what the group would see when they reached the side terrace, what they would think—but his mind shied, refusing to dwell for more than a split second on the images burned into his brain.

Without conscious direction, his eyes hunted for his beloved. He spotted her through a gap in the crowd.

From across the room, she stared pointedly at him; although he couldn't see the question in her eyes, he knew what it would be. Why hadn't he said anything? Why hadn't he raised the alarm?

The answer was simple: He couldn't think. Shock and more still had him reeling. He didn't know what anything meant.

Given the secrecy of their betrothal, a connection that not even their nearest and dearest knew of or even suspected, and given the implications of what he and she had seen...

He needed to think, but he couldn't yet think.

If, in the meantime, the authorities could learn anything about the murderer....

He didn't want to be—simply couldn't be—the one to point the finger.

* * *

*B*arnaby crouched beside the body, which was lying sprawled face up, with limbs twisted a little to the left, on the gravel path below the side terrace. An older lady, unquestionably one of the Fairchilds' guests and therefore a member of the ton's elite, her life had ended when a stone ball had fallen—or, more accurately, been dropped—on her head.

The size of a cannonball, the stone had come from the top of a pillar in the terrace's balustrade, specifically the pillar at the head of the steps leading down to the path. The ball had formed the finial but, apparently, had not been attached to the pillar's top.

The impact had crushed the upper left front quadrant of the lady's skull. "Death would, most likely, have been instantaneous." Barnaby glanced up at the men lining the terrace balustrade and looking down on the scene. "Does anyone know who she is?"

Penelope was standing behind him, peering over his shoulder. She didn't make a sound. Hugo had halted a yard behind her, unwilling to draw closer; he, too, remained mute.

Barnaby knew that his cousin was slightly squeamish; although Hugo had been in the cavalry, he'd joined long after the wars had ended, and he had never been in any battle. For his part, Barnaby had learned the knack of observing victims in an emotionally detached way—clinically, dispassionately—the better to bring them justice.

The men on the terrace glanced at each other, then stepped aside, giving way to two ladies—Lady Fairchild and Barnaby's mother, the Countess of Cothelstone. Lady Fairchild gripped the balustrade and looked over, then drew back with a faint gasp. Barnaby's mother looked and paled, but she forced herself to look long enough to see...

"Lady Galbraith." His mother glanced at Lady Fairchild. "That's who it is, isn't it?"

Lady Fairchild drew in a huge breath, held it, and briefly glanced down again. Drawing back, she nodded. "Yes. It's Marjorie Galbraith." Lady Fairchild moistened her lips. "Her husband and, I believe, all their children are inside. One son, three daughters."

"None married," Barnaby's mother added.

Barnaby rose. He turned to Penelope.

Faint moonlight glinted on her spectacles as she simply said, "Stokes."

Barnaby glanced at Hugo and nodded. Giving thanks that his father was present, he looked up at the men on the terrace. "We need to send to Scotland Yard, for Inspector Stokes."

Lord Fairchild would have equivocated, but the earl, and Devil, too, convinced his lordship that there really was no option. Lady Galbraith had been murdered, and the murderer had to be found.

With that settled, including Lady Fairchild and his mother with a glance, Barnaby said, "While it might be closing the stable door after the horse has bolted, we should ensure that no one leaves—or, indeed, arrives, at least until Stokes gets here and decides what needs to be done."

Barnaby caught his mother's gaze. After a moment's hesitation, of inner debate, the countess turned to Lady Fairchild. "Sadly, Delia, Barnaby is right—for the moment, we need to keep everyone here."

Lady Fairchild drew a deep breath. Spine straightening, she raised her head. "Yes. All right." The mantle of a great hostess almost visibly settled on her shoulders once more. "I'd best get back to the ballroom and make arrangements to ensure that everyone continues to be entertained." She glanced at her husband, then looked down at Barnaby. "After that...do you want us to round up the Galbraiths?"

Barnaby hadn't thought that far ahead.

From beside him, Penelope said, "It would be helpful if you could collect them all—in the drawing room, perhaps? Somewhere away from the hubbub. And"—she glanced at Barnaby, then looked back at Lady Fairchild—"at this point, it would be best if we all avoided saying anything to anyone about Lady Galbraith's murder. If you're pushed by the family and must say something, just say she's had an accident."

Lady Fairchild visibly quelled a shudder. "Murder. Good God."

"Indeed," Penelope said. "There's really no need to create a furor just yet."

In complete agreement, Lady Fairchild and the countess retreated into the house.

Lord Fairchild nodded to Barnaby. "I'll send for the inspector, and make sure the staff shut the doors and know to discourage anyone thinking to leave—although, thankfully, it's a bit early yet for that."

"Thank you." Barnaby glanced around. The gardens were extensive. "Is there a garden gate?"

Lord Fairchild waved to the right. "In the wall that way, but it should be locked."

"We'll check it," Barnaby said. "We'll keep an eye on things out here until Stokes arrives."

Lord Fairchild nodded. "Thank you." His lordship turned away.

The earl and Devil grimly nodded to the three of them still standing on the grass by the path, then followed Lord Fairchild into the house.

Hugo drew in a short breath, shook himself like an overgrown dog, then turned away. "I'll go and look at the gate."

Barnaby glanced down at the corpse, fixing all the details of the scene in his mind, then he looked along the path. "We can all go." Sliding his hands into his pockets, he walked past the body. Stepping onto the path, he started ambling, with a glance confirming that Penelope was all right and that she was coming. Slipping a hand into the crook of his arm, she fell into step beside him. Looking ahead, he said, "I think we can rely on the pater and Devil to ensure that no one comes outside to gawp."

Pacing on Barnaby's other side, Hugo shook his head. "They could, for all I care, but I take your point. Hysteria at a ball might be memorable, but is unlikely to be pleasant."

They found the gate and confirmed that it was locked, but a

quick survey of the stone wall surrounding the huge garden showed that any man of reasonable agility could have scaled it in several spots. They wandered further, through areas cultivated in various styles, eventually reaching an ornamental lake with a marble folly set to one side. Continuing on via yet another path, they traversed a walled rose garden and ultimately emerged on the other side of the house.

Walking back along a promenade running parallel to the rear façade of the huge house, Barnaby looked up at the long windows of the ballroom. "Anyone who approached the side terrace from this direction, or left this way, would have risked being seen by people in the ballroom."

"Hmm. And I've been thinking." Penelope glanced up and met his eyes. "The murderer had to be standing on the terrace to pick up the ball and drop it on Lady Galbraith. I have difficulty imagining someone coming from this direction, much less a man climbing over the garden wall and stealing through the gardens, then somehow managing to walk up the terrace steps all the way to the top and pick up that stone ball without Lady Galbraith noticing. And she hadn't noticed, had she?"

"But she'd looked up," Hugo said.

"Yes," Penelope conceded, "but only at the last moment. She hadn't tried to move away—she was struck down where she stood. If someone she hadn't known had walked from the path to the terrace, she would have heard and seen them. She would have been watching them. She would have been suspicious."

"Which is to say," Barnaby dryly concluded, "that the murderer is almost certainly another of Lady Fairchild's guests."

After rounding the corner of the house, they returned to the side terrace and the body. All three of them looked up at the terrace, back at the path, around at the gardens.

Returning her gaze to the terrace, Penelope grimaced. "The murderer could not have come to the terrace via the paths or the garden. They had to have come via the house."

"If they were another guest," Barnaby said, also looking up, "Lady Galbraith wouldn't have seen any reason to move—not until it was too late."

A stir in the corridor beyond the terrace doors proved to be Stokes, accompanied by one of his sergeants, along with Barnaby's father and Lord Fairchild.

Leaving the men to confer over the body, Penelope climbed the terrace steps. Pausing beside the pillar from which the lethal ball had been taken, she examined its top. The pillar ended in a stone hemisphere set round side down, but instead of being flat, the upper surface contained a shallow depression in which the ball had sat. There was no evidence of any additional fixture to hold the ball in place. A cushion of lichen had grown around where the ball had been, thickest on the side closest to the house. "Protected from the sun by the ball," Penelope muttered.

She looked up as Hugo, having already been questioned by Stokes and then released, climbed the steps.

Halting beside her, Hugo looked down at Barnaby, then he met Penelope's eyes. "I don't know how you two do this."

Penelope thought of telling him why they did—because they could help. There was, she was convinced, a great deal of good in Hugo, as in all the rest of his family, but he was still bumbling about, trying to find his way.

Instead of explaining, she smiled understandingly and patted his arm. "Go and have a brandy."

Hugo blew out a breath. "Thank you. I rather think I'll have three."

With that, he headed into the house. Penelope turned and walked along the terrace balustrade. Pausing at each pillar topped by a stone ball—there were four in all, three still with balls—she confirmed that all were the same, with nothing actually anchoring the balls to the pillars' tops.

Returning to the head of the steps, she heard Stokes say, "It seems clear enough. Someone—almost certainly some guest—lifted the ball from the pillar at the top of the steps and dropped it on Lady Galbraith." Stokes paused, then added, "Which means this is murder."

Lord Fairchild and the earl winced at the bald statement, but no one argued.

"We need to find out who did this and why," Barnaby stated. "And with all possible speed."

Again, there was general consensus. Looking over the balustrade, Penelope watched while Stokes, supported by Barnaby and the earl, and, however reluctantly, assisted by Lord Fairchild, discussed ways and means of achieving those goals. All agreed that there was no sense in even attempting to interview all the guests—there were far too many. It was determined that Stokes's sergeant, O'Donnell, aided by the constables who would have arrived at the house by now, would collect the guests' names and then let them go.

"That's the best we can do regarding the who, at least for now." Stokes looked down at the body.

Penelope bided her time while Lord Fairchild and the earl came up the steps and went into the house, followed by Sergeant O'Donnell, who recognized her and tipped his head respectfully. She waited until Barnaby and Stokes finally left the body and climbed the steps toward her.

As if sensing she was waiting with some purpose in mind, both halted two steps down, their faces level with hers.

She smiled a touch grimly. "There's another question we need to ask, and I rather think it comes first."

Barnaby and Stokes both raised their brows invitingly.

"Why did Lady Galbraith come outside?" Penelope glanced at the deserted gardens. No lanterns had been strung; it was too early in the season, the weather too often inclement to bother with such amenities. Looking back at Barnaby and Stokes, noting that both looked struck, she elaborated, "She's been dead for how long? An hour or so before she was found? Why on earth would she leave one of the premier events of the Season, which had only just commenced, and come out here?"

Stokes slowly nodded. "Even I know that's odd." After a moment, he glanced at Barnaby, then looked at Penelope. "Our first step, I think, should be to interview her family. All those present."

"According to Lady Fairchild and Barnaby's mother," Penelope said, "all Lady Galbraith's immediate family is here."

Stokes grimaced. "I'm not looking forward to breaking the news, but..." He drew breath. "After that's done, we should see if we can turn up anyone who saw her ladyship leave the ballroom with anyone, or who has any idea why she left."

Her expression resolute, Penelope nodded. "I'll come and observe the family's reactions, then I'll find out who Lady Galbraith's bosom-bows are and see if they know anything."

"Right." Clearly metaphorically girding his loins, Stokes turned to the house.

Penelope slid her arm through Barnaby's and they followed Stokes inside.

* * *

*T*hey re-entered the ballroom to find it abuzz. People had gathered in tight groups, talking in subdued tones and looking about as if searching for further enlightenment; clearly, the news of the murder had got out. Penelope hoped that Lady Fairchild and the countess had managed to corral the Galbraiths before the whispers started.

Stokes paused to consult with his men and to liaise with Lord and Lady Fairchild over how best to funnel the guests past the constables waiting to take down names and then to urge the guests to leave.

The earl and Devil had been joined by Honoria and the countess; all four offered their services in assisting with the guests. "Especially," Honoria crisply stated, "in tactfully suggesting that the most appropriate action would be to climb into their carriages and depart."

Very few of those present were likely to argue with the Duchess of St. Ives. Aware of that, Stokes inclined his head gratefully. Then, gathering Barnaby and Penelope with a glance, Stokes followed Lord Fairchild to the drawing room.

Lord Fairchild reached for the drawing room doorknob. Stokes stopped him. "If you could give me the names, my lord? It would help."

Lord Fairchild nodded. He frowned. "William, Lord Galbraith. The son is Mr. Hartley Galbraith. He's the oldest child. The eldest daughter is Geraldine, then next..." Faltering, Lord Galbraith cast a hopeful glance at Penelope.

Penelope pushed her glasses higher up her nose. "Primrose is the middle daughter, and Monica is the youngest. Monica isn't formally out yet. This is...was to be her first Season."

"Thank you, my dear." Lord Fairchild looked at Stokes. "Ready, Inspector?"

Stokes nodded.

Lord Fairchild opened the door and led them inside. Entering on his heels, Stokes swiftly took in the assembled company gathered on and about a pair of sofas set facing each other before the hearth. All looked apprehensive. Three young ladies, ranging in age from perhaps twenty-five to a bare eighteen, sat clustered on one sofa—Geraldine, Primrose, and Monica, Stokes supposed. Hartley Galbraith proved to be a well-dressed gentleman of about thirty summers. He was standing behind the youngest girl, one hand resting comfortingly on her shoulder; she appeared overwhelmed, her gaze fixed on her hands, clasped tightly in her lap.

Stokes shifted his gaze to the older gentleman occupying the corner of the second sofa, facing the eldest young lady. Heavyset and with tufty white hair, Lord Galbraith wore an openly bewildered expression. From the gap left beside him—from the way his hand reached to that space as if seeking a comfort that wasn't there—it appeared that the family, or at least Lord Galbraith, hadn't yet realized that Lady Galbraith wouldn't be joining them.

Hearing the door quietly shut behind him, Stokes halted a pace behind and a little to Lord Fairchild's right; his lordship had stopped just inside the glow cast by the lamps sitting on the side tables flanking both sofas. Stokes might have wished for better light, but could understand the instinctive impulse to grant the soon-to-be-grieving some shadow.

All eyes fixed on Lord Fairchild. His lordship hesitated, then simply said, "I fear there's been an accident. This is Inspector Stokes from Scotland Yard." Indicating Stokes with a wave, Lord Fairchild stepped back.

Of all his duties, informing innocents of the murder of one of their own was the one Stokes hated the most. Because of that, he'd paid attention to what was most effective in accomplishing that task; in simple words and short sentences, he broke the news of Lady Galbraith's death.

To say her family was shocked would have been a gross understatement.

Stokes was a policeman. He watched closely, but the initial disbelief, the insistence that he had made some mistake, followed by denial and eventually superseded by a form of chilling shock, were all too familiar and appeared entirely genuine.

Perhaps unsurprisingly, the youngest girl, Monica, was the first to burst into tears. On a series of deep, wrenching sobs, she finally raised her head, only to fling herself into her sister Primrose's arms. Primrose caught her and clung, then all three girls were weeping.

For his part, Hartley Galbraith's face had set, but he'd focused on his father. Leaving the girls clinging to each other, he swiftly rounded the sofa and crouched beside Lord Galbraith; gently, he took the old man's hand. "Papa?"

William Galbraith didn't reply. He stared at a spot in the middle of the room. He looked...unable to take the information in. He appeared utterly lost, as if his tether to the real world had snapped.

Stokes knew he couldn't not question the family, at least to ask them what they knew of their mother's movements, if they knew of any reason that would have taken her out of the ballroom. He couldn't let them go, couldn't leave them to their grief, without asking at least that much.

But he didn't have to ask straightaway. Stepping back, out of the lamplight, he turned to Lord Fairchild and Barnaby.

From the shadows by the door, Penelope continued to study the Galbraiths. Victims were most often murdered by people close to them, and no one was closer than family, but even though she'd scrutinized the Galbraiths from the moment she'd entered the room, she'd seen not one hint of any falsity or misplaced emotion. Hartley was the most difficult to read; like most gentlemen, he'd been trained to hide his emotions, but his concern for his sisters, Monica especially—and then once he'd heard the news, his flaring concern for his father—seemed utterly genuine.

If Penelope was any judge—and, increasingly, she was—Hartley would focus on helping everyone else through this difficult time, and only confront his own grief much later. He wouldn't have time to dwell on his loss while his family needed him. For men like him, dealing with the grief of everyone else was often the way they coped with their own; by the time they allowed themselves to look inside, their own grief had ebbed. So she understood Hartley, and nothing about him rang false.

As for his father, William Galbraith was shattered. Any suggestion that he might have had any hand in his wife's murder was simply untenable; the man looked as if his soul had been ripped from his body.

As for the girls, Geraldine was trying desperately to regain some measure of dignity and control, but she displayed much the same stunned reaction as her father and seemed helpless to be of much comfort to her younger sisters. Primrose and Monica were beyond distressed, but of the three, Primrose looked to be finding her feet the fastest; she didn't seem as overwhelmed as her sisters, yet her grief was etched in her face too clearly for anyone to doubt it.

On entering the room, Penelope had been unable to form any firm view about Monica Galbraith. With her gaze down and her hands tightly clasped, Monica had appeared already highly wrought, but with this being her first major ball, her not being out yet, and her mother having to all intents and purposes deserted her in a setting where most girls her age would be at a loss…in such circumstances, it wasn't hard to excuse Monica's self-absorbed tension. The subsequent implosion when she'd heard of her mother's death…given that she might well have been harboring dark thoughts over her mother having left her to the ton's not-always-gentle mercies, her reaction was not necessarily surprising and, by Penelope's estimation, was very much in character. Young girls of Monica's age were often exceedingly uncertain—of themselves and many other things.

Having finally reached through Lord Galbraith's fugue and exchanged several low-voiced words of comfort, Hartley Galbraith released his father's hand and rose.

Stokes had been waiting; he turned and met Hartley halfway.

Deciding she'd gleaned all she could for the moment, Penelope left Stokes to his work, with Barnaby as support. After quietly opening the door, she slipped out into the corridor.

She closed the door, then turned toward the ballroom. "Now let's see what I can learn from Lady Galbraith's friends."

CHAPTER 2

𝐴 quick question posed to Honoria and the countess and Penelope had
learned who she needed to question.

"They're the biggest whisperers, of course, and the most insistent
over being told what's going on. We've left them until last." Honoria
pointed to a group of five ladies clustered by the windows, their
husbands loosely grouped nearby. "That's them over there—Lady
Howatch is the redhead. She'll introduce you."

With a word of thanks, Penelope crossed the ballroom. As it
transpired, she hardly needed an introduction; her connection to
Barnaby, whose association with Stokes and the police was well
known, ensured she had the immediate attention of all the ladies, as
well as their husbands.

"My dear Mrs. Adair, what can you tell us about what has
happened?" When Penelope didn't immediately respond, the lady who
had spoken lowered her voice. "Is it true that dear Marjorie was
attacked and violated and then beaten to death by some itinerant who
had taken refuge in the gardens?"

Penelope fixed the silly woman, whose name escaped her, with a
direct stare and, borrowing her tone from Honoria, stated, "No."
Realizing that she needed to hold on to the conversational reins, she
continued, "My husband's cousin, Hugo Adair, found Lady
Galbraith's body in the garden several hours ago. She had already
been dead for some time." Hugo would have been among the first to
depart; Penelope had no compunction in throwing his name, at least, to
these wolves. "I am not at liberty to disclose further information, and a
surgeon has yet to view the body and determine the cause of death."
All of which was perfectly true. "However, what the police need at

this juncture is information. We need you to tell us whether you know of any reason or have any notion whatsoever as to why Lady Galbraith left the ballroom this evening."

The ladies exchanged glances; it was easy enough to see that, while each of the five wished to claim some knowledge, none could.

Penelope swallowed her impatience. "Do you know of anyone who was present at the ball with whom her ladyship might have wished to meet with privately?"

Again, the ladies exchanged glances. This time, they looked back at Penelope and shook their heads.

"Do you know anything at all that might prove helpful?"

That caused some shifting and quick glances, then Lady Howatch ventured, "Well, there's the feud, of course."

Penelope blinked. "What feud?"

"Why, the feud over Lady Latimer's shoes."

Even Penelope, with her constitutionally low level of sartorial interest, had heard of the style of ladies' shoes—dubbed Lady Latimer's shoes—that had been a fervent craze since the beginning of the previous Season. Covered in crystals, the shoes were held to have a magical quality and were lusted after by scores of young ladies but, as far as Penelope knew, had thus far remained exclusive to the Latimer family, hence the name. As the Latimer household included four young ladies of marriageable age, the exclusivity was, at least in ton terms, understandable; it gave all four girls a way to stand out among the horde crowding the marriage mart.

Penelope vaguely recalled hearing that the eldest Latimer girl had married at the end of last Season, and that a second very favorable engagement was pending. In the same conversation, Lady Latimer's shoes had been given another moniker: Cinderella shoes.

She fixed Lady Howatch with an impatient look. "I repeat, what feud?"

What tumbled out from Lady Howatch, with supporting comments from the four other ladies, was a tale of childhood friendship between Hester, now Lady Latimer, and Marjorie, subsequently Lady Galbraith.

"Their families were neighbors in the country—in Somerset, I believe," Lady Howatch explained.

Of similar age, the two girls had shared all the experiences of their formative years, and as young ladies had made their come-outs together. "Thick as thieves, they were," one lady said. "I can remember them from that time."

Hester and Marjorie had married within a month of each other and had settled down to raise their families.

"And the families shared everything," Lady Howatch declaimed. "Simply *everything*. Even their husbands are—or at least were—the closest of friends."

"Their children," another lady put in. "Well, it's as if they are—were—just one big family."

"And then came the feud." Lady Howatch exchanged glances with the other ladies, then returned her gaze, now somber, to Penelope. "It was the shoes. They'd shared everything all their lives, but when Hester found those shoes and bought the exclusive license, well, Marjorie assumed Hester would share with her and her girls."

"But Lady Latimer didn't," Penelope said.

"No." Lady Howatch compressed her lips, but then grimaced and said, "I wish I could hold that against Hester, but the truth is, with the marriage mart so crowded, there's not one of us who has or has had girls to establish who could say we wouldn't have done the same thing."

Another lady quietly confided, "I know—well, we all do—that Hester swore that the instant her girls were all spoken for, or even close to it, she would give Marjorie and her girls access to the shoes, passing on the advantage as it were."

"Indeed," another lady averred, "but Marjorie wouldn't have it. She wanted those shoes *now*—then and there—and nothing else would do."

"She dug in her heels and no amount of reasoning would sway her." Lady Howatch shook her head. "One does not wish to speak ill of the dead, but if there was one characteristic Marjorie embodied, it was boneheaded stubbornness."

"Marjorie broke with Hester and all the Latimers." The oldest lady in the group drew her shawl tighter about her shoulders. "Worse, she insisted all her family did the same. And that was a cruel shame." The lady met Penelope's eyes. "Those children had grown up together—they were as close as, if not closer than, a single family—but Marjorie insisted on splitting them apart, on cutting every single tie."

It was as if a pall of sadness had descended on all five ladies.

Eventually, Lady Howatch straightened and put the feeling into words. "The past twelve months have been a sad time in both those households. Indeed, it's been rather painful to watch."

The others all murmured their agreement.

Realizing that she now had somewhere else to be, Penelope briskly nodded. "Thank you. You've been a great help." She glanced around. "Are the Latimers still here?"

"Yes. They've hung back, too. Hester will be aching to know...well, she'll be wishing to comfort the others, but how can she?" Lady Howatch indicated a small knot of ladies and gentlemen on the other side of the room. "That's their party over there."

Penelope repeated her thanks and quickly crossed the room, but she didn't immediately approach the Latimers. Under the direction of Honoria, Lady Fairchild, and the Countess of Cothelstone, the crowd was gradually leaving the ballroom, but the exodus was by inches, as all the guests had to pause to give their names and directions to the policemen at the doors, and, of course, speculation was rife, with the hum of voices a steady thrum; everyone was busy talking.

Spotting Gerrard Debbington and his wife, Jacqueline, toward the rear of the ebbing crowd, Penelope swooped in front of them and halted. Gripping Gerrard's sleeve, she drew him around so that she could appear to be talking to him and Jacqueline while she observed the Latimers. Longtime friends of Barnaby and by now well acquainted with Penelope, Gerrard and Jacqueline laughed and asked who she was watching and why.

They sobered when she told them.

Aware that she was perfectly capable of carrying on a conversation while doing something else, the pair asked after Oliver, and Penelope in turn asked after their children—Frederick, nearly six years old, Miranda, a playful four, Alice, barely three but going on ten, and William, the baby of the family, who was a year older than Oliver.

The Latimers stood only a few yards away. Penelope scanned their faces, searched their expressions. Every member of the family— Hester, Lady Latimer, her four daughters, and the older gentleman Penelope took to be Lord Latimer—were unquestionably deeply shaken. All wore looks of helpless confusion, of welling horror, sadness, and incipient sorrow entirely consistent with the tale of the feud and the news of Lady Galbraith's death. The only members of the group relatively unaffected were the two gentlemen of about thirty or so, each of whom hovered at the elbow of one of the younger ladies— the new husband of one and the prospective fiancé of the other. Penelope recognized both men—Lord Fitzforsythe and Mr. Herbert

Brandywell respectively. Both were openly concerned and solicitous, which, she reflected, augured well for the Latimer family as a whole, and spoke well of the two gentlemen themselves.

Penelope took several moments to work out her strategy, then she refocused on Gerrard and Jacqueline, thanked them for their help, touched cheeks and squeezed hands, and with a shared promise to meet again soon, parted from them.

The Latimers were among the last groups of people remaining at the end of the ballroom; most guests were nearer the doors. Penelope suspected that by dallying the family had hoped to learn more—to learn something beyond the news that Lady Galbraith had died. But as Penelope neared, it appeared that hope had faded; the ladies were resettling their shawls and preparing to join the departing tide.

Gliding up, Penelope halted directly before the group. Fixing her gaze on Lady Latimer's face, she said, "I cannot imagine what you and your family must be feeling, but you have my sincere sympathy."

Lady Latimer was a tallish woman, with a spare figure and fairish blonde-brown hair pulled back to emphasize the strong bones of her long face, the plainness of which was overcome by a pair of fine pale blue eyes. From her rigidly controlled expression, Penelope had pegged her as a very reserved woman even before she spoke.

"Thank you." Lady Latimer paused, then said, "I'm sorry. I know I've seen you about, but at this moment, I can't place you."

Penelope inclined her head graciously. "I'm Penelope, Mrs. Adair. My husband, Barnaby Adair, is a consultant to the Metropolitan Police and is assisting with the investigation into Lady Galbraith's death."

The interest from the entire group was immediate. All the others crowded closer.

"Can you tell us anything more?" the married daughter asked.

Penelope pushed her spectacles higher. "Sadly, no. All I can say is that Lady Galbraith was found dead on the path below the side terrace. The police surgeon has yet to determine how she died."

"Have you—" Lady Latimer pressed her lips tight and didn't go on.

Penelope met her pale blue gaze; even though her ladyship's features remained set and uncommunicative, anguish was plainly writ in her delicately hued eyes. Penelope lowered her voice. "I have seen the body."

Lady Latimer was of the sort who had been taught all her life to control her emotions, to never let them show. Her fists clenched; it took effort for her to ask, "Did she...suffer?"

"I don't believe so." Penelope chose her words with care. "It would appear she died instantly."

Lord Latimer closed a large hand about one of his wife's tightly clenched fists. He gave Penelope a short nod. "Thank you, Mrs. Adair."

"Before you leave," Penelope said, "and please understand that of all those here, you as a group, having known the Galbraith family for so long, are the only ones who might be able to assist us with this, do any of you"—with her gaze she included the entire group—"know of anyone who might have wished Lady Galbraith dead? Did she have any enemies?"

A pause ensued. The younger girls looked at each other, but from their expressions, while all were clearly racking their memories, none were finding any answer.

Eventually, Lady Latimer said, her tone again showing the strain of fighting against a deeply entrenched reluctance, "I know of no one who wished Marjorie ill. She was, generally, a likeable soul."

Lady Latimer paused. A sudden tenseness gripped her; her features contorted as if in pain, and she turned her hand and gripped her husband's tightly. "If anything, Mrs. Adair, the shoe was on the other foot. Marjorie had developed a marked enmity toward me over those wretched, *wretched* shoes."

The degree of emotion invested in those last words was, from one such as Lady Latimer, utterly shocking. Her family reacted, immediately drawing closer, all the girls reaching to touch their mother in unspoken comfort.

Appreciating the moment, Penelope inclined her head and stepped back. "Thank you." She stopped herself from wishing them a good night and glided away, allowing the family to gather themselves and, after a moment, fall in at the rear of the crowd moving toward the doors.

Halting by the side of the ballroom, Penelope stood and stared after them, fixing in her mind all she'd learned. Then, deciding it was time to rejoin Barnaby, she turned—and all but ran into Lady Horatia Cynster.

On a soft laugh, Horatia caught Penelope, tugged her the last inches into a fond embrace, then released her. "Well met, my dear." Horatia's shrewd eyes took in Penelope's expression. "And how do you go on?"

Pushing her spectacles, dislodged by the embrace, back onto the bridge of her nose, Penelope grimaced. "I greatly fear this will not be an easy case. There are a lot of emotions involved."

"As is generally the case whenever the ton is a part of things." Horatia nodded and, in matronly fashion, folded her arms in her shawl. "Is there anything I—" She glanced around as three others joined them—Helena, Honoria, and Horatia's daughter-in-law, Patience Cynster. Horatia smiled and amended, "Is there anything we can tell you that might help?"

The other three ladies bent inquiring—ready to be helpful—looks on Penelope.

Rapidly, she gathered her thoughts. "I've learned about the feud over Lady Latimer's shoes. I've seen the Galbraiths—William, Lord Galbraith, Hartley, the son, and the daughters, Geraldine, Primrose, and Monica. Barnaby and Stokes are interviewing them, and doubtless I'll learn more about them later. So…" She raised her gaze to the faces of four of the best sources of information in the ton. "What can you tell me about the Latimers?"

Helena blinked. "You don't think they're involved?"

"I really don't know," Penelope said. "But courtesy of the feud, at this point the Latimers stand out as the only obvious source of discord in Lady Galbraith's life. We need to know more about them, if only to eliminate them from our deliberations."

Honoria nodded in understanding. "While I don't know the family intimately, I have met them and can certainly give you my impressions. Hester Latimer is one I would label a 'good sort.' Fundamentally a good person. She's very contained—that's both her character and her upbringing. She was always the quiet one, while Marjorie Galbraith was the bubbling, vivacious, outgoing one of the pair."

"Until last year," Penelope said.

"Indeed." Patience nodded. "The Latimer girls are also straightforward and, relatively speaking, unremarkable. Georgina, the eldest, is now married to Lord Fitzforsythe, and the second girl, Cecilia, is, I understand, about to become formally betrothed to Herbert Brandywell, another excellent match." Patience paused, then went on, "The third girl, Cynthia, is rather like her mother in that she's quiet and contained. I haven't heard anything yet about a match for her. The youngest girl, Millicent, is not formally out, so I don't know much about her."

Penelope looked inquiringly at the others.

Honoria shrugged lightly. "The only information I have to add is that Georgina is twenty-five years old, Cecilia is twenty-three, Cynthia twenty-one, and Millicent is just eighteen, I believe, and none of the four are in any way outstanding. In appearance, all are passable, but nothing more. However, they are well brought up and have nice, steady characters."

"Of course," Helena said, "while the Latimers are not paupers, with four daughters to establish, none of the girls have the advantage of large portions. That, to my mind, is the critical point that makes Hester Latimer's stance over the shoes so very understandable."

"What is the ton's view of the feud?" Penelope asked.

Honoria grimaced. "There's not one lady with daughters to establish—especially in number, as is the case with the Latimers and the Galbraiths—who does not understand and, indeed, sympathize with Hester Latimer's decision. In essence, Marjorie forced Hester to choose between Hester's daughters' best interests and Hester's best friend's interests." Honoria held Penelope's gaze. "Hester's daughters won."

"That can hardly have been a surprise," Penelope remarked.

"It was apparently a rude shock to Marjorie Galbraith." Patience's expression was firmly disapproving. "We all knew how close she and Hester were. Marjorie forced a break, and although Hester hides it well, having to deny her friend and then having that friend turn her back on her deeply wounded Hester. As for the rift Marjorie then forced between the two families...that was a level of vindictiveness no one had anticipated."

Penelope considered that information, then asked, "Are Lady Latimer's shoes really that influential? I've heard that some are referring to them as Cinderella shoes."

Patience nodded. "I would have to say that I do think that they serve a purpose, and that Hester Latimer was inspired in securing the exclusive license and using the shoes as she has."

Seeing Penelope's puzzlement, Helena said, "You must understand, my dear, that at present, the marriage mart is dreadfully crowded, and it is very hard for any young lady to stand out—to attract the attention of gentlemen."

"Precisely." Horatia added, "The shoes do one thing and one thing only—they make gentlemen curious enough to come and look, and, really, that's all any mother wants. If gentlemen come and look, then the chances are that at least one eligible is going to notice the girl standing in the shoes, and one excellent suitor is all one needs."

Penelope frowned. She herself had assiduously avoided the marriage mart in all its many forms; she and Barnaby hadn't met and grown to appreciate each other in any ballroom. But the four ladies before her understood that world in all its various aspects; she accepted their judgments without question. She turned her mind to what she hadn't yet asked. "I understand the husbands—Lord Galbraith and Lord Latimer—were also close friends. How has the feud affected them?"

"Much less than their families, I suspect," Horatia cynically replied. "I daresay you'll discover that they still meet regularly at their club, where their wives—or, more particularly, Marjorie—couldn't know."

Penelope nodded. "Thank you." Glancing around, she saw that most of the guests had departed; they were among the last in the room.

She turned and walked with the others toward the doors beyond which three constables stood, still taking the names and addresses of the stragglers.

Looking more frazzled than Penelope had ever seen her, Lady Fairchild was standing by the doors. She smiled weakly and touched cheeks with the four older ladies, thanking them for their sterling support.

At the last, she turned to Penelope and squeezed her hand. "My dear, I do hope you and your husband and that handsome policeman of yours can solve the mystery of how Marjorie died with all speed, for I have to tell you that if you do not, then I greatly fear that the weight on Hester Latimer's shoulders will grow so great it will crush her."

Penelope was puzzled. "Because of their falling out over the shoes?"

Lady Fairchild looked at her as if she were being woefully obtuse. "No, dear—at least not directly. But surely you know the ton well enough by now to know what the whisperers will say."

Penelope blinked. "Oh." Then she frowned. "Frankly, I would have thought that, if any murder arose out of this feud, it would have been Lady Latimer dead, with Lady Galbraith our prime suspect. *That* would have made sense."

"Indeed." Lady Fairchild nodded rather grimly. "But when has sense had anything to do with gossip? The inconvenient fact that there is no connection between the feud over Lady Latimer's shoes and Marjorie's death will matter not at all."

* * *

*T*he carriage rocked over the cobbles. With her head resting against the edge of the window frame, she kept her gaze fixed on the streetscape outside while her mind churned, alive with questions, possible answers, and potential reasons, all swirling in a sea of overwhelming emotion.

Why hadn't he raised the alarm?

She suspected she knew the answer—the darling idiot was protecting her.

And hers.

He had and always would see her family as his; that was a part of what had drawn them together, a crucial strand in the rope that now bound them so tightly that neither could imagine ever drawing apart.

But did she agree with his stance?

She wished she could simply decide that she did and leave it at that, but...

Surreptitiously raising a hand, she rubbed at her forehead. Uncharacteristically, she was finding it difficult to think. She couldn't remember ever being so shocked, so stunned, so...unable to follow any line of thought for more than two seconds.

The unprecedented difficulty was disconcerting, and only fed an escalating worry that his actions in trying to protect her and shield her and hers from the investigation, while perfectly understandable, would, nevertheless, only lead to worse complications.

She didn't know what the explanation for what he and she had seen was. Her mind simply froze whenever the images replayed in her brain. Yet she was perfectly certain of *what* they had seen. And...

It took effort to fight the constriction about her chest, but she managed to draw in a deeper breath—and the fogs clouding her mind cleared sufficiently for one certainty to shine through. The one thing she knew beyond all doubt, the one thing in which her faith could never be shaken. She seized that certainty, clung to it, felt it like a rock beneath her mental feet, and, feeling more secure, set her mind to examining the situation again.

She knew that the truth behind what they'd seen wasn't anywhere near as simple as the obvious conclusion he and she had initially leapt to, that the authorities would leap to if they knew.

But he and she couldn't simply forget and hide the matter; such a path was unthinkable, for her as much as him.

The carriage tilted as it rounded a corner. They were nearly home. Soon she would be in the quiet of her room, in the silence of her bed.

She was going to have to give serious thought to how to turn the situation about.

But until she'd determined what their best path was, she would have to continue to keep her own counsel.

* * *

𝒫enelope stood beside Oliver's cot and looked down on her sleeping son. After a moment, she bent and placed a soft kiss on his ruffled curls, guinea gold just like his father's.

Straightening, a soft smile curving her lips, she turned away.

Barnaby was lounging in the doorway, waiting and watching as he usually did; Penelope wasn't sure why he accompanied her to the nursery, yet he always did.

Reaching him, she looked into his face, at the clean angles and planes and the depth of understanding behind his brilliant blue eyes that had drawn her from the first. After several seconds, letting the words flow from her mind without restraint, she said, "Every time we stumble on a murder, just looking at Oliver underscores for me why we need to help Stokes find the killer."

Meeting her eyes, Barnaby let his thoughts follow hers. Two heartbeats later, he offered, "I think it's something along the lines of balancing the scales, of needing to see justice done."

Her gaze steady on his face, she tipped her head. "So that the world he grows up in will be—"

"The best place we can make it." Taking her hand, he straightened from the door frame. Drawing her over the threshold, he closed the door.

Side by side, hand in hand, they went down the stairs to their bedroom.

In the carriage on the way home, she had told him of all she'd learned about the Galbraith and Latimer families, about Lady Latimer's shoes and the resulting feud. She had, as he'd informed her, managed to collect a great deal more pertinent information than he and

Stokes had. The Galbraiths, collectively and individually, had all been so overset that he and Stokes had been able to glean very little—nothing beyond vague and distracted assurances that none of the family had gone out to the terrace, and none had any idea of when or why Lady Galbraith had left the ballroom, much less why she had ventured outside.

Barnaby unbuttoned his coat, shrugged out of it, and set it aside, then, presented with Penelope's buttoned back, he obligingly slipped the tiny jet buttons from their moorings while letting his mind freely sift through the facts.

"I wonder," Penelope said, "what possible motive anyone might have for killing Lady Galbraith."

It was, he realized, the point about which his mind, too, was revolving. Finishing the buttons, he straightened.

"Thank you." Penelope glided away, stripping the gown off her shoulders. They hadn't bothered to light a lamp, and the moonlight washing through the uncurtained window turned her alabaster skin pearlescent.

"I'm having difficulty," she continued, "imagining it to be a crime of passion, or jealousy, or something of that nature." She stepped out of her gown and, her hands rising to the ties of her petticoat, glanced at him. "She was a touch too old, don't you think?"

He blinked; it took a second to realign his thoughts with hers. "She definitely didn't seem the type." He set his fingers to the buttons of his waistcoat. "And it's unlikely to be money, either. I imagine all that will be in her husband's name—although we should ask Montague to look into the financial side, just to be sure."

"Indeed." Tossing her petticoat aside, Penelope grasped the hem of her chemise and whisked it off over her head. After sending the delicate garment wafting to join the pile of her clothes on her dressing-table stool, entirely naked she walked to their big bed, lifted the covers, and slid beneath.

"Still," she said, wriggling as she settled on her back, staring—slightly frowning—up at the canopy, "I can't help wondering if, somehow, Lady Galbraith's murder has something to do with this feud—that it's somehow connected to Lady Latimer's shoes—and no, I haven't the foggiest notion how that might be so."

Having dispensed with his clothes, Barnaby lost no time in joining his wife beneath the sheets. Shifting over her, letting their legs tangle and their hips meet, he propped his weight on his elbows and looked down into her face. And let his cynical skepticism show. "Murdered over a pair of shoes?"

Her grin flashed. "Trust me"—she twined her arms about his neck—"among the female half of the ton, that thought is not *at all* far-fetched."

He chuckled, then bent his head and kissed her. Ardently.

Penelope tightened her arms about his neck, kissed him back with equal fervor, and, setting aside all consideration of shoes and murder, gave herself up to the heady delights of being Barnaby Adair's wife.

CHAPTER 3

$\mathcal{A}$t ten minutes past nine o'clock the next morning, Barnaby followed Stokes through the doors of Montague's offices.

Slocum, Montague's senior clerk, recognized them instantly. "Good morning, Inspector, Mr. Adair. I'll let Mr. Montague know you're here."

"Thank you, Slocum." Stokes had his policeman's mask in place, sober and serious.

Slocum headed for the door to Montague's office.

Glancing around, Barnaby noted that, like Slocum, all the rest of Montague's staff working at their various stations around the large outer office had recognized them and had deduced the likely reason for their arrival; all were watching with expectant expressions.

Slocum returned and waved them to the door of Montague's office. "Mr. and Mrs. Montague will see you immediately, sirs."

With nods of thanks, Stokes and Barnaby crossed to Montague's office.

Montague met them just inside the door. He, too, looked expectantly intrigued. "Well met. Come in."

The three men shook hands, then Barnaby and Stokes turned to greet Violet, who had risen from the chair behind the small desk on the opposite side of the room from Montague's.

Smiling softly, she pressed Barnaby's and Stokes's hands and planted light kisses on their cheeks; she was a close friend of both their wives. "What an unexpected pleasure." She waved them to the chairs angled before Montague's desk. "Please, sit."

She led the way, moving to take the chair to the left of the massive desk. As Montague sank into the admiral's chair behind it, Violet fixed her gaze on Stokes and Barnaby. "Given the hour, I take it you have a case with which we might assist?"

Since her marriage to Montague several months previously, Violet had divided her days between being Montague's secretary and being Penelope's; in both positions, she organized people who had a tendency to become overly immersed in their work. Certainly, Penelope was much happier these days, and Montague was patently more relaxed; he smiled frequently, far more than he ever had.

At Violet's eager question, Stokes wryly smiled. "Business at the moment must be boring."

Montague feigned shock. "Business is *never* boring." His features relaxed. "However, at times, it can be very predictable." He scanned their faces. "You do have a case."

Barnaby nodded. "A murder. Rather an odd one." He outlined the bare bones of what they knew.

"There's no reason to suppose that there's any financial angle," Stokes said. "The chances are it's a purely personal motive. However, if you would check to see if there is anything unusual about the Galbraiths' finances, we could eliminate that prospect with greater certainty."

Montague was taking notes. He nodded. "It'll be easy enough. Given who they are, I can ask directly, and discreetly. Slocum will know who the family's man-of-business is." Glancing up, Montague met Barnaby's and Stokes's gazes. "I should have an answer by tomorrow at the latest. I'll send word if there's anything of possible relevance."

"Excellent." Stokes rose.

"So what's your next move?" Violet rose, too, as did Barnaby and Montague.

Barnaby glanced at Stokes. "We're off to interview the Fairchilds' staff."

Stokes grimaced. "Just pray that someone noticed something, because otherwise, as things stand, we have no place to start."

"No loose thread to tug on to unravel the mystery." Barnaby cocked a brow at Violet. "Wish us luck."

Violet smiled, and they parted.

Montague accompanied Stokes and Barnaby to his office door; he watched them cross the outer office and leave, then he called in Slocum and requested the Galbraiths' man-of-business's name and direction.

Turning back to his desk, he saw that Violet had again sat in the chair beside it.

Glancing up, she met his eyes. "I do hope Penelope is working on her translation and hasn't been distracted by the lure of this investigation."

Dropping into his chair, Montague considered, then humphed. "What are the odds, do you think?"

Violet's brows rose. "I honestly don't know. She is making a considerable effort to be stricter over allocating her time. Her 'balance,' as she calls it." Standing, Violet shook out her skirts, then glided back to her desk. "Still, we haven't had a case—not one we ladies might help with—for some time, and this Galbraith case certainly sounds like one of those."

We ladies. Montague realized he'd frozen at the words. The instinctive reaction was novel, not something he recognized, much less understood. As, directly across from him, Violet settled again at her desk and gave her attention to the letters that were now her domain, he wondered at his odd feeling... He couldn't be *jealous* over the time Violet spent with Penelope and Stokes's wife, Griselda, could he?

Inwardly frowning, he studied Violet—his wife—as she worked; he drank in the calmness, the sense of serenity and simple contentment she projected, at least to him.

After a moment, he mentally shook himself, picked up his pencil, and returned to the column of figures he'd been checking.

Feeling put out over Violet spending time with Penelope and Griselda, even if they plunged into another investigation, was just plain silly.

* * *

"*I*'m not yet certain of where the best place to start in this new investigation will be," Penelope informed Oliver. Holding his hand, she walked very slowly, one step to several of Oliver's short and still uncertain ones, along the strip of lawn bordering the flower beds in Berkeley Square.

The square and its gardens were a few minutes' walk from their town house. Noting that Oliver was eager to explore not just their garden but the sights, sounds, and colors of people and carriages, other children, nursemaids, and even dogs, Penelope had decided that whenever the weather permitted, an hour in the square was an excellent diversion. For Oliver, and for her, too.

Restraining Oliver, now a sturdy fifteen-month-old, from diving headfirst into a flower bed sporting a few last daffodils and jonquils among burgeoning pansies and violas, Penelope went on, "Of course, there's that wretched translation to be finished. Why they couldn't find a more legible copy of the original I can't imagine—I've had to use a magnifying glass over most of it. And even then, I've had to use my imagination in several places." She frowned. "I might even have to ask Jeremy Carling for a second opinion."

Spotting a dog being walked on a lead, Oliver chortled and waved. "Ma, ma, ma!"

Which, Penelope knew, translated to *Mama, take me over there!*

She obeyed; halting, she exchanged a greeting with the dog's attendant human, a footman from Lord Ferris's household, who obligingly held the dog, a poodle, so Oliver could clumsily pet it. The dog accepted the attention with a resigned air.

As she and Oliver moved on, Penelope wondered if they should get a dog of some sort. Although they lived in a town house, they did have a decent-sized garden. Putting the notion aside for later discussion with Barnaby, and with her mother and his, Penelope refocused—not on the translation that was plaguing her but on the case that had so unexpectedly fallen into their laps the previous evening. "Who would have thought," she said to Oliver, "that someone would be murdered at such an event? The premier ball opening the Season, and immediately someone is murdered. Much as I enjoy investigating, I do hope that that isn't an omen." She paused, looking ahead, then added, "Especially as we have the coronation coming up later in the year. Not a good time for members of the haut ton to end up dead. Not, I suppose, that there is a good time."

She'd grown accustomed to talking freely to Oliver, more or less letting her mind ramble and the words tumble out without restriction. Upon reaching the northern end of the long oval that was the gardens, they turned and started back down the other side of the central court, toward where Oliver's nursemaid, Hettie, sat on a bench enjoying the weak sunshine and a welcome break.

"I suppose," Penelope went on, "that we—Violet, Griselda, and I—will have to wait for Stokes and Barnaby to establish what leads exist before we can pick one and start following it." Glancing down, she saw Oliver looking up at her, curious and—at least as she interpreted his look—interested. "There's nothing that, at present, stands out as an obvious place to start pushing and prodding."

Oliver smiled a wide, five-toothed smile, then looked ahead and tugged at Penelope's hand.

"Yes, you're right. We should get back." Penelope exhaled gustily. "And I suppose I must spend at least a few hours on that translation, or Violet will shake her head at me, and we can't have that." At the mention of Violet's name, Oliver looked up eagerly. Penelope smiled back. "Yes, I know—you like Violet. But she's not coming today. She'll be in tomorrow..." Raising her head, Penelope grimaced. "Blast! I just remembered I have to attend that lecture at the Royal Society this afternoon. I promised Mrs. Fischer that I would be there to lend her and her son my support, and she'll notice and be upset if I don't appear."

Oliver chortled and, with Hettie now in his sights, tugged her on.

"Back to what awaits." Penelope obliged by walking slightly faster. "Sadly," she said, keeping an eye on Oliver to make sure he didn't overbalance, "it seems there's little prospect of me being able to accomplish anything investigation-wise today. Regardless, I have to admit that I'm thoroughly fascinated by this feud over Lady Latimer's shoes. And, just between us, I have a niggling suspicion that, somehow, in some way, we will find that the feud and the shoes had something to do with Lady Galbraith's murder."

Although Hettie was now only a few paces away, Oliver slowed and—somewhat to Penelope's surprise—directed a wide-eyed, clearly questioning look up at her.

She blinked. "Why do I think that?" Although Oliver didn't reply—his grasp of words was not that advanced—he did seem to wait, so she answered, "I suppose because it's such a curiously odd situation that it really would be terribly disappointing if Lady Latimer's shoes *weren't* involved."

* * *

*B*arnaby and Stokes arrived at Fairchild House with Sergeant O'Donnell and Constable Morgan, two of Stokes's more trusted men, in their train. Leaving the uniformed men in the front hall, Barnaby and Stokes met with Lord Fairchild in his library.

"Terrible business." His lordship frowned. "And so senseless. I didn't know Marjorie Galbraith well, but I cannot imagine she would

have posed any sort of threat to anybody. She simply wasn't the type."
Having foreseen the necessity, Lord Fairchild had already
warned his butler that Stokes would need to question the staff.

"Primarily as to what they saw," Stokes said. "Especially what
they saw of Lady Galbraith. Neither Lord Galbraith nor Mr.
Hartley Galbraith were with her ladyship around the time she must have left
the ballroom, and sadly, her daughters are so overset that we've been
unable to ascertain anything from them of their mother's movements
beyond that, at some point in the proceedings, she moved from the
spot where they had parted from her. As yet, no one has been able to
tell us exactly when, or by what route, her ladyship left the ballroom."

"Are those details significant?" Lord Fairchild asked.

"As we don't yet know either the when or the how," Stokes
replied, "at this point, we can't say."

Lord Fairchild nodded. "Yes, of course. Well, I sincerely wish
you both swift success—occurring as it did on what was essentially the
opening night of the Season, this has cast something of a pall over the
entire haut ton. Any murder would have been bad enough, but to have
one of our own taken, and in such an incomprehensible fashion...well,
it's unnerving."

Stokes glanced at Barnaby, then said, "I've brought two
experienced officers to assist Mr. Adair and myself, so we'll keep the
disruption to your staff and their duties to a minimum."

"Thank you. My wife, especially, will appreciate that. She's still
in a state of disbelief bordering on outrage that such a thing could have
happened at an event of hers, in our house." Lord Fairchild summoned
his butler and gave orders for the staff to be assembled so that Stokes
and Barnaby could question them.

Following the butler, rigidly disapproving but scrupulously
correct, Barnaby and Stokes entered the servants' hall to find the staff
already gathered.

Barnaby glanced at the butler, who unbent enough to explain,
"Elevenses, sir. We usually come together briefly at this time."

Halting at the head of the long deal table about which the staff
were now standing in their places, Stokes introduced himself and
Barnaby, then nodded at the staff to retake their seats. Once they had,
Stokes described in plain terms what was known to that point—that
Lady Galbraith had left the ballroom and gone outside, onto the path
below the side terrace, and that someone had then dropped a stone
ball-cum-finial from the terrace balustrade onto her ladyship, killing

her. Subsequently, her body had been discovered by Mr. Hugo Adair when that gentleman had gone outside to smoke a cheroot.

Barnaby stepped forward and, with an easy air, explained that Lord Fairchild had given orders that the staff should cooperate with the police and should answer all questions put to them truthfully. He glanced at the butler, who with a brief nod and a terse "Indeed, sir" verified those statements.

Then they got down to business. Stokes divided the staff into three groups—the senior staff, who he and Barnaby would interview, the other males on the staff, who O'Donnell would question, and the rest of the female staff, from whom the engaging, baby-faced Morgan was best qualified to extract information.

A hum of conversation enveloped the room as questions were put and answers were offered and noted. In addition to the inquiries Stokes had mentioned to Lord Fairchild, the questions the investigators put to the staff were also designed to eliminate any member of the staff as a suspect. As it transpired, the latter wasn't difficult; the previous night's event had been a major ball, and every staff member had had specific duties and a strict schedule.

Stokes had never before appreciated the logistics of putting on a major ton ball; he was impressed and said so, which somewhat eased the butler's and housekeeper's resistance. Subsequently, they grew steadily more helpful, explaining where this staff member, then that, had to have been at any particular time. Given that the butler had been on duty in the front hall throughout the evening, and the housekeeper had been acting as major-general in the kitchen, neither of them had seen anything pertinent, nor could they have been involved in any way. As—according to Hartley Galbraith—the Galbraiths had arrived after nine o'clock and Lady Galbraith's body had been discovered at eleven o'clock, the period over which the investigators needed to account for the staff and their movements was relatively short.

Eliminating the staff was, in Stokes's view, a necessary first step; he'd been involved in too many ton cases where the upper class assumed that any villain naturally hailed from some class lower than their own. Masters always looked to their staff, and staff looked to those lower than themselves. From experience, Stokes knew that eliminating all chance that any member of the Fairchilds' staff was involved in the crime was the fastest way of clearing his path so he could focus on the Galbraith family and their ton acquaintances. In ton murders, the murderer was almost always a member of the same set, if not the same family.

Stokes wasn't at all surprised that none of the staff were likely to have played any role in the crime, and he was pleased that striking them all from the suspect list was proving so straightforward. What he wasn't so pleased about was the dearth of information on Lady Galbraith and her movements.

Eventually, the housekeeper looked him in the eye and stated the matter plainly. "We all had things to do, minute by minute, and so all of us were concentrating on what we were doing and not on what any of the guests were doing. We don't get paid to do that."

Stokes grimaced but inclined his head in acceptance.

Just then, Sergeant O'Donnell, who had been interviewing the male members of the staff in the far corner of the room, came up, a tall young footman somewhat nervously trailing behind him. O'Donnell tipped his head to Barnaby and to the butler and the housekeeper, then addressed Stokes. "Sir—Robert here remembers seeing Mr. Hartley Galbraith leave the ballroom early in the evening."

O'Donnell stepped back, exposing Robert to Stokes's and Barnaby's now very interested gazes.

After taking rapid stock, Stokes evenly asked, "Are you sure it was Mr. Galbraith?"

Robert swallowed and glanced at the butler. Receiving an encouraging nod, he looked back at Stokes and replied, "I didn't know it was him then—when I saw him go out onto the side terrace—but I saw him later, when we were ushering the family into the drawing room. The Galbraith family. The man I saw earlier was the younger man—well, he'd be about thirty—who we ushered into the drawing room with the young ladies and the older gent."

That was as definitive an identification as they could hope for. Stokes glanced at Barnaby.

His gaze resting deceptively gently on the footman's face, Barnaby asked, "What time was it when you saw Mr. Galbraith go out onto the side terrace?"

Robert blinked, then glanced at the housekeeper. "It was early-ish, soon after the ball started. We were still ferrying about the salvers with glasses of champagne. My tray was empty, so I left the ballroom and headed for the kitchen, and ended up following the gent down the corridor for a little way. I saw him turn off toward the little hall that gives onto the side terrace. When I passed the opening of that corridor, I glimpsed him just starting down the terrace steps."

Barnaby cocked a brow at the housekeeper. "Can you give us an approximate time?"

The housekeeper narrowed her eyes on Robert. "We did two rounds each footman of the champagne. Was that the first time you came back—after your first tray was emptied?"

Robert nodded.

"Well, then." The housekeeper looked at Barnaby and Stokes. "That would've been a trifle before half past nine. First round went out at ten past the hour, and second from about half past."

"Right." Stokes looked at O'Donnell, then looked down the room to where Morgan, with his harem of females, had stopped talking and had been listening, too. Stokes raised his voice and addressed the room at large. "We have a sighting of Mr. Hartley Galbraith leaving the house via the side terrace at just before half past nine. Did anyone see Lady Galbraith leave the ballroom, or see her go outside, via the side terrace or by any other route?"

Silence and a general shaking of heads.

"Next question," Stokes went on, "did anyone see Mr. Hartley Galbraith talking with anyone in the ballroom before he left the house—in other words, soon after he arrived?"

Again, nothing.

"Did anyone see Mr. Hartley Galbraith return to the ballroom?"

No answer came. The butler shifted. "But he was in the ballroom when, with his lordship and her ladyship, we gathered the family and took them to the drawing room. He was standing with his sisters when we found them."

Stokes nodded. "All right. Now go back to Lady Galbraith. Did anyone see her speak with anyone earlier in the night—any comment, discussion, argument—before she must have left the ballroom?"

Silence reigned.

Barnaby broke it to ask, "Did any of you notice any other guest leaving the ballroom for the gardens, or returning from that direction, at any time before the body was found?"

Heads shook all around the room.

Barnaby exchanged a glance with Stokes, who nodded, then Barnaby addressed the gathering. "Is there anything else that you noticed, or heard, over the hours of the ball that struck you as odd? Anything at all."

Several seconds passed, then the butler stirred. "Actually, the one thing that strikes me as…well, unusual, was Mr. Galbraith, and Lady

Galbraith, too, going outside so early." The butler met Stokes's interested gaze, then looked at Barnaby. "In my experience, it's unusual for guests to go wandering the gardens that early. They've only just arrived, and they have all their friends to find in the crowd and speak with. Normally, they don't start into the gardens until after midnight, once the ballroom begins to heat up. And it is March, after all—it was chilly outside, and the ballroom hadn't had time to get stuffy."

Barnaby inclined his head. "Indeed. That's a very valid point."

Stokes looked around the room. "Thank you, everyone—I believe that's all we need at this point. You've been very helpful."

With a general air of relief—everyone assumed dealing with a police investigation would be an ordeal and was pleased that nothing harrowing had occurred—the gathering broke up.

The butler, now much more at ease, conducted Barnaby and Stokes back through the house to the front door. O'Donnell and Morgan had elected to leave via the kitchen door; while the butler no doubt assumed that was due to them knowing their place, Barnaby suspected that, experienced men that they were, the two officers had gone out that way to get a better look at the layout of the house and grounds.

Waiting with Stokes by the police carriage in the drive for O'Donnell and Morgan to join them, Barnaby started putting the pieces of information they'd gathered together in his mind; to him, cases were like jigsaws, solved by fitting fact after fact into place. "Leaving aside any leaping to conclusions over Hartley Galbraith—whatever reason took Lady Galbraith outside, could she have surprised someone, seen something they didn't want her to witness, and been killed because of that?"

Stokes grunted. "At this point, anything's possible. But the question I keep coming back to is why she went outside at all—and, as the butler pointed out, at a time in the proceedings when you toffs don't generally amble on the lawns."

Barnaby grinned at the "you toffs."

O'Donnell and Morgan strode up, and the four climbed into the carriage.

By the time the wheels were rolling, Barnaby had sobered. Across the carriage, he met Stokes's eyes. "The butler's observation, which is entirely accurate, highlights even more the oddity of Hartley Galbraith leaving the ballroom so early. What possible reason had *he* for going outside at that time?" Barnaby frowned. "*And* he denied it later. Why?"

Stokes returned Barnaby's gaze steadily. "I suggest we go and ask him."

* * *

*A*fter reporting to the chief commissioner, then enjoying a quick ploughman's lunch at a public house not far from Scotland Yard, instead of immediately pursuing Hartley Galbraith, Stokes and Barnaby returned to the City and Montague's offices.

It was early afternoon when they walked in—only a few hours since they'd steered Montague and his team in the Galbraiths' direction—yet when Montague spotted them walking in the door, he grinned in clear triumph and beckoned them to join him in his office.

"I've found something that might be of interest," he said, as they ambled to the chairs before his desk.

"And we've found someone whose finances might bear investigating." Stokes sank onto a chair. "But"—he waved—"you first."

"No Violet?" Barnaby asked, taking the other chair.

"She's upstairs. She'll be down in a moment." Folding his hands on his blotter, Montague fixed them with a self-satisfied look. "It's about Hartley Galbraith."

Stokes blinked. So did Barnaby.

Montague noticed. "What?"

"Hartley Galbraith was the person we came here intending to point you toward," Stokes said. "We've discovered that he left the ballroom and went out via the terrace early in the evening, but he lied about it later. So what have you found?"

Montague took a moment to digest that news, then refocused. "First, you need to know that since Hartley reached the age of twenty-five, his share of the income from the family's estate has been split from the income paid to Lord Galbraith. That's a common arrangement and one I applaud—one doesn't want to give young men access to their fortunes at too early an age, yet you do want them to learn how to manage money before they marry and have children of their own. The firm who handles the Galbraiths' interests, meaning the estate of Lord Galbraith, is well known and all is aboveboard there. However, Hartley moved his business to another firm—also a common and reasonable arrangement. Hartley's chosen firm is less well established, but is reputable and well regarded. Thus far I have only inquired of the Galbraiths' firm, and while they assure me that there is nothing out of the ordinary with the Galbraith accounts, they have recently been asked by Hartley's man-of-business for an assessment of Hartley's share of the estate—essentially an accounting of what he stands to inherit."

Montague paused, then clarified, "Such an accounting might be thought to be contingent on the details of Lord Galbraith's will, but with an entailed estate such as the Galbraith estate, the scope of the minimum that Hartley will inherit is defined. It's possible, therefore, to put a figure on that minimum worth at any given time."

Meeting first Barnaby's gaze, then Stokes's, Montague concluded, "In common parlance, Hartley Galbraith is putting his affairs in order."

Stokes frowned. "What reason would a gentleman like him have for doing so?"

"In my experience," Montague replied, "there are only two reasons a gentlemen of Hartley's ilk seeks to put a value on his fortune. He's either going into business and requires the backing of some other party and he needs the financials to get that party's approval—for instance, a loan. Or—and for someone of Hartley's style and age, this sounds more feasible—he intends to get married and needs the details of his worth to negotiate the settlements."

Montague paused, then his lips quirked in wry grin. "Indeed, for a gentleman like Hartley Galbraith, you could say that going into business and getting married are more or less the same thing."

Barnaby snorted.

Stokes looked amused, but he quickly sobered. "So he might be about to offer for some lady's hand—and something to do with that might have taken him outside."

"The only other possibility is that he's making his will," Barnaby said, "but as he's not yet thirty, that's hardly likely." Barnaby cocked a brow at Stokes. "Shall we go and ask him which it is—business or pleasure, as the case may be?"

Stokes grinned wolfishly. "Yes. Let's." He rose.

Barnaby got to his feet. He and Stokes shook hands with Montague, who promised to let them know if any other interesting financial tidbits about the Galbraiths came to light.

Montague rose, too, and watched the pair walk out.

After the door closed behind them, feeling buoyed by a sense of accomplishment, however minor, he turned back to his desk and the investment reports spread across its surface. Sitting again, his gaze went to the smaller desk across the room and the empty chair behind it. Violet would be down soon. He hesitated, then made a definite mental note to tell her of Stokes and Barnaby's visit, and of the investigation's new focus on Mr. Hartley Galbraith.

CHAPTER 4

*T*he address Hartley Galbraith had given was of a lodging house in Jermyn Street. Prior to his marriage, Barnaby had lived several doors down on the opposite side of the street.

Stokes knocked on the door of the narrow house. A manservant opened the door, but on being asked for Mr. Galbraith, he shook his head. "Not here at present. He's had a death in the family."

"Do you know where he is?" Stokes asked.

"I'm sure I couldn't say, sir." The man started to edge the door closed.

Barnaby, who had been getting his bearings, turned to face the man. "Does Lord Carradale still own this house?"

The man paused. "Why, yes, sir."

Reaching into his coat pocket, Barnaby drew out a card and handed it to the man. "Knowing Carradale, at this hour he's still having breakfast. Give that to him and tell him Adair would like a word."

Having studied the embossed gold lettering on the thick ivory card, the man nodded. "Yes, sir. Ah…"

"We'll wait here," Stokes said. "Just leave the door open and fetch Carradale."

Reacting to Stokes's tone of reined patience, the manservant did as he was bid; a minute later, a long, lanky figure swathed in a multicolored velvet dressing robe came ambling out of the shadows of the hall. Carradale nodded to Barnaby, then eyed Stokes, transparently waiting for an introduction.

Barnaby obliged. "Inspector Stokes of Scotland Yard."

With only the most infinitesimal of pauses, Carradale inclined his head. "Inspector." Lounging against the door frame, he looked at Barnaby and arched his brows. "I'm only half here, but what can I do for you?"

Fleetingly, Barnaby grinned; Carradale was about Barnaby's age, but he had remained unmarried and, clearly, had not changed with the years. Sobering, Barnaby said, "We're looking for Galbraith."

Carradale winced. "I heard about the murder. The news did the rounds of the clubs last night."

"Have you seen Hartley since?" Barnaby asked.

Carradale nodded. "I came home after I heard, and he was here—it was the early hours by then. He was…well, holding it in, of course, but he was cut up and in something of a state underneath. Well, who wouldn't be? He was packing—"

"Packing?" Stokes said.

Carradale looked at Stokes curiously. "Yes, packing." Carradale met Barnaby's eyes. "He told me his father and his sisters were in a dreadful way, and so he was moving back home for a while to lend them his support."

Barnaby nodded. "Home as in Galbraith House in Hanover Square?"

Carradale's brows rose. "So I assumed. I can't imagine he'd be thinking of transporting three females all having hysterics down to Sussex anytime soon. Regardless, he took a hackney. I had my man get it for him." Turning, Carradale called, "Johns! What address did Mr. Galbraith give the hackney driver?"

From the rear of the hall, Johns replied, "Hanover Square, m'lord."

"So there you are." Carradale looked at Barnaby, then at Stokes. "I hope you find whoever did for Galbraith's mother, Inspector. I didn't know her at all, but Galbraith is a decent chap, and things like this shouldn't happen to such as him."

Studying Carradale's steady, if faintly bloodshot, gaze, Stokes inclined his head. "With luck and help from the right quarters, we will."

Carradale's lips lifted in a fleeting—stunningly beautiful—smile, then he straightened and reached for the door. Pausing, he looked at Barnaby, then his lips lifted once more and he drawled, "Marriage clearly suits you, Adair. No doubt I'll see you around the traps."

Barnaby raised a hand in salute. He and Stokes turned away as Carradale shut the door.

"Hanover Square?" Stokes said.

"Indeed," Barnaby replied.

* * *

$\mathcal{G}$albraith House was a substantial family home that communicated a sense of quiet prosperity. Sitting in the middle of a long line of similar houses lining the west side of Hanover Square, the only feature that distinguished it from any of its neighbors was the fact that the curtains in all the windows facing the street were drawn. That and a sense of stillness, of the lack of any movement within.

Despite the pervasive feeling that they were intruding unforgivably, Stokes and Barnaby climbed the steps to the porch and rang the bell. They could hear it echo hollowly inside.

Several minutes passed before footsteps neared, then an elderly butler who looked as if he hadn't slept all night opened the door and tiredly asked, "Yes?"

Stokes showed his police identification, and Barnaby handed over one of his calling cards. They were left to wait in the front hall for less than a minute before being shown into a room that was plainly the library.

Behind a desk, Hartley Galbraith rose to his feet. "Thank you, Millwell," he said to the butler, then waved Barnaby and Stokes to the chairs before the desk. "Mr. Adair. Inspector." As Barnaby and Stokes sat, Hartley said, "I'm afraid my father is currently indisposed."

Subsiding into the chair behind the desk, Hartley went on, "My mother's death has been a huge blow to us all, of course, but to my father most of all. He—they—were devoted, and he's taken it very hard. The doctor has given him a sleeping draft, and he's lying down upstairs…" Hartley dragged in a tight breath; his hands, linked on the blotter, clenched tight. "So if there's anything you need to know, perhaps you'll allow me to stand in his shoes for the moment, at least until he recovers enough to…well, make sense."

Hartley's voice was passably even, but a tremor of exhaustion, compounded by shock and sorrow, lay beneath. His face—handsome with long planes and well-set features—was wan and etched with concern, and the expression in his eyes was harrowed.

Both Stokes and Barnaby had been studying Hartley, absorbing each sign, every little clue projected by how he looked and moved, how he spoke, his tone.

His gaze steady on Hartley's face, Stokes quietly said, "Actually, Mr. Galbraith, it's you we've come to see."

Hartley's eyes widened. "Oh?" There was an instant's pause, as if Hartley looked beyond them and debated how to respond; both Barnaby and Stokes noted it. But then Hartley refocused, raised his chin fractionally and, his gaze steady again—indeed, more controlled than previously—said, "In that case, how may I help you?"

Stokes glanced at Barnaby. Understanding the implied suggestion, Barnaby opened his mouth—

A rap on the library door had him pause.

Hartley grimaced. "Excuse me." Looking faintly harassed, he called, "Come!"

The rumpled elderly butler came in, a black silk shawl overflowing his hands. "I'm sorry to interrupt, Mr. Hartley, but Mrs. Forecastle is insisting we must put black ribbon on the knocker—that it's scandalous that we haven't already done so—but we don't have any black ribbon in the house. Tabitha, Miss Geraldine's maid, wondered if this might do." The butler held up the shawl.

Hartley stared blankly at the shawl…then, weakly, he waved. "Yes, Millwell." His voice sounded distant and somewhat strained. "Use that for now, and ask Mrs. Forecastle if she can send one of the maids out for…however many yards of black ribbon she thinks we need."

"Yes, sir. Thank you, sir." Millwell bowed, turned, and plodded toward the door. "Oh." Pausing, the old butler turned back to Hartley. "And Miss Primrose and Miss Monica's elocution master has arrived." When Hartley looked even more blank, Millwell added, "For their weekly lesson, sir. We—Mrs. Forecastle and I—wondered if you wanted them to be summoned, although I don't know what good that will do, as both are exhausted, what with all their weeping, and can barely speak at all. Or should we send Mr. Phineas away?"

"Send him away," Hartley said.

"Very good, sir." The butler bowed, straightened, but then simply stood there, staring vaguely into space.

Hartley drew in a steadying breath. "Is there anything else, Millwell?"

There was—a veritable litany of minor household decisions, ranging from how many Cook should expect to sit down to dinner that evening, to the advisability of getting in an extra dozen bottles of the port Lord Galbraith favored.

Barnaby watched Hartley Galbraith keep a tight rein on his own emotions and deal with the old servitor with a degree of patience that was remarkable under the circumstances. That Hartley's presence was essential in providing a steady hand on the household tiller was demonstrably true.

At last, Millwell's querulous queries were all dealt with, and he plodded out of the room.

As the door closed, Hartley exhaled, then he refocused on Barnaby and Stokes. "My apologies. As you can see, the household is at sixes and sevens. The staff are as shocked as the family. While my father and sisters are prostrated, the staff seem paralyzed and unable to deal with all the minor matters they would normally take in their stride."

It was a compassionate exculpation, one neatly made without drawing attention to the fact that Hartley was the only member of his family making any effort to hold the fort.

Clasping his hands before him, Hartley settled his somewhat grave attention on Barnaby. "I'm sorry. You were about to say…?"

Barnaby wasn't sure that he was happy the interruptions had occurred—and given him and Stokes a better understanding of Hartley Galbraith's position in the family—but Barnaby was certain that the interruptions and their inevitable coloring of Hartley's character hadn't been staged. After a second's consideration, he said, "We wanted to ask whether you had had any recent disagreements with your mother."

Hartley's eyes widened fractionally, but he shook his head. "No. None." He paused, then added, "I'm nearly thirty years old. I haven't lived under this roof for quite some time."

Which was something of a non sequitur.

"But you're residing here now," Stokes observed.

"For the moment." Hartley paused, then said, "It's only temporary. I just threw a few things in a bag last night—well, early this morning—and came here." He gestured to the door. "As you saw, someone has to deal with things. My father wouldn't be able to, anyway, and my sisters aren't up to coping."

Barnaby searched, but found no hint of anything resembling guilt in Hartley's demeanor. Of course, Hartley might have a very good poker face. To test that hypothesis, Barnaby ventured, "We were given to understand that you're in the process of organizing your affairs."

Hartley was stunned, yet the only change in his near-blank expression—Hartley's way of hiding the emotions evoked by his mother's death, Barnaby realized—was a faint widening of his eyes and a slackening of his otherwise rigidly controlled jaw. After a long moment, Hartley blinked, then, refocusing on Barnaby, he nodded. "Yes. I'm expecting to make a formal offer for a lady's hand very soon." He paused for only a second before adding, "And, please, do keep that under your hats for the moment. I haven't yet told my family or, indeed, anyone else, other than my man-of-business. My intended and I..." Hartley paused, then gave a faint sigh. "There are reasons she and I have thus far kept our attachment a secret, although we consider ourselves betrothed."

An awkward silence ensued while the obvious question hung in the air, then Stokes simply voiced it. "Why the secrecy? Do you have any reason to believe that your family wouldn't approve?"

Frustration flashed briefly in Hartley's face, then he considered them again, but as if he were examining them, evaluating and deciding whether or not he could trust them. Barnaby got that impression quite clearly, that he and Stokes were being weighed with regard to their discretion.

Then Hartley grimaced; his features eased, his shoulders and spine slumped from their previous rigidity. He sighed, rubbed his eyes with one hand, then said, "I know I should have told you this straightaway—as soon as it happened—and even more later, when you questioned us...my only excuse is that I was so shocked I couldn't think. I couldn't decide what to do for the best." His gaze now openly weary, he met Stokes's, then Barnaby's eyes. "It wasn't only me— wasn't only Mama—involved, you see."

Stokes frowned, but kept his voice unchallenging as he asked, "Involved in what?"

"What happened last night in Lady Fairchild's garden." Re-clasping his hands on the blotter, Hartley went on, "Let me tell it from the beginning. I arrived at the ball with my family. My intended was already there with her family. We'd arranged to meet in the folly overlooking the ornamental lake. As soon as we spotted each other in the crowd, she left the ballroom. I waited for five minutes or so, then I followed her out to the garden."

"So a tryst," Stokes said.

"No." Hartley's lips firmed. "At least, not in the sense you're implying. We met to discuss what our next steps should be. As you've already learned, I was getting my affairs in order preparatory to making a formal offer. She, too, has had to keep our attachment a secret from her family. We decided a few weeks ago that we'd had enough of secrecy. We've been working out, step by step, how best to break the news to both our families..." Hartley paused, then, voice firming, went on, "We decided some time ago that we wanted to be married by my thirtieth birthday, which now is only a few months away. We decided to hold to that date, to use it as a deadline by which to achieve what we've set our hearts upon."

Hartley stopped. Then his expression hardened. "But you need to know what happened last night, and I'm rambling. As I said, my intended had left the ballroom, and I went out to meet with her. She and I both know how events such as the Fairchilds' ball unfold—we knew we'd be safe if we met in the garden early. Later, and there would have been more people about, so that's why we'd arranged to meet at that particular time."

"When you got to the folly," Barnaby asked, "was she there?"

Hartley nodded. "Yes. She was waiting, as I'd expected." He looked at Barnaby. "You'll understand that she could only safely be out of the ballroom for about twenty minutes without risking someone noticing and commenting, raising questions we would rather not have asked, so we had to make the moments count. We talked. We went over where we were and what our next steps needed to be, then we headed back to the house."

Stokes's brows rose. "Together?"

Hartley hesitated, then, lips tight, inclined his head. "Our families are acquainted. If I was seen escorting her in from the garden, it wouldn't cause any great consternation. The assumption would be that I was being chivalrous."

"Family friends?" Barnaby slipped in.

Hartley nodded before he could catch himself. Lips twisting, he confirmed, "As you say. Regardless, no one would expect to hear of our betrothal."

Before Barnaby could think of the right question with which to pursue the identity of Hartley's intended, Hartley continued, "So we walked back to the house together." His gaze grew distant, as if he were back in the garden, seeing what he had then. "We came over the bank above the lake, still well away from the house but following the path to the side terrace—we'd both come out that way. We looked ahead..." Locked in the vision only he could see, Hartley paled. After a second, he swallowed and, his voice growing hollow, went on, "My mother was standing on the path below the terrace. We could see her quite clearly—she wasn't in shadow, as we were. We were under the trees bordering the path at that point, and there was an overhanging branch that blocked the terrace itself from our sight, but Mama was down on the path, and we could see her."

Neither Stokes nor Barnaby said a word. Neither so much as blinked.

Without prompting, his expression no longer blank but instead filling with mounting horror, Hartley continued, "Just as we saw her, she turned to look up at the terrace, toward the top of the steps..." Hartley's voice suspended. After a second, still patently lost in the awfulness of the memory, he dragged in a breath and, his voice hoarse, said, "We saw the ball fall and strike her down."

He'd only just managed to get the words out. Neither Stokes nor Barnaby interrupted; neither shifted their sharp gazes from Hartley's face.

Hartley bowed his head for a moment, then dragged in another tortured breath and, raising his head, looked at them, anguish etched in his eyes. "We froze. Both of us. You know how it is, in that instant when something you can't believe could possibly happen occurs before your eyes. Then both of us started forward. We rushed out of the trees. But there was nothing we could do. She was already dead."

Hartley's gaze dropped to his hands, the fingers tightly clenched, knuckles showing white; he stared at them, but Barnaby doubted he was seeing anything, at least nothing in the here and now.

Glancing at Stokes, Barnaby found his friend looking his way. He read the question in Stokes's eyes and nodded. Returning his gaze to Hartley, Barnaby gently asked, "Did you see anything—hear anything—of the person who dropped the stone ball?"

Hartley blinked. Slowly, he raised his eyes, but his gaze remained distant as, frowning, he grimaced. "We both did—and more than anything else, that's why I didn't raise the alarm or say anything to anyone last night. I simply couldn't understand what it meant." He paused, then, in an empty voice, added, "I still don't."

Stokes had his notebook out and was scribbling. He glanced pointedly at Barnaby.

Quietly, Barnaby asked, "What did you see?"

"I saw—we both saw—a lady's shoes and the swish of her hem as she went quickly back inside." Hartley finally refocused on Stokes and Barnaby. "You have to remember we were on the bank, above the stone steps leading down to the path in front of the side terrace. Our eyes were level, more or less, with the terrace's flagstones. The glimpse we caught was through the stone balusters. There was moonlight at the time, enough to see anyone on the terrace itself, but the shadow of the house closed in around the door and the little hall beyond, and the corridor, too, were unlit. The woman—the lady—was disappearing into darkness, but the last thing to pass into shadow was the flicking hem of her gown and the backs of her shoes."

Barnaby was frowning. "You said you couldn't understand what you saw. It seems plain enough. A lady dropped a stone ball onto your mother's head and killed her."

Hartley met Barnaby's eyes; Hartley's gaze was direct and rock steady. "No—or, rather, yes, but that's not all. Not the part that's so confounding." He paused, then said, "The shoes. They were Lady Latimer's shoes."

* * *

*I*t took the combined descriptive powers of Barnaby and Hartley Galbraith a good ten minutes to impart to Stokes the full meaning of the term "Lady Latimer's shoes."

Even then, Stokes remained incredulous. He stared at Hartley. "So although you saw a lady wearing a pair of these Lady Latimer's shoes leaving the scene of the murder less than a minute after you had seen your mother struck down, that doesn't mean that it was Lady Latimer who murdered your mother."

"No." Lips compressing, Hartley paused, then conceded, "But as far as I know, logically speaking, the lady must have been either Lady Latimer or one of her four daughters, but even that I can't—simply *don't*—believe."

Settling back in his chair, Barnaby studied Hartley's face. "Why?" When Hartley glanced at him, Barnaby elaborated, "Why do you find that so hard to believe?" Blessing Penelope's investigative skill and the fact that she had not only learned all about Lady Latimer's shoes and the resulting inter-family feud but had also thought to explain the whole to him, he added, "I understand that there's no love lost between your families."

Hartley blinked, then slowly shook his head. "That's…not really the case." He met Barnaby's gaze, then briefly glanced at Stokes, before looking back at Barnaby. "You need to understand that the feud, as people call it, was entirely of my mother's making. Aunt

Hester—Lady Latimer—is the kindest soul, but Mama's demand to be given access to the shoes placed her—Aunt Hester—in an invidious position. Mama refused to see that. She and she alone was the architect of the feud. For the rest of us?' Hartley shrugged. "Even my sisters weren't all that concerned. Yes, they would have liked to have had Lady Latimer's shoes, but they were happy enough to wait. Aunt Hester told them from the first that of course she would make them— my sisters and my mother, too—gifts of Lady Latimer's shoes as soon as her own daughters were on the way to being settled." Hartley glanced at Stokes. "In ton terms, that was fair dealing."

Stokes still wasn't sure he fully appreciated the importance of Lady Latimer's shoes and, indeed, wasn't at all sure he wished to— shoes, for heaven's sake—yet when it came to the ton and matters of family, he was long past the age of being surprised. "You refer to Lady Latimer as Aunt Hester. Why?"

Hartley's jaw tightened. "We're not related by blood, but if anything, the ties go deeper. Mama and Lady Latimer—Aunt Hester— grew up together in the country. They were neighbors. They made their come-outs together, were chief attendant at each other's wedding, and through all the years, our families have been very close. We—the children—were one big tribe. We were in and out of each other's houses all the time." Hartley angled his head toward the front of the house. "The Latimers' town house is just across the square, almost directly opposite. And in summer we were always together, either at their country house in Surrey or at ours in Sussex." He paused, then added, "I consider the Latimers family. So do my sisters and my father. In instigating and then perpetuating the feud, Mama trampled rough-shod over all our feelings. We tried to remonstrate, but she refused to listen. She'd caught a bee in her bonnet and was not about to let it go. Courtesy of my mother's actions, my sisters have been cut off from their closest friends for the past year and more."

Hartley hesitated, then more quietly said, "The feud hurt us all, us just as much as the Latimers, but caught in her obsession, Mama refused to even see that, much less consider it."

A short silence fell, then Hartley stirred and looked at Stokes.

Glancing down at his notebook, Stokes asked, "The young lady—your intended. Her name?"

Hartley debated; Barnaby noted that Hartley's expression had grown easier to read the more he focused on facts and not emotions. Eventually, Hartley said, "If it should become necessary, I will give you her name, but until that time, I would prefer not to reveal it. As I mentioned, we are striving to break the news of our betrothal to our families in the least disruptive way, so…no. Not at this moment." His gaze on Hartley's face, Stokes considered that.

Hartley didn't wilt. Instead, he offered, "The most she can do is corroborate all that I've told you. She was by my side throughout those minutes, so saw no more than I did. Unless you truly doubt my word, there's little point in me telling you her name." He hesitated, then added, "And regardless of all else, I see no reason why she should be subjected to an unnecessary inquisition."

Stokes's lips quirked cynically at that "inquisition," but after a second of further deliberation, he inclined his head. "Very well. For the moment, I will allow you your veil of secrecy. However, if we do need her testimony, and most likely at some point we will, then we will ask again, and you will need to answer."

Hartley acknowledged the concession with a nod. "Thank you, Inspector."

Barnaby unfolded his long legs and rose.

Stuffing his notebook into his pocket, Stokes got to his feet, too. They parted from Hartley Galbraith on equable terms. Millwell, appearing even more distracted than he had earlier, showed them out and shut the door on their heels.

Glancing back at the door, Barnaby saw that the knocker was now decently swathed in black silk. Facing forward, he said, "I have to own to a rabid curiosity over who Galbraith's intended is."

Halting on the pavement, Stokes humphed. "Just ask your wife. I'm sure she'll work it out in three blinks." A second passed, then he glanced at Barnaby. "Speaking of which…"

Barnaby grinned. "Indeed. We may as well accept the inevitable and head directly to Albemarle Street. There's no sense in going all the way back to the Yard just to read the note-cum-summons that, no doubt, is by now residing on your blotter."

Stokes sighed and raised an arm to hail the hackney just rounding the square. "Any bets that Griselda and Megan are already there—and Violet and Montague, too?"

"Not Violet and Montague." Barnaby opened the door of the hackney as it drew to a halt before them; waving Stokes in, he met his gaze. "It's too early for them, but I'm sure they'll arrive in good time for dinner."

Stokes laughed and climbed in. Grinning, Barnaby looked up at the jarvey. "Number twenty-four, Albemarle Street." Then he followed Stokes into the carriage.

CHAPTER 5

𝒫enelope felt positively virtuous. She had spent most of the day slaving diligently over the translation the British Museum had commissioned. She was making good progress; Violet would be pleased.

Her mother, the Dowager Viscountess Calverton, had called early in the afternoon, and Penelope had allowed herself to be distracted enough to take tea and to have all she'd learned about the Galbraiths and Latimers confirmed by her most trusted source on such matters. Yet after seeing her mother into her carriage, she had dutifully returned to her desk and her Greek scribe; in the late afternoon, she had attended the Royal Society lecture as she had promised, before returning once more to her desk.

Now, her metaphorical halo glowing, she settled on one of the twin sofas in her drawing room and prepared to indulge in her reward—dissecting all the information Barnaby, Stokes, and Montague had thus far assembled, ferreting out what clues they had found, and deciding where next to search. "Right, then." She looked around eagerly—at Griselda, sinking onto the sofa beside her, at Montague and Violet seated on the sofa opposite, and, finally, at Stokes in one of the armchairs flanking the fireplace and Barnaby in its mate. "Where should we start?"

"At the beginning," Montague said. "Neither Violet nor I—nor, I suspect, Griselda—have heard a full accounting of the murder." Even as the words left his lips, Montague wondered at himself; there he was, seated alongside his lovely wife and inviting others who were long accustomed to dealing with crime to sully her ears with gruesome details. Then he glanced at Violet's face, took in her expression—every bit as eager as Penelope's—and reminded himself that Violet's happiness was his principal goal, conservative protectiveness be damned.

"I think that's my cue." Stretching out his long legs, Barnaby collected his thoughts, then began. "One of my cousins, Hugo, found the body when he went outside to smoke. He came and found me." Concisely, Barnaby described the body and all he and Penelope had noted about the site and the body itself, and what they had consequently deduced.

Stokes was nodding. "So whoever the murderer is, they were almost certainly one of Lady Fairchild's guests."

"But her guest list for that evening is enormous," Penelope put in, "so combing through it trying to identify the murderer isn't a way we want to go."

Stokes grunted. "We've made some advance on the murderer's identity, but as we're not up to that yet, let's continue with our recapitulation."

Barnaby duly described the Galbraith family and what he and Stokes had learned from the interviews carried out in the Fairchilds' drawing room.

"Precious little," Stokes muttered.

Barnaby inclined his head and continued, ending with, "However, all of them did deny going outside at any time." Having completed that section of their report, he cocked a brow at Penelope.

She sat straighter and lifted her chin. "I stayed in the drawing room long enough to confirm that all the Galbraiths' reactions rang true. I didn't detect anything unexpected in the way they responded to the news. Subsequently, I went back to the ballroom and questioned a group of Lady Galbraith's friends."

In short order, she outlined what she'd learned about the feud between the Galbraith and Latimer families. "After that, I made straight for the Latimers." She briefly described the family and all she'd observed and deduced about them. "And later I had a chance to speak to some of the grandes dames, and they gave me the ton's view on Lady Latimer's shoes, Lady Latimer's stance regarding Lady Galbraith's demand, and the resulting feud."

Frowning slightly in concentration, Penelope recounted the pertinent details of the conversation. "And finally," she concluded, "Lady Fairchild pointed out that, despite there being no connection between Lady Latimer's shoes and Lady Galbraith's murder, society being what it is, fingers will soon enough be pointed at Lady Latimer and her family."

Ending with a brisk nod, Penelope looked around the group—and discovered that Stokes and Barnaby were regarding her rather grimly. "What is it?"

Stokes grimaced. He glanced at Barnaby, then said, "Let's continue to take this step by step." Stokes looked at Montague. "As our first foray this morning, Barnaby and I called on Montague and asked him to check the Galbraith's finances, thinking to at least eliminate money as a motive." Stokes looked at the others. "While Montague was doing that, Barnaby and I returned to Fairchild House and interviewed the staff. No one saw Lady Galbraith leave the ballroom, or go out onto the terrace, and none of the staff noticed her having any altercation or even a conversation with anyone. However, thanks be, we turned up a footman who'd been serving champagne in the ballroom and had seen Mr. Hartley Galbraith leave the ballroom and go outside via the side terrace."

"So Hartley lied about going outside." Griselda frowned. "Did he go outside before or after his mother?"

"Before." Stokes glanced at the notebook he'd extracted from his pocket and was balancing on his knee. "This was quite early in the evening—about half past nine."

Violet asked, "Do we have any idea of when, exactly, her ladyship met her end?"

Stokes looked at Barnaby. "From your description when you first found her and what I saw when I got there, I'd say she was killed around ten o'clock."

Fingers steepled before his face, Barnaby nodded. "I agree. But as it happens, we got confirmation of the time later." He looked at Penelope and Griselda. "After learning that Hartley had gone out via the terrace yet had denied doing so during our interview in the Fairchilds' drawing room, a second interview with him was in order, but first we stopped at Montague's to steer him more specifically toward Hartley." Barnaby looked at Montague. "And…"

"It so happened that I had already received information on Hartley Galbraith's recent financial activity." Montague paused, amused by the way both Penelope and Griselda hung on his words, waiting…

Violet flicked his arm with her fingers. "Stop teasing." She looked at Penelope and Griselda. "Hartley Galbraith was putting his affairs in order, most likely either in pursuit of a business venture or because he planned to make an offer for some lady's hand."

Penelope blinked, then swung her gaze to Stokes. "And..."

Stokes grinned at her imperious tone. "And so we went and asked him which it was. But first we had to track him down." With a nod, Stokes passed the reporting baton to Barnaby.

"Hartley had given an address in Jermyn Street." Barnaby glanced at Penelope. "Near where I used to live. As it transpired, Hartley wasn't there, but his landlord, Lord Carradale, was." Briefly, Barnaby recounted their conversation with Carradale. "For all his faults, Carradale is someone I would class as acutely observant and very hard to gull. If Carradale says Hartley was deeply cut up over his mother's death, then he was."

"I also got the impression that Carradale liked Galbraith—that he would consider him a friend," Stokes put in.

Barnaby nodded. "Indeed. Which tells us something of Hartley's character." Barnaby paused, then went on, "As Hartley had gone to stay in Hanover Square, we trundled around there and soon had his stated reason for returning home confirmed—Hartley is holding the household together entirely by himself."

Stokes snorted. "I wasn't expecting to approve of the man, much less respect him, but unless he's the greatest actor ever born, he truly is struggling to hold his family together over what is unquestionably a terrible time. His father is prostrate, and so are his sisters."

"I would have to agree," Barnaby said. "I went there thinking that Hartley might be our murderer, but by the time we left...even his excuses for not speaking at the Fairchilds'—that he was in shock and couldn't think and was stunned by the implications—rang true. And, of course, there was the tale he had to tell, which is simply so dramatic and fits the other facts we've learned so well that, despite wanting to be suspicious of him and his account, I found myself believing it."

Stokes reluctantly nodded.

Penelope looked from one to the other. "What tale? *Was* Hartley out in the garden when his mother was murdered?"

"Yes, he was." Succinctly, Barnaby recounted all that Hartley had divulged.

The others stared.

Predictably, Penelope recovered first. "So he saw his mother murdered?"

Barnaby nodded. "And assuming he's telling the truth, so did his intended."

All six fell silent, dwelling on what Hartley and his mysterious intended must have seen.

After a moment, frowning, Montague looked at Penelope. "It would help if I knew what these Lady Latimer's shoes looked like." Stokes grunted in agreement.

Penelope grimaced. "I really should have thought to take a closer look when I spoke with the Latimers last night, but from all I've heard, in style the shoes are ordinary ballroom pumps, but their fabric is embroidered with metallic thread, and then crystals are stuck on in various patterns. As I understand it, getting the crystals to stick is the difficulty—normally crystals don't stay stuck on fabric or leather, especially not in the atmosphere of a ballroom and with the flexing of shoes while dancing. At the beginning of last year when Lady Latimer's shoes first became all the rage, others tried to copy the effect, but their crystals fell off and got under everyone's feet and scratched the floors. Ultimately, all such attempts ended in disaster."

Violet tilted her head, clearly visualizing such shoes. "So imagining what Hartley and his intended saw, given there was moonlight, I could see the crystals flashing on the shoes and drawing their eyes as the lady disappeared into the house."

"Actually," Penelope said, "that's another point—did Hartley notice what color the shoes were?" Immediately upon voicing the question, she grimaced. "He didn't, did he?"

Barnaby met her gaze. "Given the quality of the light at the time, even had he noticed, I doubt he could have distinguished any color beyond 'light' or 'dark.'"

"We might get more information from his intended," Penelope said. "Clearly at some point you will have to interview her." Seeing Stokes's and Montague's puzzled looks, she elucidated, "Generally, ballroom pumps are covered in the same fabric as the gown with which they're worn. A light-colored gown could be worn by anyone, but a dark material would not be worn by a young lady, and only certain matrons wear darker hues, so if we knew the color, it would reduce the suspects."

Griselda shifted to look at Penelope. "Can you remember the colors of the gowns the Latimer ladies were wearing last night?"

Penelope closed her eyes and reeled off the names, along with the relevant color and style of gown.

When she opened her eyes again, Griselda grinned. "I see your point."

"Indeed, but as we don't know the color of the shoes, and as Barnaby says, the quality of the light wasn't conducive to identifying any hue accurately—" Penelope broke off as Mostyn entered. She arched her brows. "Dinner?"

Mostyn bowed. "Indeed, ma'am. Dinner is served."

The six had developed the habit of putting aside their investigative deliberations over their shared meals, the better to appreciate the food and each other's company. By general consensus, the next hour and a half was filled with conversation on more pleasant subjects.

But immediately the meal was over, and they were settled once more in what had rapidly become their accustomed positions in the drawing room, all refocused on the crime that lay before them, waiting to be solved.

"Can I suggest," Stokes said, "that we take our usual approach and list what we feel we know about the events leading up to and immediately following the murder?"

"And then see what questions that leads to." Penelope nodded. "I second the motion."

Along with the others, she looked at Barnaby, who was usually the most concise in drawing the disparate threads of an investigation together. Settling in his armchair, he accepted the unvoiced invitation. "The first relevant fact is that Hartley Galbraith left the Fairchilds' ballroom at about half past nine. He was seen going out onto the side terrace and down the steps into the garden. We don't know when Lady Galbraith left the ballroom—earlier or later—but if it had been earlier, her daughters would most likely have noticed." Brows rising, Barnaby met Stokes's eyes. "Indeed, it's unlikely that Lady Galbraith *could* have quit the ballroom before Hartley. That would have meant her disappearing very soon after she'd arrived, and with three unmarried daughters present, one of whom is not even formally out, that would certainly have been noticed, by her daughters if no one else."

Stokes lightly shrugged. "I'll take your word for that."

Fleetingly, Barnaby grinned. "So…Lady Galbraith most likely left the ballroom sometime after her son. We don't know why she left, what reason she had for going out onto the terrace and subsequently down onto the path. We have no sightings of anyone else leaving the ballroom, but it's entirely possible that someone could have."

"Someone did," Penelope said. "From our wander around the garden, it's difficult to see how anyone could have come from outside and calmly climbed up to the terrace in order to drop that stone ball on Lady Galbraith. But *someone* must have met Lady Galbraith outside, either on the terrace or on the path below."

Barnaby nodded. "And all indications are that that someone came from the ball, from the ballroom."

"But," Penelope said, "surely the critical point is what moved Lady Galbraith to go outside. Was she alone when she left the ballroom? Or was her killer with her?" Penelope glanced at Stokes. "She couldn't have been killed in the manner she was if she hadn't been out on the path—so why was she there?"

Violet frowned. "Might she have followed Hartley?" She met Penelope's eyes. "To see where he was going, who he was meeting in the gardens."

Penelope blinked. "You mean she noticed... Well, yes, that's possible, isn't it?" She glanced around the circle. "Lady Galbraith might well have noticed Hartley slipping away to meet secretly with someone. If she suspected something of a clandestine nature was going on—and she sounds like the sort to leap to the conclusion that he'd formed a tendre for someone entirely unsuitable—then at the Fairchilds' ball, she might have been watching him, and when she saw him slipping away so very early, she naturally went after him." Behind her spectacles, Penelope's eyes gleamed. "*And* that would explain why she so cavalierly abandoned her three daughters, leaving them to fend for themselves. In Lady Galbraith's eyes, Hartley, her firstborn and her husband's heir, and who he is to marry, would unquestionably take precedence over her daughters' futures."

Barnaby frowned. "All right—so now we have Hartley leaving the ballroom at about half past nine to meet with his intended, who is already waiting in the folly by the lake. And Lady Galbraith follows him...why didn't she go further? Because Hartley saw her and stopped and confronted her?"

Stokes stirred. He caught Barnaby's eye. "That raises a rather disturbing possibility. At present, we have only Hartley Galbraith's word for what he says happened. What if, instead, Lady Galbraith came after him and caught up with both him *and* his intended on the path below the terrace, or even as they were returning to the house. There's a confrontation—there's some reason Hartley and his intended have kept their attachment a secret, after all—and Lady Galbraith declares that she will never allow Hartley to marry the lady—over her dead body and all that. Leaving Hartley and his mother on the path, the lady involved storms up the steps, then, in a fury, she pauses at the top, picks up the stone ball, and drops it on Lady Galbraith's head."

Feeling rather pleased with his hypothesis, Stokes refocused on Griselda and Penelope, then, when they said nothing but just looked steadily back at him, he glanced at Violet, but she, too, remained silent. Unconvinced. "What?" Stokes said, straightening in his chair.

Rather primly, Penelope said, "I really don't think any young lady would imagine that killing her mother-in-law-to-be in front of her prospective husband was likely to smooth her path into matrimony."

"Ah." Stokes held up a hand. "But we don't know what Hartley's relationship with his mother was. We do know that he hasn't lived at home for years—perhaps there was some deep antipathy between them? Regardless, I can't see him as being the sort to kill his own mother, but perhaps his intended knew how the land lay, and that removing Lady Galbraith wouldn't, ultimately, turn Hartley against her—especially if his mother was determined to stand in the way of their marriage."

"And we have to remember," Montague said, "that Hartley did not report his mother's death. He left the body lying on the path, returned to the ballroom, and kept mum."

The ladies remained patently unconvinced, and even Barnaby didn't look swayed. "Hartley," Barnaby said, "claimed that he didn't report finding the body because he was so shocked by what he'd seen that he couldn't think past the conundrum posed by the lady fleeing the terrace wearing Lady Latimer's shoes."

"I would think," Penelope said, tilting her head as she considered, "that given his lifelong connection with the Latimers, for him, seeing a lady wearing those shoes in that setting would create something of an emotional clash." She paused, then added, "I can understand why he might have been unable, then and there, to decide what to do."

"But," Violet said, frowning slightly, "returning to Stokes's point about us only having Hartley's word about what he saw, do we even know that he and his intended saw Lady Latimer's shoes at all? Or is that pure invention, in the circumstances the perfect suggestion to divert the investigation into an arena that will likely be rife with possibilities, given that all the Latimer ladies were at the ball?"

"Come to that," Stokes said, "if you entertain the notion that what Hartley told us is a fabrication, we also have no reason to believe that his intended exists, and that it wasn't he, himself, and no one else, who murdered his mother."

A pause ensued, then Penelope grimaced. "Well, against that we have yours, Barnaby's, and Carradale's readings of Hartley as an honest and honorable man. On the other hand, no one else was seen leaving or returning to the ballroom, but that hardly means no one did."

Montague stirred. "I feel compelled to point out that Hartley's tale of having an intended meshes with him putting his affairs in order."

"True," Penelope said. "And, what's more, there's another hole in the theory that either Hartley or his intended felt moved to kill his mother. Namely that, as Hartley is nearly thirty years old, who he decides to marry is not subject to his mother's approval." Penelope looked at Montague. "I assume Hartley is independent enough financially to marry whom he pleases?"

Montague nodded. "That would be my understanding."

"So," Penelope expounded, "although Lady Galbraith might have created a great deal of unpleasantness and fuss, she couldn't have prevented Hartley from marrying his intended. Thus, from either Hartley's or his intended's point of view, killing Lady Galbraith would not have been in their best interests. Indeed, it's hard to see what might have motivated them—and if one is involved, then both are—to do such a thing."

Barnaby shifted, stretching out his long legs and crossing his ankles. "I would have to agree. However, that said, we all know that the motive for murder can be, at first glance, very obscure." Meeting Penelope's eyes, he said, "As much as I'm inclined to believe Hartley, at this point I don't think we can accept his version of events as uncontestable fact."

Penelope wrinkled her nose. "All right." She paused, her gaze growing distant as she rapidly reviewed their findings, then she refocused. "Either Hartley is lying, or he's telling the truth. If he's lying, then either he or his intended killed his mother—for some as-yet obscure reason—and subsequently Hartley concealed the crime. If that is the case, then his story of seeing a lady wearing Lady Latimer's shoes leaving the terrace immediately after his mother had been struck down is pure invention, a distracting smokescreen with no basis in fact."

Barnaby nodded. "Thus far, that's sound."

Penelope inclined her head. "Which leaves us with the

alternative—that everything Hartley told you and Stokes is the unvarnished truth."

"And that means," Griselda said, "that the murderer is a lady wearing Lady Latimer's shoes who followed Lady Galbraith out of the ballroom and onto the side terrace. From there, the lady dropped the stone ball on Lady Galbraith's head, then turned and walked quickly back into the house."

"Ah—but did the lady in Lady Latimer's shoes commit the murder?" Violet asked. "Or did she follow someone else—or perhaps she came out intending to speak with Lady Galbraith but someone else was before her—and so she, the lady in Lady Latimer's shoes, saw the murderer drop the ball on Lady Galbraith's head? That might have been why the lady in the shoes rushed back into the ballroom and said nothing about the murder—she might have recognized the murderer and been frightened. As for the murderer..." Violet paused, then asked, "I know you said it was unlikely that the murderer could have reached the terrace above Lady Galbraith if the murderer had come via the gardens, but could the murderer have come from the ballroom and left via the gardens?"

Penelope, Stokes, and Barnaby exchanged glances, then Penelope pulled a face at Violet. "I hate it when we have a multitude of perfectly believable but entirely different scenarios for a murder."

Violet shrugged. "The question had to be asked."

Stokes was frowning. "If the lady in the shoes saw the murderer and was frightened of him, surely the safest thing she could do is tell the authorities what she saw."

A pause ensued while the others considered, then Penelope sighed. "In any other case, yes, but in this one? We have to assume, as I believe Hartley has, that the lady he and his intended saw fleeing the terrace is one of the Latimer ladies. And that being so, then no—to her, telling the authorities would not feature as her wisest course. If she speaks up, she stands a very good chance of being accused of Lady Galbraith's murder, and regardless of any facts, that *would* be the ton's verdict."

Stokes growled, "Why is it that murders within the ton are *never* straightforward?"

Barnaby grinned fleetingly. "You love the challenge."

Stokes grunted. "So what are our questions, and what do we do next?"

A lively discussion ensued. It was decided that Stokes and

Barnaby would check with the police surgeon to verify the time of Lady Galbraith's death and also that it was, as everyone had assumed, the ball falling on her ladyship's head that had crushed her skull enough to kill her. Such details, Penelope pointed out, were important. Montague was delegated to look more deeply into Hartley Galbraith's finances to eliminate any other possible motive lurking there. He also volunteered to confirm the financial bona fides of the Latimers, given that, quite aside from the existence of the feud, the lady on the terrace, assuming she was real, had drawn the family into the investigation.

For their part, Penelope, Violet, and Griselda exchanged glances and merely agreed to meet on the morrow to define what investigative areas they might best address. Their husbands eyed them with a certain wariness, but did not venture any comment.

The evening broke up shortly afterward. A sense of camaraderie and expectation, of shared purpose and determination, followed the six into the front hall. Hettie, who had been watching over Megan, Stokes and Griselda's barely one-year-old daughter, in the nursery, was summoned and brought the swaddled, peacefully sleeping bundle down. Griselda took Megan, and Penelope and Violet gathered around to peek and then drop soft kisses on one delicate rosy cheek.

Stokes looked proud and hovered protectively. Barnaby and Montague smiled.

Eventually, Penelope and Barnaby stood at the top of their front steps and waved the other couples, each in their own carriage, away.

Returning into the warmth and light of the front hall, Penelope paused, head tilted; her gaze grew abstracted, a frown slowly crimping her dark brows.

Barnaby halted beside her. He studied her expression, then reached for her hand and twined his fingers with hers. "What is it? Don't try to tell me you're not thrilled to have another case you can help investigate."

Penelope blinked. "Heavens, no—it's not that." Glancing up, she met Barnaby's eyes. "I was just thinking that my maxim about such investigations is continuing to hold true—a case is invariably more complicated when a romance is involved."

Lips quirking, Barnaby arched his brows. "In this case, that's proving to be an entirely valid observation."

* * *

*A*t eleven o'clock that night, Hartley Galbraith strode down the pavement bordering Hanover Square. Shoulders hunched against the chill breeze, he kept his head down and continued south into George Street. Glancing forward, he noted the dark bulk of St. George's church ahead on his left.

Lips thinning, Hartley inwardly owned to amazement verging on disbelief at how many hurdles life had managed to strew in the path of what should have been the most straightforward of romances.

Drawing level with the church, he glanced around, then crossed the street and went quickly up the steps into the dark shadows of the pillared porch. At this hour, with the church closed for the night and no lamps burning along its façade, the porch was wreathed in near darkness and helpfully deserted except for the lady he had come to meet.

He'd sent her a note that morning, telling her of his change of address and stipulating this time, this place; she'd replied confirming the meeting, and had also urged him to reveal all to the police, regardless of the implications and possible repercussions. The truth, as she'd so eloquently stated, had to be paramount. Had to be their guide through this maze.

He glanced around as he strode to join her where she waited on one of the stone benches set in alcoves flanking the main doors. Her maid should have been somewhere nearby, keeping watch over her mistress, but Hartley couldn't see anyone else.

His intended rose as he neared. He slowed and opened his arms, and she came to him with her usual directness. Halting, he closed his arms around her. She lifted her face, inviting his kiss, but he held back. Peering deeper into the shadows, he asked, "Where's your maid?"

"She and Samuel, the undergardener, are standing just around the corner where they can't see us, but they will hear if I call." Through the dimness, his beloved searched his face. "Now kiss me."

Thus adjured, Hartley complied, bending his head and covering her lips—lips of soft rose just made to be kissed—with his. She responded as ardently as she always did, and for several long seconds—which could have been minutes for all he knew—his senses spun, giddy with the taste of her, with the unvoiced promise not just conveyed but underscored by the svelte female form pressed so firmly, so trustingly, and so deliberately provocatively against his harder body.

They had always been intended for each other. That was why the phrase "my intended" leapt so readily to his lips when referring to her. From their earliest years, they had known there was a link, some special connection between them. Despite the closeness of their families and the fact that they thought of all the others as sisters, neither he nor she had ever viewed what lay between them, even in the years before it had fully blossomed, as anything even vaguely sibling-like.

From the very first they had known that, at some point, they would wed. Had known that their futures were inextricably linked, that them getting married wasn't a possibility but rather a certainty. Yet even as they'd matured and the link had only grown stronger, more assured, they'd realized and had accepted that they would have to wait—that he would have to wait until she was deemed old enough to make her choice. Which had meant until she'd had her first Season and had seen what the ton had to offer in terms of eligible gentlemen.

Her affections had never wavered, any more than his had with the passing years.

He'd expected to ask for her hand at the beginning of last Season. That had been their plan.

Until the falling out—ridiculous and unnecessary but so very *real*—that had separated their families.

So they'd waited again, hoping, expecting, that it would blow over, that the rift was temporary and would soon enough be healed.

But that hadn't eventuated; if anything, the situation had only grown worse.

Two weeks ago, they'd decided that they had waited long enough, that they could not put their lives and the future they were determined to share in abeyance forever. That they had a responsibility to themselves and that future to secure it.

He'd asked his man-of-business to get all in readiness for him to make a formal application for her hand. Neither he nor she foresaw any difficulty in gaining her parents' permission, indeed, their support.

It had been his parents, his mother in particular, who would have planted herself firmly in their way.

And then they'd seen her killed.

Not even the sweetness of his beloved's kiss could yet counter the horror, sadness, and sorrow of that memory.

Hartley drew back from the kiss; raising his head, he drew in a tight breath.

Her palm cradling one lean cheek, Cynthia Latimer searched his face, then softly said, "I am so very, very sorry. No matter how difficult she was being, she didn't deserve to die."

Catching her hand, Hartley gently squeezed her fingers, then pressed a kiss to her fingertips. "I know. I'm still..." He grimaced. "Well, I *would* still be reeling if I had the time to do so."

Releasing her, he waved her to the bench in the alcove. He glanced around, but there was no one passing, no one to see them. "I hate this," he muttered. "All this sneaking around in the shadows."

Gathering her skirts, Cynthia sat and sighed. "I know, but we can put up with that—we have for the last year and more." They'd previously met at his lodgings, before he had moved back to Hanover Square, the better to take care of his family. She fully understood and accepted that necessity, but neither she nor, she knew, he was in any way accepting of the utterly unexpected turn of events. Quite aside from having to deal with the shock and the grief occasioned by his mother's death, her demise would mean an unavoidable setback to their plans, but how much of a setback—how much of an obstacle it might prove to be—they had yet to divine; it was the latter uncertainty that weighed on them both. She studied Hartley's face as he settled beside her. "How difficult has it been?"

"More or less what you would expect. Geraldine and Primrose ended in near-hysterics, and the doctor had to give them something to calm them. They're still keeping to their beds. The pater, too, has been...unable to cope, but he's starting to rally." Clasping his hands, leaning his forearms on his thighs, Hartley went on, "But it's Monica who worries me the most. She's been weeping uncontrollably, and in between bouts, she just stares blankly at the wall."

After a moment, he softly swore. "What Monica needs—what they all need—is your family. Your father, your mother, you, and your sisters. But even though Mama is dead, the stupid feud she started still stands like a brick wall, cutting us off from the comfort and relief all of you would willingly offer and bring us."

Reaching over and inserting one of her hands into his clasped ones, Cynthia stated, "The wall will come down. You and I will make sure of it."

Hartley grimaced. "Perhaps in time, but for the moment, Mama being murdered as she was means we must keep the wall in place." He looked at her. "The last thing we need to do is suggest any link between the feud and Mama's murder, much less connect that with our betrothal, and if immediately after she's been..." He swallowed and, facing forward, continued, his tone rougher, "Been removed, everything instantly goes back to the way it used to be...you know what the ton is like. People will talk, and you know how damaging such talk can be."

Cynthia studied his profile, then gently said, "I'll be very surprised if there isn't a degree of talk anyway."

Hartley dipped his head. "Perhaps. But there's a difference between vague gossip with no foundation and the sort of talk when people have something definite to point at and whisper."

Cynthia couldn't argue that.

Turning his head, Hartley captured her gaze. "That's part of what I need to warn you about. An Inspector Stokes is handling the case, along with Mr. Barnaby Adair, who I had heard of but not previously met. They interviewed us all briefly at the Fairchilds', and they called to see me this morning." He paused, then said, "They had learned—I have no idea how—that I'd been getting my affairs in order and had come to ask why. I told them I was intending to make an offer shortly, but I didn't tell them for whom. Adair, and Stokes, too, seem decent enough sorts, but—and this is the pertinent point—they are neither of them fools. Not by a long shot. In the circumstances, and given your encouragement, I told them the truth—why we were in the garden and where we met, and then what we saw—all of it."

Cynthia nodded approvingly. "I'm glad you did. I have to admit I was surprised when you didn't raise the alarm last night."

He pulled a face. "I meant to, but...I couldn't make head nor tail of what we'd seen and...I suppose I was in shock or something. I just couldn't seem to think—to put two thoughts together." He shook his head.

Cynthia squeezed his fingers. "Never mind what you did last night—it was a frightful experience all around. Today you rectified yesterday's mistakes and told the police all you could to help them find out who did this."

He studied her, trying to read her eyes in the poor light. "I accept that we had to tell the truth, but aren't you anxious over having your mother and sisters viewed as the prime suspects?"

"I would be if I thought there was the faintest possibility that any of my sisters or my mother could have been the lady we glimpsed on the terrace—the lady who dropped that stone ball on your mother and killed her." Cynthia held his gaze steadily. "But I know my mother and my sisters. No matter that she was being difficult, we all still loved Aunt Marjorie. My sisters and I have a wealth of fond memories of her. We remember how she used to sit with Mama and brush and plait our hair—years of little things like that. Until recently, we considered her our closest female family, after Mama. As for Mama…if she didn't still love your mother, she wouldn't have been so hurt by the feud, as we all know she has been." Cynthia paused, then, her gaze still locked with his, she gripped his fingers more tightly and said, "I *know* my family. None of them could *possibly* have done it. And as I see it, the sooner the police look into their alibis and discount them as possible suspects, the better off we'll all be."

He read the determination in her eyes, in the firm set of her chin; it was one of the reasons he was so in love with her—her trenchant devotion to those she held dear. She and he were the quiet, watchful protectors and defenders, each in their own families; it was one trait that had drawn them together from the first—that stalwart, protective stance.

Prompted by her words to consider the likelihood that her sisters and her mother almost certainly would be able to produce alibis for the relevant period, sound ones supported by a small army of other members of the ton with whom they had been dancing or conversing in the ballroom, he felt a lightening of the weight that, after his talk with Stokes and Adair, had settled on his shoulders. Slowly, he nodded. "I daresay you're right about them having alibis."

Cynthia softly snorted. "Georgina was parading proudly—and being proudly paraded—around the ballroom on Fitzforsythe's arm. Cecilia was dancing with Mr. Brandywell and otherwise chatting with his acquaintances. I was with you, and Millicent was absorbed with a group of her friends. As for Mama, she was in a group with Lady Lachlan and Mrs. Ferris the entire time." She grimaced, wryly, self-deprecatingly. "I checked when I returned to the ballroom, and Georgina and Cecilia were still fixed with their beaux, and neither Mama nor Millicent appeared to have shifted from where they'd settled earlier, before I slipped away to go outside."

Drawing in a deeper breath, she definitively stated, "So I *know* the lady we saw on the terrace wasn't one of us. But I have no idea who she was, much less where she had found a pair of Lady Latimer's shoes."

After a moment, Hartley nodded. "All right. So the police now know what we saw, and all we can do is fervently hope that they quickly discover who the lady was, why she had those shoes, and why she killed my mother." He refocused on Cynthia's face. "So to return to our own affairs, ours and our families', given the situation with the murder, with my family's need for comfort and your family wanting to help, what's the best way forward?"

Cynthia considered, weighing their options. Hartley watched her, but his gaze grew abstracted; he was thinking, assessing, evaluating, too.

Eventually, she stirred and glanced at his face. "Much as I would like to ignore that brick wall and just pretend it had never been, I agree that we can't do that, can't move that fast without occasioning a great deal of misinformed gossip. Likewise, matters being what they are, it would be inviting trouble to announce our engagement now, prior to the funeral and a decent period of mourning. Regardless, our first goal should be to remove your mother's murder, and both our families, from the ton's most-talked-about list. So correct me if I'm wrong, but as far as I can see, the best thing we can do to advance all our interlinked common causes is to do whatever we can to assist the police to bring their investigation to a speedy and successful conclusion. Indeed, that's possibly the only tack we can effectively take at this point."

Hartley was nodding. "Once the police apprehend the real murderer, thus proving that it wasn't one of your family, the case will be closed, and the ton will quickly move on to the next scandal."

"Exactly." Cynthia's tone was definite and determined. "So the question is: What can we do to hasten that much-desired end?"

Hartley wracked his brains. Eventually, he offered, "The shoes are the key—they're what ties your family to the murder. Perhaps if we nudge the police into looking into how the lady got such shoes..." He broke off on a grimace. "Frankly, my mind boggles at trying to convince Stokes, or even Adair, to look into the supply of ladies' shoes."

Cynthia held up a hand. "Wait—Adair. Last night toward the end, just before we left the ballroom, a Mrs. Adair came up—rather boldly, I thought—and spoke with us. She was very direct, almost shockingly so, but...she was also sympathetic." Cynthia met Hartley's gaze. "She said she was Adair's wife."

Hartley thought back. "There was a lady who followed Stokes and Adair into the Fairchilds' drawing room. Dark-haired. Short in stature, but quite striking. I can't remember the color of her gown, but it was darkish—perhaps purple or blue—and she wore spectacles and a diamond necklace."

Cynthia nodded. "Yes—that was her."

Hartley frowned. "Now I think of it, I've heard that Adair's wife is an original and occasionally assists with investigations, among other rather unusual pastimes. She's Calverton's sister, so very well connected."

"Indeed?" Cynthia's expression turned calculating. "Adair might be difficult to convince, but I wonder if his wife might be interested in learning more about Lady Latimer's shoes?"

CHAPTER 6

The next morning, Barnaby and Stokes ran the police surgeon to earth in the morgue.

As it happened, Pemberton had just finished re-examining Lady Galbraith's corpse. Wiping his hands on a towel, he joined them in the outer office.

A highly experienced practitioner, large-boned, a trifle rotund, and with an air of being worn about the edges, Pemberton fixed them with a jaundiced eye. "Very timely. Young Quale did the examination on your corpse, meaning Lady Galbraith. I read his report and just checked something that struck me as…not quite what we might have been expecting from the description of the means of death you'd noted." He paused, but before Stokes or Barnaby could demand to know what he'd been checking and why, Pemberton said, "It would help if you described the scene."

Stokes cast his own jaundiced glance at Barnaby, but complied.

Barnaby added several details for clarity.

Pemberton nodded as if ticking off the elements of the scene in his mind, then proceeded to interrogate them over how the body had fallen.

They tried as best they could but, dissatisfied with their inexactitude, Pemberton stumped over to a battered desk set against the wall, rummaged and found a piece of unmarked paper, slapped it on the top of the reports scattered over the desk's surface, and beckoned Stokes over. "Draw it—how the body was lying when you first saw it. Pay particular attention to the relative positioning of the body on the path, and also with respect to the terrace."

Stokes grunted but drew out his pencil and obliged; he was,

Barnaby judged, now too curious not to. Barnaby, certainly, was eager to learn just what it was Pemberton had discovered that ran counter to what they'd expected.

When Stokes had completed his sketch, Pemberton looked at Barnaby and arched his brows.

Barnaby studied what Stokes had drawn and nodded. "Yes. That's as I remember it, too."

Pemberton studied the sketch for half a minute, then said, "In that case, gentlemen, I have to inform you that I will be adjusting Quale's report to read: The findings were inconsistent with the ball having been dropped from above onto the victim's head. Instead, from the position of the primary impact of the ball on the skull, it appears that the ball was thrown down at the victim, presumably from the terrace, with some degree of force."

"Thrown?" Stokes frowned. "You mean the murderer picked up the ball and threw it down at her ladyship?"

"Precisely." Pemberton continued, "No matter how you imagine she was holding her head, if the ball had simply been picked up, extended, and dropped strictly vertically, it would have struck higher on the skull. Instead, the point of impact and, even more telling, the line along which the damage lies both show quite clearly that there was some degree of angle away from the vertical to the trajectory of the ball."

"In short," Barnaby said, "it was thrown."

Pemberton nodded. "And if you can get me the exact measurements of the height of the terrace relative to the spot on the path where Lady Galbraith was standing, and the horizontal distance between the edge of the terrace and the point where you estimate her ladyship's feet must have been when she was struck—essentially the same spot in which her feet were when you found her—then I might even be able to give you some idea of the height of your killer, whether they are short, of average height, or tall." Pemberton's eyes gleamed. "If that sort of information is of any interest to you?"

"Oh, it is," Stokes assured him. "In this case, we'll be grateful for any crumbs that fall our way."

"Right then." Pemberton turned away. "Get me those measurements, and I'll see what I can do for you. I've already got the height of the impact point, and that's the only other measurement I need."

Pemberton headed back into the examination room. Stokes

turned to Barnaby, who had noticed the murder weapon, the stone ball, sitting balanced on a nearby bench. Barnaby was holding it between his hands and frowning.

"What?" Stokes asked.

"I hadn't picked it up before—it's heavy." Barnaby extended the ball to Stokes.

Stokes gripped the ball—and nearly dropped it; he had to use both hands to hold it. "It's heavier than it looks."

"Because, contrary to what we thought, it's not stone. I think it's an ex-cannonball, perhaps from the unused ordnance that was made just before the wars ended and the stockpiles became obsolete. Presumably some enterprising gardener looking to replace worn finials came up with the idea to use surplus cannonballs and to paint them to look like stone."

"So our murderer must be strong enough to hoist one of these." Stokes returned the ball to the bench.

"Indeed—which leads to my next question." Barnaby met Stokes's eyes. "Could a woman have lifted that? More, could a lady have not just lifted that ball, but thrown it? It takes less strength to lift a weight, extend it, and drop it, than to deliberately throw that same weight at someone." Barnaby grimaced. "Given the weight of that thing, I'm honestly not sure any lady *could* have been the murderer."

Stokes looked faintly disgusted. "Before we eliminate the only person we've succeeded in placing at the scene in the moment the murder occurred purely on her gender, I suggest we take ourselves to Fairchild House and revisit the scene of the crime. And this time, I'll take a measuring tape."

Barnaby waved Stokes to the door. "Lead on."

* * *

Penelope and Violet were working through Penelope's translation for the museum, noting where she still had queries as to the original scribe's true meaning, when the front doorbell pealed.

Looking up and across Penelope's desk, Violet met Penelope's eyes. "Are you expecting anyone?"

Penelope frowned. "No." She looked at the papers spread before her, then waved dismissively at the door. "None of my acquaintances would call at such an hour—everyone knows I never host morning at-homes. Mostyn will handle it."

"In that case," Violet said, "we're up to page sixty-three of your copy."

Penelope humphed. "I will have to clarify that passage at the bottom of the page with Jeremy Carling. It's an obscure use of words, as far as I can tell, but—"

The door opened. Penelope glanced up.

Violet turned to look as Mostyn entered.

Shutting the door, he approached the desk. "I'm sorry to trouble you, ma'am, but there's a caller asking to consult with you, and I rather think you might want to see her."

Penelope pushed her spectacles higher. "Her who?"

"She says she's Lady Latimer, ma'am." Mostyn proffered his salver, on which rested an embossed calling card.

Penelope all but pounced on the card. She read it, then handed it to Violet.

"Well, well." Penelope's eyes gleamed brightly behind her lenses. "I wonder, Violet dear, if in the circumstances, we shouldn't take a short break from this boring Greek scribe and find out what her ladyship wishes to consult with me about?"

Violet grinned and started tidying the sheaf of papers in her lap. "Yes, I definitely think we should. In the interests of furthering your dear husband and Stokes's investigation, if nothing else."

"Indeed." Glancing at Mostyn, Penelope smiled. "Thank you, Mostyn. Where have you put her?"

"Anticipating your interest, ma'am, I have shown her ladyship into the drawing room."

"You are a gem among majordomos, Mostyn." Rising, Penelope headed for the door. "Violet?"

"Right behind you." Smiling, Violet followed her friend, employer, and colleague out of the door.

Penelope paused in the front hall to straighten her gown and check her hair, then after a nod to Mostyn to open the drawing room doors, she swept into the room, Violet gliding in her wake.

Lady Latimer rose from one sofa. She clutched a reticule rather tightly at her waist. Her gown was a subdued gray, not a color that particularly suited her but clearly donned as a measure of mourning. In Penelope's eyes, the most telling point about her ladyship's appearance was that she had come alone, with no daughter or friend to support her—or to bear witness as to what she might say.

Assessing the above in a single glance, Penelope kept her smile muted and advanced; she held out her hand. "Lady Latimer. I would say that it's a pleasure to see you again, but I suspect the matter that brought you here is a somber one."

"Indeed, Mrs. Adair." Lady Latimer touched Penelope's fingers. Her gaze deflected to Violet as, courtesy of Mostyn, the doors softly clicked shut.

"This is Mrs. Montague. She's my secretary and works on all my projects, including our investigations. You may speak before her as you would before me." After her ladyship and Violet exchanged polite nods, Penelope gestured for Lady Latimer to resume her seat. She and Violet moved to sit on the opposite sofa.

Once they were settled, Penelope and Violet with politely inquiring gazes fixed on Lady Latimer, her ladyship's expression, rarely communicative, seemed to harden. For a moment, Penelope wondered if, after all, Lady Latimer would balk, but, all but visibly stiffening her resolve, her chin rising a fraction, her ladyship began, "I have heard, Mrs. Adair, that—as you mentioned—you engage from time to time in investigations. Of crimes. Especially those within the ton."

When her ladyship paused, Penelope nodded. "Yes. That's correct."

Lady Latimer drew a tight breath and confessed, "I have come to inquire whether you would be willing to undertake to investigate Lady Galbraith's murder with a view to apprehending her killer."

Penelope blinked. She'd expected to hear some incriminating revelation. After a moment of staring, she asked, "Why? Why are you so keen to have the murderer of a lady who, as I understand it, had broken with you entirely, caught?"

Lady Latimer's lips pinched, but after a second's hesitation, she replied, "The why is simple enough. The disagreement between Lady Galbraith and myself is common knowledge. I'm perfectly certain— and no doubt you are, too—that the whispers have already started, rumors that this tragedy is somehow linked to that falling out. Cynthia—one of my daughters—mentioned this morning that she had even heard some speculation last night, and, of course, this being the ton, speculation and more are inevitable."

Her ladyship paused, her blue gaze steady on Penelope's face, then went on, "My daughters—the three still at home—and I discussed the matter over breakfast this morning. My husband was there, too, of course. We felt that, although the loss is the Galbraiths', we, too, are very likely to be badly damaged by this situation. We all agreed that the best way forward—the only way to limit damage to ourselves and, along the way, cut short this dreadful ordeal for the Galbraiths—is to do all we can to assist the authorities in finding the murderer and bringing this distressing situation to an end."

Penelope nodded. "I see."

"Indeed." Lady Latimer drew in a deeper breath and, transparently steeling herself, continued, "And as for breaking with the Galbraiths—that, I assure you, was no doing of mine."

When Penelope, her gaze locked with Lady Latimer's, raised an encouraging brow, Lady Latimer paused, then, lips thinning, went on, "I am sure you have heard that Marjorie and I were children together. We..." Her gaze growing distant, Lady Latimer proceeded to impart a more detailed, more personal account of the long friendship between her and Lady Galbraith and, eventually, their entire families, and the rupture over Lady Latimer's shoes and the subsequent cutting of all ties by Lady Galbraith.

Despite the rigid control over her expression Lady Latimer habitually maintained, through the course of her lengthy recitation, in looking back at past comforts and contrasting them with the present pain, her control slipped and her features reflected both the deep contentment of earlier years and the emotional hurt occasioned by the recent rift. "As I'm sure you've heard, Marjorie had grown extremely...contentious toward me. While that distressed me, knowing her as I did, it wasn't entirely unexpected. She had always been given to fits of quite rancorous pique. What did surprise and shock me was her...prohibition of any contact between our families."

Lady Latimer paused, battling emotion, searching for words. Eventually, she said, "To use our children—hers as well as mine—to strike at me...I hadn't expected that." After a moment, she went on, "If there had been any other way, but"—Lady Latimer straightened her spine and raised her head—"I had to do what was best for my girls. For me, they came first."

Penelope nodded; a year ago, she might not have understood the imperative behind that statement, but with Oliver in her life, she had no difficulty understanding Lady Latimer's stance.

Before she could frame her next question, Lady Latimer said, "You are of the ton yourself, so you know how these situations can play out. An investigation may stretch for months, or even years. While my family, and the Galbraiths, too, can weather a few days, perhaps even a week or so, of whispers and rumors, the longer those are allowed to run unchecked by fact, the more entrenched and accepted they will become…until the rumors become fact in society's mind—to the lasting detriment of my family, certainly, but the other direction in which people will look for any murderer is at the Galbraiths. Both our families will be damaged by this. In the first days, perhaps only slightly—but the longer the case goes unsolved, the damage will mount and will eventually be irreparable." Lady Latimer looked directly at Penelope. "Which brings me to my purpose in calling, Mrs. Adair—to ask for your help in ensuring that Marjorie Galbraith's murderer is identified and apprehended as soon as may be."

Penelope studied her ladyship, then said, "You must be very sure that none of your family is involved."

Lady Latimer held Penelope's gaze. "As you say. Indeed, I *know* that none of my family—not my husband or my daughters—could have been involved. Aside from all else, we were all in the ballroom and had been for some time before Marjorie's body was found."

"So you all remained in the ballroom from the time you arrived until the police arrived?" Penelope asked.

Lady Latimer went to nod, then stopped herself. Frowning slightly, she said, "All except Cynthia. But that was virtually immediately we arrived—her hem had come down and she went to the withdrawing room to pin it up. In the end, she sewed it up, so she was absent for…perhaps half an hour. But she had returned to the ballroom long before the murder."

"What time did you arrive?" Penelope saw no reason to explain that the murder had taken place at least an hour before the body was found.

"A trifle after nine o'clock." Lady Latimer appeared to cast her mind back. "After that, Humphrey was with his cronies, but they were nearby—I could see him the entire time. My younger girls were chatting with their friends—they will be able to tell you with whom—and Georgina and Cecilia were strolling with Fitzforsythe and Mr. Brandywell." Lady Latimer focused on Penelope's face. "None of them went out onto the side terrace."

Violet, seated beside Penelope and absolved of any part in the exchanges, had used the time to carefully study their unexpected guest; she found Lady Latimer's certainty—her unshakeable confidence that none of her family had been involved in the murder—interesting.

Violet had to wonder if that certainty stemmed from her ladyship knowing—or having guessed—who the murderer actually was. Regardless, Lady Latimer's certainty was utterly categorical, projected in her tone, her demeanor, in the very way she was sitting, facing them directly with not so much as a glance aside.

When Penelope, frowning slightly, remained silent, Lady Latimer studied her in turn; briefly, her ladyship's gaze shifted to Violet's face, taking note of her focus, then Lady Latimer looked back at Penelope. "Although I elected to come here alone, as I mentioned, my family as a whole is aware of these issues. Indeed, my daughters are entirely supportive—they, too, see the dangers for our family and also for the Galbraiths. Cynthia—as you might have heard, she's my quiet one, but she's also a rock of practicality and clear-headedness—remembered you from last night and had heard about your interests. She suggested that asking for your assistance in this matter was, at least, something we could actually do." Lady Latimer paused, then added, "I'm sure you comprehend, Mrs. Adair, Mrs. Montague, that an adverse situation is more easily borne if one can tell oneself that one has taken some active step to deal with whatever the problem is."

Penelope nodded. "Indeed."

"So." Lady Latimer gripped her reticule more tightly. "Will you act for us in this case, Mrs. Adair?"

No one had actually asked Penelope to consult before; now that someone had, she discovered she had to stop and think matters through. That said, the invitation from Lady Latimer was entirely too good to pass up. "I would be happy to assist, but such assistance must be subject to certain caveats." Meeting Lady Latimer's gaze and encountering a questioning look, Penelope elaborated, "I and my colleagues"—she gestured to Violet—"Mrs. Montague, and also Mrs. Stokes, the inspector's wife, who always works alongside us in our investigations, will need an assurance of cooperation from you and your family. We will need to interview you and your daughters. Interviewing your husband I am sure can be left to our husbands, and that brings me to my second caveat." Penelope held Lady Latimer's gaze. "You will need to accept that any pertinent information we discover will be communicated directly, without any limitation, to the authorities in the persons of Inspector Stokes and my husband."

Lady Latimer inclined her head. "I and my family would expect nothing less. Indeed, as our sole purpose in contacting you, Mrs. Adair, is to help bring the police's investigation to a speedy and successful conclusion, I see no clash whatever in our agendas."

Penelope gave a decisive nod. "Excellent." She pushed her spectacles higher, then said, "In that case...you've told me of the feud over Lady Latimer's shoes. I have heard of the shoes, but have never examined any—all I know is derived from descriptions given by others. If you would, could you describe the shoes themselves for us?"

Lady Latimer frowned. After a moment, she said, "I can't see how it is relevant, however, they are ballroom pumps with a Louis heel, embroidered with either silver or gold thread, with lead crystals, small ones, attached to the metal embroidery." She shrugged. "We have a pair made for each ball gown, using the fabric of the gown as the base for the embroidery."

"And the shoes are made by...?" Penelope asked.

"That is a secret, Mrs. Adair." Lady Latimer's expression turned bleak. "A secret I wish I had never discovered—it's been the source of so much pain and discord."

"Perhaps," Penelope said, "but that's water under the bridge, and you can't be sorry over the shoes helping you settle two of your daughters so well." She paused, then said, "Will you at least tell me this: Is the shoemaker who makes Lady Latimer's shoes located in London?"

Lady Latimer nodded. "Yes. In town."

"Very well. Next question. Could another lady have learned your secret or, in any other way, gained access to a pair of Lady Latimer's shoes?"

Her gaze steady on Penelope's face, Lady Latimer frowned. "I don't believe so, but I'm unclear as to why you're asking. As I stated earlier, there can be no connection between the feud and Marjorie's murder."

Looking into her ladyship's blue-gray eyes, Penelope made an executive decision; the only way they could learn about the shoes was through Lady Latimer, and so her ladyship needed to know the reason for their interest. "As to the feud itself, you may well be right, but as for the shoes...I have to inform you that the authorities have a witness who saw a lady wearing Lady Latimer's shoes fleeing the side terrace within seconds of Lady Galbraith being struck down."

Lady Latimer paled. She didn't move; she didn't blink. Violet wasn't even sure her ladyship breathed.

A long moment passed. Then, her gaze growing distant as if trying and failing to picture the scene, Lady Latimer said, "Oh." But then she shook her head, clearly bewildered. "No—that can't have been. How...?" Two seconds later, she refocused, somewhat severely, on Penelope's face. "That witness, whoever they are, must have been mistaken. Or...or someone is seeking to deflect attention from the real murderer by fabricating a clue, one the ton, and presumably the police, will leap on far too readily."

Penelope's glasses glinted as she nodded. "Indeed. That occurred to us, too—that the sighting of the shoe was a deliberately placed red herring."

Something of Lady Latimer's obdurate defensiveness eased. "I commend your common sense, Mrs. Adair." After a moment, as if speaking to herself, her ladyship murmured, "Clearly Cynthia was prescient in suggesting I contact you."

Lady Latimer paused, then looked at Penelope. "So, Mrs. Adair, will you and your colleagues"—her ladyship inclined her head to Violet—"accept my commission?"

"Yes." Penelope straightened. "But just so we have it clear, we do not work for any fee, but we will agree to use our best endeavors to identify who killed Lady Galbraith. Any information we discover will be communicated directly to the police, and we will not censor or in any way conceal any facts we find." Penelope paused as if replaying her words, then looked at Lady Latimer. "Are those terms agreeable to you?"

Lady Latimer met Penelope's gaze and nodded. "Yes. I want Marjorie's murderer caught, and I know the villain isn't me or mine."

* * *

*A*fter Lady Latimer had departed, Penelope and Violet returned to the garden parlor and settled once more on either side of Penelope's desk. Neither made any move to refocus on the translation on which they'd been working; instead, rather absentmindedly, both started gathering the scattered pages, neatening them into two piles.

Her gaze abstracted, Penelope murmured, "It's both curious and interesting that her ladyship—encouraged by her daughters—thought to engage us."

"True. But that has handed us the perfect invitation to interview all four girls." Violet was looking forward to assisting in her first investigation—one in which she wasn't personally involved.

Penelope nodded. "As well as speaking with her ladyship again. I did wonder if giving her until this afternoon to gather her daughters to meet with us was a good idea or not, but..."

"Well, one could see her point. And that will also give us time to think of all the questions we should ask—" Violet broke off as the front doorbell pealed.

When the sound of distant voices reached them, Penelope and Violet exchanged delighted smiles, set the manuscript for translation safely to one side, and rose.

The door opened and Griselda came in, balancing little Megan on her hip. One swift glance, and Griselda noticed the neat piles on the desk—the neat desk. She touched cheeks with Penelope, then surrendered Megan to her so Griselda could greet Violet. "I thought," Griselda said, straightening and nodding at the desk, "that I would find you both hard at work—at least until I got here." Looking from Violet's face to Penelope's, Griselda asked, "Has anything happened?"

They told her; immediately, Griselda had Penelope ring for Hettie, Oliver's nursemaid, who arrived with Oliver in tow. Settling both Megan and Oliver with Hettie on a rug by the long windows, with a bag of toys to keep the toddlers amused, the ladies retreated to the sofa and armchairs before the fireplace.

"So!" Eyes bright, Griselda settled into one armchair, facing Penelope and Violet, who'd sat on the sofa. "Combining yesterday's conclusions with what you learned from Lady Latimer, what are our current thoughts, and how should we proceed?"

"We agreed to call on the Latimers at half past two." Penelope glanced at the clock. "It's barely eleven—" She broke off as Mostyn arrived with the tea tray.

Once they were supplied with tea and tiny cakes and the children had been given a ginger biscuit each, they returned to their deliberations. "As to our current stance," Penelope said, "while we have reserved judgment on whether Hartley Galbraith is telling the truth—whether there was any lady on the terrace, whether she was wearing Lady Latimer's shoes, and whether he actually had his intended by his side—Lady Latimer's request has emphasized that, regardless of Hartley's tale, society will and, indeed, already is directing suspicion and disapproval, which will gradually escalate into opprobrium, at the entire Latimer family."

"More, as Lady Latimer also mentioned," Violet put in, "suspicion will eventually be directed at the Galbraiths themselves, no matter how undeserved."

Griselda nodded. "Yes—I can see that." She sipped and looked at Penelope. "And even if Hartley Galbraith is telling the truth on all points, there is still a chance that some other lady—not a Latimer—has duplicated Lady Latimer's shoes."

"Hmm. And if you think about that," Penelope said, "it's perfectly possible, knowing of Lady Galbraith's avid interest in the shoes, that said lady might have followed her ladyship onto the side terrace to show off her find."

Violet shrugged. "That doesn't tell us why Lady Galbraith was killed, or even whether the lady with the shoes was to blame or saw who did it, but all those possibilities are certainly there."

"So." Griselda set her cup on its saucer. "What's our next step? Go and interview the Latimers and see what more we can learn?"

"We'll do that, yes." Penelope was frowning slightly. "But first, I suggest we revisit the scene of the crime." She met Violet's gaze, then Griselda's. "I think we should verify the details of Hartley's account— he described where he and his intended were on the path and why they couldn't see the terrace itself, and he also mentioned that when they rushed forward, their gazes were level with the terrace flags. We can check those three points, at least. I also want to examine one of the stone balls—the one dropped on Lady Galbraith is with the police, but there are others along the terrace balustrade that we can look at. And before we start checking the alibis of anyone in the ballroom, it will help to have a clear understanding of the possible routes between the ballroom and the terrace—how long it would have taken to go back and forth, for instance—and that might give us a better idea of whether the lady on the terrace might simply have seen the murder committed, then turned and fled."

"And, for whatever reason, not raised the alarm." Griselda nodded. "That all sounds very logical." She grinned. "As usual."

Violet smiled, too. "So we're agreed. First, we'll go to Fairchild House, and I will admit to being intensely eager to study the scene, and then, armed with whatever we learn, we'll go on to the Latimers'."

The other two nodded.

All three ladies turned as a pair of wobbly toddlers came chortling—trying to run—around the end of the sofa. Each child made a beeline for their respective mother's knees, shrieking with glee and burying their faces in their mother's skirts as Hettie came hurrying up.

"I'm sorry, ma'am, Mrs. Stokes." Even as she said the words, Hettie was grinning. "We were playing hide-and-seek."

The next few minutes went in play and communion between the four women and the chattering, laughing babes.

Then Hettie stood and held out her hands. "It's nearly time for luncheon. I'll take them upstairs."

Penelope, Oliver lolling in her lap, looked across at Griselda. "Perhaps, before we set out for Fairchild House, we should take an early luncheon, too. In the nursery?"

Griselda grinned and hefted Megan. "Yes. Let's."

The ladies stood, and with Penelope carrying Oliver, Griselda with Megan once more on her hip, and Violet—Auntie Violet—walking between, they headed for the stairs.

CHAPTER 7

𝒫enelope, Violet, and Griselda were in buoyant moods as they climbed the steps to Lady Fairchild's door. They were admitted by the butler; after inquiring of his mistress, he conducted them into Lady Fairchild's presence. Her ladyship was seated writing letters at a delicate escritoire, in the conservatory attached to the great house.

"Penelope, dear!" Rising, Lady Fairchild enveloped Penelope in a scented embrace, then looked with patent curiosity at Violet and Griselda.

Penelope made the introductions, not in the least surprised that Lady Fairchild showed no consciousness of the difference in classes.

"My dears," her ladyship declared effusively, "had I the time, I swear I would be quite prostrate. This business is not at all how I intended to start this Season—everyone is talking of my ball for entirely the wrong reasons."

"Sadly, that's true," Penelope stated. "But we've come hoping to winkle out a clue or two to help the authorities—Barnaby is assisting Inspector Stokes, you see."

"Indeed," Lady Fairchild said, "and I believe you will find both those gentlemen somewhere around the house. I was told they had called. Edmund is with them."

Penelope, Violet, and Griselda exchanged glances, then Penelope turned to Lady Fairchild. "We were wondering if we might study the ballroom and the corridors around it, and the terrace and the gardens, too."

"Yes, of course." Lady Fairchild spread her arms. "You may have carte blanche, my dears. Go anywhere you please, and by all means, should you so wish, feel free to speak with any of the staff. They are all as eager as I am to have this grisly matter cleared up—it's

not the sort of thing anyone expects in a household such as ours."
Lady Fairchild glanced at her desk. "I regret I cannot accompany you,
however. I must get these letters out."

Penelope assured her that they were quite happy to wander and
explore on their own. Taking their leave of her ladyship, they duly
headed for the ballroom.

Accessed via a foyer at the rear of the front hall, the ballroom
was a massive rectangular chamber, with one long wall devoted to
windows and French doors that gave onto a paved area bordered by
lawns; the latter rolled down to a graveled path with landscaped
gardens beyond. Both shorter walls at each end of the room boasted a
central ornate fireplace flanked by two doors; the doors in the wall
shared with the entry foyer were clearly the ballroom's main entrance.
The other long wall, opposite the windows, was paneled and hosted a
single door set centrally, with two much narrower doors, one at either
end of the wall, all but concealed in the paneling.

Halting under the central chandelier, Penelope looked around the
empty, echoing space. "Ballrooms feel so strange when there's no
ball." She turned in a circle, noting all the exits. "Other than the staff
entrances"—she pointed to the two narrow doors set into the
paneling—"and the doors back to the foyer, there are only three ways
anyone could have left the ballroom."

Griselda glanced at the windows. "That's not the terrace in
question, is it?"

"No," Penelope said. "That's the patio, and because it was chilly
on the night of the ball, none of those French doors were open. No one
went out there, and if they had, they would have been in full view of
all those in the room." She pointed to the wall at the end of the
ballroom. "There are rooms beyond on that side, between the ballroom
and the side of the house where the terrace in question lies. We'll go
that way in a moment, but first, I wanted to check how many
reasonably direct routes there are between the ballroom and the
terrace."

Going to the door in the center of the long paneled wall, she
opened it and stepped through. Violet and Griselda followed and found
themselves in a corridor that ran the length of the ballroom.

"I think," Penelope said, strolling down the corridor away from
the foyer, "that the withdrawing room was just along here."

Pausing by a door, she opened it and looked inside. "Yes, this is
the room that was used as the ladies' withdrawing room that night."

Peering past Penelope, Violet saw a large parlor-like room. "So." Closing the door, Penelope walked on. "Quite aside from anyone else who might or might not have come out of the ballroom, we know that at least four guests did—Hartley Galbraith's intended, Hartley himself, Lady Galbraith, and the lady seen fleeing from the terrace."

Together with Griselda, Violet followed Penelope down the long corridor to where a second corridor, running parallel to the end of the ballroom, crossed it. Penelope turned left, walked a few paces on, then halted at the entrance to yet another corridor, this one running perpendicular to the one they were currently in; leading away from the ballroom, it passed between two rooms to end in a small hall. As Violet and Griselda joined her, Penelope pointed down the corridor to where it ended in a wall of tall windows with a central glassed door. "The side terrace is out there—you can see the stone balustrade. That's the door through which Hartley, and most likely also Lady Galbraith and Hartley's intended, left the house. The lady on the terrace also almost certainly came this way—she certainly returned via this route."

After looking down the corridor for several seconds, Penelope glanced at Violet and Griselda. "To reach the side terrace via any other exit would have taken considerable time, and would also have required a certain knowledge of the house. If I had been Hartley's intended, I would have excused myself to go to the withdrawing room, but instead of stopping there, I would have continued along the way we just walked, slipped into this corridor and so outside."

Violet nodded. "And it being so early in the evening, she wouldn't have been likely to encounter any other guests."

"*And*," Griselda said, "with that schedule the staff adhered to so strictly, she could easily have walked out as the footmen started serving the champagne, in the period when all the staff on this level were in either the ballroom or the foyer."

Penelope nodded. "Yes, exactly. And once he'd seen her go, Hartley followed, but he left the ballroom via that door." Penelope pointed further along the corridor in which they stood, to the door near the end that gave access to the ballroom. "He had to have come that way, because the footman who saw him was leaving the ballroom and heading back to the kitchen, which is that way." She pointed along the corridor past the intersection through which they had come. "The footman followed Hartley from the ballroom, saw him turn down this corridor, and when the footman reached this intersection, he glimpsed

Hartley outside on the terrace, just going down the steps to the right."

Griselda looked down the corridor. "*Could* the footman have seen Hartley?"

Penelope considered. "Good question, but yes, I think he could have. This corridor was unlit—Hartley gave that as the reason he and his intended didn't get much of a look at the lady as she fled back inside."

A quick survey confirmed that the corridor was devoid of lamps. Penelope nodded. "So that adds up. There was moonlight outside, and Hartley would have been illuminated enough for a sharp-eyed footman to spot. So we can accept that, indeed, that is what happened." She glanced again at the glassed door at the end of the corridor. "So how did Lady Galbraith leave the ballroom?"

"If we accept that she was following Hartley," Violet said, "then presumably she left the ballroom via the same door he did."

Penelope was nodding. "And if we posit that the lady, whoever she was, followed Lady Galbraith, then presumably she, too, came via that door." Satisfied, Penelope met Violet's and Griselda's eyes. "If it comes to having to question any guests, be they Galbraiths, Latimers, or any others, then *that* is the exit we need to focus on. We'll need to ascertain who left the ballroom early in the proceedings via that door."

"What about when the lady returned?" Griselda asked.

Penelope grimaced. "That's going to be more difficult, especially as she could have used any door, including the main doors from the foyer, and there were lots of other guests entering the ballroom at that time." She tilted her head. "Of course, the lady—and, later, Hartley's intended—might have paused in the withdrawing room to recover their composure. Remind me to speak with the maids who were on duty in the withdrawing room before we leave."

Violet nodded.

"Now—onward." Penelope set off down the corridor toward the side terrace.

Opening the glassed door, she heard the rumble of male voices rising from the area below the terrace. With Violet and Griselda at her back, she walked to the balustrade and looked over.

Barnaby, Stokes, and Lord Fairchild were standing on the grass bordering the path where they had found Lady Galbraith's body. Their hands sunk in their coat pockets, the men appeared to have been staring moodily at the gravel, but, hearing Penelope's heels on the flags, all three glanced up.

They watched as Violet and Griselda appeared beside Penelope, then the three men smiled—Stokes and Barnaby in wry resignation, Lord Fairchild with open delight.

"Penelope, my dear." His lordship beamed. "What brings you and your companions here?"

"We came to check the routes between this terrace and the ballroom, and also to check that the information we've been given makes sense." Penelope fixed her gaze on Barnaby and Stokes. "But what brings you two back?"

The pair exchanged a glance, then Barnaby looked up and said, "Fresh evidence from the surgeon. As it happens, we were wanting to conduct an experiment—one you three can help us with."

Penelope wanted to ask what fresh evidence the police surgeon had found, but she was equally curious over the—intentionally distracting, she was perfectly sure—carrot Barnaby had dangled; she decided to play along. "What experiment?"

As if appreciating her dilemma, Barnaby grinned. "You first." He pointed to the stone ball resting on the top of one of the pillars in the balustrade. "Go to that pillar, stand directly behind it, and see if you can lift the ball."

Obediently walking to the pillar, Penelope examined the ball; it was indistinguishable from the one that had rested on the pillar at the top of the steps, which had been the ball used to kill Lady Galbraith. Because Penelope was so short, the ball was almost level with her shoulders. Obediently setting her hands to its sides, she gripped and lifted—or tried to, but although not anchored to the pillar's top, the ball was far heavier than she'd imagined. Lips setting, she tried again, but... Exhaling, she let go of the ball. "I can't lift it. Why is it so heavy?"

"They're old cannonballs, you see," Lord Fairchild said. "The original finials had quite worn away—deuced ugly, they were—so the gardener sawed them off, ground down the tops of the pillars, and set old cannonballs on top."

"How...enterprising," Penelope said.

Stokes waved. "Violet—you next."

Taller than Penelope but shorter than Griselda, Violet took Penelope's place. For Violet, the ball was at mid-chest height. She gripped the ball and strained to lift it, but she could only just shift it. Setting it back, she shook her head. "I can move it a fraction, but I can't really lift it clear."

Barnaby nodded. "Thank you. Griselda?"

Taller and larger-boned than either Violet or Penelope, and with the strong hands of a professional milliner, Griselda stepped up; for her, the ball was almost at waist-height. She grasped the ball and lifted it several inches off the pedestal, but then she let out her breath in a *whoosh* and set the ball down hard. She looked at Stokes. "Yes, I can lift it, but truly, even in a rage, I doubt I could hold it well enough to reach out and drop it on someone."

Penelope frowned. "Perhaps the ball that used to be there"—she pointed at the empty pillar at the top of the steps—"is lighter."

"It isn't," Stokes said. "We've checked—they're all the same."

Penelope blinked. "Then...that means no woman—well, short of a strong-woman from some circus—could have lifted and extended that ball and dropped it on Lady Galbraith's head. So there had to have been someone else—some man—who actually murdered her."

Stokes grimaced and looked at Barnaby.

Barnaby grimaced back. He looked up at the ladies. "I think we might be getting a trifle ahead of ourselves."

Penelope opened her mouth to ask why, but at that moment, the butler arrived with a summons for Lord Fairchild.

His lordship excused himself, shook hands with Barnaby and Stokes, paused on the terrace to gallantly kiss all three ladies' hands and thank them for their assistance, then followed the butler back into the house.

Once his lordship had disappeared inside, Penelope narrowed her eyes on her spouse. "What have you learned?"

Barnaby glanced around, then tipped his head toward the gardens. "Come down and join us while we check out the lie of the land, so to speak. We can talk while we do."

Perfectly ready to do just that, the three ladies quickly went down the steps and met Barnaby and Stokes on the path. "This way." Barnaby waved to another set of steps cut into the raised bank opposite the terrace. "Essentially we'll be retracing the route by which Hartley said he and his intended returned to the house."

Penelope linked arms with Barnaby, while Stokes took Griselda's hand.

Violet led the way up the steps. "Hartley and his intended met in some folly by a lake, didn't they?"

"Yes," Barnaby said, "but we don't need to go that far. Let's see if we can find the spot where Hartley and his intended first saw Lady

Galbraith standing below the terrace."

"The spot where their view of the terrace itself was obscured by some overhanging branch," Stokes said.

Gaining the top of the bank, they set out along the path that led deeper into the gardens, more or less directly away from the house.

"So," Penelope said, "what did you learn from the surgeon that brought you back here? It was something about the cannonball, I take it."

"In a way," Stokes replied. "According to the surgeon, the ball wasn't dropped on Lady Galbraith—at least, not as we'd envisioned. The trajectory was wrong for that—according to Pemberton, the ball hit her ladyship's head too much to the side. He concluded that the ball was thrown, but, as we've just confirmed, no woman could have lifted that ball and then thrown it at someone."

Penelope frowned. "So…we're now looking for some gentleman who we otherwise have found no evidence for?"

"Well, no," Barnaby said. "Pemberton also asked for various measurements—the height of the terrace above the path, the horizontal distance of Lady Galbraith from the terrace. He thought to estimate the height of the murderer—or at least how high the murderer lifted the ball. However, while we were measuring, we worked out some angles on our own." Glancing at Penelope, meeting her dark eyes, Barnaby said, "We now think the ball was *pushed* off its pillar—shoved hard toward Lady Galbraith. When we get back to the terrace, we'd like you to try it with one of the other balls."

"Hmm." Penelope's frown hadn't lifted. "All right."

Walking just ahead, Violet had been glancing back at the terrace every few yards. Now she halted and turned to face the house. "This is the spot, or close to it."

The others gathered around. Standing behind Violet, Stokes studied the limited view of the terrace, then he took one step back. When the others glanced at him, he said, "Hartley Galbraith is close to my height. If I had been standing here, on this spot, that evening, I would have been able to see exactly what Hartley described—his mother clearly visible on the path below the terrace, and that branch there"—Stokes pointed at the thick branch extending over the path—"completely blocks my view of the terrace itself."

Penelope bustled back to stand just behind Stokes's shoulder; she studied the house, then looked at Violet. "Violet—you're about average lady height. Can you come and stand here beside Stokes and see what you can see?"

Violet obliged, and duly reported, "I can almost see the terrace surface, but not quite."

Penelope sighed. "So it's likely that Hartley's intended saw no more than he."

She eyed the house, then touched Stokes's and Violet's shoulders. "Why don't you two lead the way back and stop when you can see all of the terrace?"

They discovered that, due to the curves and dips in the path, and interference from the stand of trees growing alongside, they had to go more than ten yards closer to the house before the view of the terrace was sufficient for Hartley and his intended to have been able to glimpse the lady fleeing into the house.

"What about the steps leading down to the garden?" Griselda asked. "Would they have seen someone fleeing that way?"

Violet and Stokes shook their heads. "There are several tree trunks in the way," Stokes said.

"So," Barnaby concluded, "a gentleman doing the deed and leaving that way is still—at least theoretically—a possibility."

Penelope pushed her spectacles higher on her nose. "By my estimation, the lady on the terrace would indeed have had time to shove the ball off the pillar at Lady Galbraith, then rush back across the terrace and be stepping into the dark of the corridor by the time Hartley and his intended glimpsed her."

"Indeed." Stokes sounded grim. "Theoretical possibilities aside, it looks like we truly are looking for a lady murderer."

"And it does seem," Penelope continued, "that all Hartley told us is true. If he hadn't been here, on this path, when his mother was struck down, he wouldn't have known about that branch obscuring the view, and, well"—she gestured to the distance they'd had to come before they could clearly see the terrace—"everything else fits, too."

Barnaby nodded. "Despite his panic and his not reporting the crime at the time, everything he's told us is not only true, but it proves he's not the murderer."

"And," Stokes said, "that a lady who was wearing those Lady Latimer's shoes is."

"Hmm." Penelope was not yet convinced about the latter. "Let's go back and try your suggestion with the ball. Meanwhile," she went on, as they all fell into step, "we have to inform you that we—me, Violet, and Griselda—have been commissioned by Lady Latimer to investigate and assist the authorities in whatever way we can to find Lady Galbraith's murderer."

Barnaby and Stokes turned to stare at the three ladies—whether in awe, stunned surprise, or both wasn't clear.

Then Barnaby said, "But you would have done—are doing—that anyway."

"Yes, but Lady Latimer wasn't to know that," Penelope replied. "And, of course, her agreement to fully cooperate means we can ask about the shoes—which we clearly need to learn more about. Although *supposedly* no lady bar the Latimer ladies has access to those shoes, we need to confirm that that is, in fact, the case, and that someone else hasn't either bribed Lady Latimer's secret shoemaker, or alternatively, found another shoemaker who knows the trick of creating those shoes."

Stokes grunted. "Better you three than we."

Grinning, Griselda patted his arm. "Indeed. And we'll also relieve you of the burden of interviewing the Latimer ladies and taking down their alibis."

Penelope was nodding. "And, if need be, checking those alibis."

Slowly, Stokes smiled. He met Barnaby's eyes. "It's like having another group of constables, only this lot wear skirts."

Penelope and Griselda hit Stokes's arms in mock-umbrage, but everyone was smiling.

"I should also point out," Penelope said, "that by requesting our assistance in this, Lady Latimer is making something of a statement."

Barnaby nodded. "An unspoken declaration that neither she nor any of her family are guilty and they have nothing to fear from an investigation."

"Indeed," Violet said. "And, at least to me, Lady Latimer was very convincing in her confidence and certainty that she and hers had nothing to hide."

"Interestingly," Penelope said, "her ladyship brought up the point that, after the Latimers, the other group the ton's suspicious minds will focus on will be the Galbraiths themselves. While that's not a pretty thought, it is an accurate prediction."

Stokes humphed. "Sadly, the ton's view has some justification. Most murders are committed by family members, or at least those close to the victim."

"And in this case," Barnaby pointed out, "all the Galbraiths were present at the ball, just as much as the Latimers."

They reached the steps in the bank and descended to the path below the terrace. Barnaby slid his arm free of Penelope's, squeezing her hand before releasing it. "Go up to the terrace and try to push that ball, the one you earlier tried to lift."

Raising her skirts, Penelope climbed the stone steps.

"Gather your strength first," Stokes advised. "*Shove* the ball as if you're in a rage with someone and want to throw something at them."

Penelope peered over the balustrade to make sure all the others were standing well back. They'd moved several yards away, onto the grass. Reassured, she stepped up to the ball, considered it, then thought of being in a temper, mustering her strength. Abruptly, she brought her right hand up and pushed hard at the ball, swinging slightly as she shoved at the face nearest her.

She had doubted the ball would even move.

Instead, it sailed off the pillar, falling quickly due to its weight, but her shove had given it the angle Stokes and Barnaby had been hoping to duplicate.

Following the flight, she rushed to the balustrade; looking over, she saw the ball land almost on the other side of the gravel path.

Stokes looked at Barnaby. "That's it. That's how it was done."

Barnaby nodded.

When no one volunteered anything else, Penelope leaned on the balustrade and stated, "Yes, but it's hardly a sound way to commit murder, is it?"

The others looked up at her, but none of them argued, so she continued following that train of thought. "I agree that's how the ball was launched at Lady Galbraith, but surely that suggests it was a spur-of-the-moment act—a sudden flaring of temper and a consequent lashing out. Pushing a ball at someone like that might cause them harm, but it's more likely to give them a scare. It doesn't suggest planning, much less premeditation, does it?"

She paused, then said, "Which brings us to the question of: Was this even cold-blooded murder? Or was it a lashing out in a fit of temper, an attempt to harm that, in this instance, actually killed?"

Stokes grimaced. He glanced at Barnaby, then looked at Penelope. "It is still murder, whether murder was intended or whether the intention was simply to harm."

Penelope regarded him, then nodded. "Yes, that's true. But apropos of the ball being pushed rather than dropped, there's something you might not have noticed." She walked back to the empty pillar at the head of the terrace steps. She examined the upper surface, then pointed. "You can still see it. Although it's dying off and flaking away now that the sun is reaching it, there was a cushion of lichen around the base of the ball, thicker on the terrace side than on the garden side because of the shadow cast by the ball." She glanced up as the others joined her, crowding around to see. Once they'd looked, she pointed to the second empty pillar; Stokes had brought the ball she'd pushed off it back up. "You can see the same growth of lichen on that one, too, but on the night of the murder, the uneven cushion of lichen on the pillar at the top of the steps was considerably thicker. I noticed it at the time."

Barnaby and Stokes examined the seating of the ball she'd pushed off, then replaced it.

When they straightened, Penelope stated, "I suspect that on the night of the murder, the ball on the pillar at the top of the steps would have been even easier to push off than that one."

No one disagreed.

"Right, then." Stokes looked at the ladies. "What's next on your slate?"

"We have an appointment with Lady Latimer and her family at half past two," Violet said. "We'll go there as soon as we've finished here." She looked at Penelope. "Don't forget we want to speak with the maids who were in the withdrawing room to see if they noticed any lady in distress."

Stokes's brows rose.

Barnaby nodded. "An excellent idea. They might have seen or even heard something relevant."

"Exactly." Penelope was pulling on her gloves. "After that, we'll head to the Latimers' house in Hanover Square and see what we can learn there."

"Hopefully we can learn about the shoes," Griselda said.

"Whatever we find, we'll share with you this evening." Penelope looked at Stokes and Barnaby. "We're meeting for dinner at Violet and Montague's apartment. Don't be late."

"And put the good Mrs. Trewick out?" Barnaby grinned. "We'll see you there."

"But where are you going?" Penelope asked.

Stokes exchanged a glance with Barnaby. "First, back to the Yard to give Pemberton his measurements and our revised thoughts on what actually occurred. Then I believe we'll go and have another chat with Hartley Galbraith. As it appears he truly did see his mother killed, it's possible that, branches notwithstanding, he actually noticed more than he's realized."

The group parted. Stokes and Barnaby set off along the path around the house, making for the carriage they'd left in the drive. After one last look at the empty pillar at the top of the steps, Penelope led the way back into the house.

She took one step into the corridor and stopped dead.

Violet nearly ran into her. "What is it?"

"Move back a bit." Looking down, Penelope stepped back, over the shallow step that marked the threshold. "Aha!" Glancing at Griselda and Violet, she explained, "I had wondered how it was that Hartley and his intended saw the shoe so clearly. Normally when a lady walks, her hems largely conceal her shoes. However, here we have a step. The lady, even fleeing, would have lifted her skirts—we all do it without even thinking. I just did." Penelope paused, head tilting. "I wonder how much of the shoe Hartley—and even more likely his intended—saw?"

Griselda followed the thought. "Do Lady Latimer's shoes have different styles?"

"I don't know," Penelope said. "We'll have to ask."

Violet had been studying the step, experimenting by raising her own hems while glancing out to where Hartley and his intended had stood. "They might, indeed, have had quite a decent view." Violet met Penelope's gaze. "In the moonlight, they might not have been able to see color, but style is a different matter altogether."

"Indeed." Penelope's eyes gleamed. "We really must learn more about these shoes—that's becoming imperative." She looked at Violet. "Do we have time to question the maids before going on to the Latimers'?"

They decided that they did. Penelope inquired of the butler, who, it transpired, had been instructed by Lady Fairchild to grant Penelope whatever she desired. Following in Penelope's wake, Violet soon found herself seated on a sofa alongside Penelope and Griselda in Lady Fairchild's elegant white-and-gilt drawing room. The two senior maids who had tended the ladies' withdrawing room on the night of the ball stood on the rug before them, nervously wondering why they had been summoned and what was to come.

Penelope reassured the maids, and Griselda's calm presence put them at ease.

But when informed of Penelope's wish to know if, early on the evening of the ball, they had noticed any lady upset or displaying signs of shock, the older of the pair shook her head. "I'm sorry, ma'am, but we see so many ladies of a ball-night, we'd be hard-pressed to remember any of them, not in particular, and there's always upsets and dramas going on." She glanced at her colleague. "I can say that I didn't see or hear anything that made me think any lady had seen the dead lady."

The second maid nodded. "Nor me. But even if we had, even if we saw them again, they'd have to be in the same gowns and with their hair done the same way, with the same jewels and such, for us to be sure of them."

Penelope swallowed a sigh and dismissed both maids with thanks.

Rising, she, Violet, and Griselda returned to the front hall where the butler was waiting to see them to Penelope's carriage.

"Off to Latimer House, Phelps," Penelope called up to the coachman. "It's in Hanover Square."

Phelps raised his whip in acknowledgment. Penelope climbed in, followed by Violet and Griselda. Conner, the groom, shut the door, and seconds later they were rolling down the Fairchild House drive.

"I can only hope," Penelope said, settling back against the squabs, "that we can persuade Lady Latimer that she really does need to entrust us with the secret of her shoes."

* * *

On arriving at the Latimers' house, Penelope, Violet, and Griselda were shown into the drawing room. It was a little after two thirty, and it was clear that the assembled ladies had been awaiting their arrival with some degree of anxiety.

Penelope intended to soothe them by apologizing for being late, but the information that she, Violet, and Griselda had just come from Fairchild House didn't really help. The tension in the room remained high.

Penelope introduced Violet—"Mrs. Montague"—and Griselda— "Mrs. Stokes"—to Lady Latimer, then her ladyship introduced her daughters. All four were present—Georgina, the eldest, married and more experienced, Cecilia, the next, about to become formally betrothed to Mr. Brandywell, Cynthia, not yet spoken for, and

Millicent, who had been expecting to enjoy her first Season and instead was coping with grief. Penelope took due note of their expressions, of their tones and the way they moved—of every little sign that testified to their frames of mind.

The overwhelming impression she received was one of sadness and regret. Sadness over Lady Galbraith's demise, and regret—very much ongoing—that the existence of the feud prevented them from comforting the Galbraiths.

Who, Penelope recalled, reminded by several glances toward the window associated with mention of that family, lived just across the square.

Seeing her comprehension, Lady Latimer said, "We bought the houses so we could remain close. That's a major reason why the children are so…intertwined. My girls were forever over there, and her girls—and Hartley, too—were forever over here." She hesitated, as if she'd intended to say more, but then she glanced at her daughters. "Very well, Mrs. Adair, ladies." As her daughters fell silent and expectantly looked Penelope's way, Lady Latimer turned to her and asked, "How may we best aid you in helping us?"

Penelope rapidly ordered her questions. "The first thing we need is, not to put too fine a point on it, your alibis. That's the easiest thing to get out of the way, and short of identifying who did kill Lady Galbraith, you having sound alibis declared and checked is the surest way to eliminate each of you as suspects."

After an instant of silence, Georgina asked, "So what do you need? A list of all those with whom we spoke at the ball?"

"Yes, but only over the first hour or so." Penelope glanced at Lady Latimer. "You told us that you and your daughters arrived at a little after nine o'clock, and we have reason to believe that Lady Galbraith was dead before half past ten."

Lady Latimer almost winced. But she nodded. "Very well." She looked at her eldest daughter. "Perhaps, Georgina, you could start?"

Georgina inclined her head and obliged. Violet had pulled a notebook from her capacious reticule and duly wrote down the names and details Georgina rattled off. Cecilia followed with another comprehensive list; the sheer number of names made it highly unlikely that either young lady could possibly have squeezed in a trip to the side terrace.

Cynthia, however, had significantly fewer people who might vouch for her whereabouts. "I felt the hem catch as we climbed the front steps. I spoke with Henrietta Martin in the foyer and, once in the ballroom, I chatted with Melinda Wyman and Mr. Chatteris, but then I realized my hem really had come down and I told Mama that I was going to fix it. I went to the withdrawing room to do so." Cynthia paused, as if remembering, then went on. "When I returned to the ballroom, the first dance was in progress, so I waited by the wall. When the dance ended, I spoke with Susan Watkins and Mr. Molloy, and the Webb sisters."

Penelope knew ton balls; by her calculation, Cynthia's alibi left over twenty minutes unaccounted for. "How was the hem?"

Cynthia grimaced. "It was properly torn. I couldn't pin it up—it was that new slinky silk, and the pins wouldn't hold—so I had to sew it up, which is why I took so long."

As Lady Latimer had said, Cynthia was the quiet one. Her recitation of what she had done and with whom she had spoken had been exceedingly spare compared to her older sisters' more detailed accounts. But Cynthia wasn't only quiet in that sense; she also sat still where others fidgeted. She projected a sense of deep and immovable calm, while her sisters appeared much more fashionably flighty, although none of them, thankfully, took that to extremes. Yet…Penelope wondered about Cynthia.

And, as if she could read Penelope's mind, Cynthia stated, with that entrenched calmness that rendered the statement a solid, uncontestable fact, "Regardless, I can assure you, Mrs. Adair, ladies, that I was not the lady your witness saw fleeing from the side terrace."

After a moment of studying Cynthia's face and detecting not the slightest sign of any degree of prevarication, much less guilt, Penelope inclined her head in acceptance. She and Violet moved on to the youngest daughter, Millicent.

As she was not yet formally out, Millicent had not danced but, instead, had been chatting the entire time with a group of similarly restricted young ladies; Millicent rattled off their names, along with several of the topics they'd discussed. The latter, more than anything else, served to convince Penelope, as well as Violet and Griselda, that Millicent's alibi resembled cast iron.

Finally, Lady Latimer gave them her own list of friends with whom she had conversed; it, too, was comprehensive. Penelope knew enough of those mentioned to feel certain that Lady Latimer had not been the lady seen fleeing the side terrace.

After writing down the last name, Violet showed Penelope her notebook. Penelope glanced down the fifty or so names and nodded. "Should it come to it and the police need to formally eliminate each of you as suspects, these lists should be more than adequate to the task." For all except Cynthia, at any rate; Penelope kept that observation to herself. "However,"—looking up, she let her gaze travel over all five Latimer ladies' faces—"this being the haut ton, it would be better all around if we could avoid having to ask others to confirm each of your whereabouts."

None of the Latimer ladies were fools; it was clear from their expressions that all of them—even Millicent—followed Penelope's reasoning perfectly.

"Consequently," she went on, "if we accept that the lady wearing Lady Latimer's shoes who was seen fleeing the side terrace immediately after Lady Galbraith had been struck down wasn't, in fact, any of you, then the tack I believe we need to take is to clarify just what the witness actually saw. As I mentioned, we revisited Fairchild House earlier. There, we confirmed that several corroborating points in the witness's statement are factually correct. Both the police and we are inclined to believe that the witness has spoken the truth. That being so, we need to account for the pair of Lady Latimer's shoes that he saw, apparently quite clearly."

Lady Latimer and her daughters exchanged glances, then Lady Latimer looked at Penelope. "In light of what you told me this morning, I asked the girls to check—none of us has lost a pair of our shoes. All are accounted for and still in our possession."

Penelope inclined her head in acceptance. "So that's one possible explanation eliminated—thank you. Let's turn to the next possibility." She looked steadily at Lady Latimer. "I understand your agreement with your shoemaker is for exclusive supply. Is there any chance whatsoever that your shoemaker, intentionally or otherwise—for instance, through being burgled—has allowed a pair of shoes to go elsewhere?"

Lady Latimer opened her lips, clearly intending to refute the suggestion, but paused. After a moment of returning Penelope's regard, her ladyship admitted, "I can't answer that. I cannot know."

Penelope nodded. "Which, given the seriousness of the situation, is why you now need to tell me who your secret shoemaker is."

Lady Latimer glanced at her daughters, then, frowning, looked back at Penelope. "I will undertake to visit and ask—"

Penelope shook her head. "You can't ask. If the shoemaker has signed an exclusivity agreement with you—which I assume they have?" Reluctantly, Lady Latimer nodded. "Then," Penelope went on, "your asking will place them in an invidious position. If they admit to losing a pair of shoes, they'll be admitting to breaking your contract. However, if we"—Penelope indicated Violet and Griselda as well as herself—"as investigators assisting the police, ask in complete confidence, we will have a much better chance of receiving a truthful answer."

Penelope paused. When Lady Latimer continued to regard her without any sign of capitulating, Penelope stated, "To determine whether the pair of Lady Latimer's shoes worn by the lady fleeing the terrace might have been lost from the shoemaker's shop, rather than being one of the pairs your family own, we will need the shoemaker's direction."

Lips thinning, Lady Latimer held Penelope's steady gaze...then her ladyship glanced at her daughters, clearly seeking their advice.

Penelope noted that, although Lady Latimer's gaze swept all four faces, it came to rest on Cynthia's.

Cynthia returned her mother's gaze, then quietly said, "Perhaps if Mrs. Adair and her colleagues would swear not to divulge the information to anyone else? We do, after all, need to discover where that pair of shoes came from, and if not from us, then..."

Penelope waited for five seconds, then offered, "I assure you that our discretion on this matter will be absolute."

Lady Latimer pulled a face, rather shocking in one who normally kept her expression so controlled. Facing Penelope, her ladyship conceded. "Very well, Mrs. Adair. Your point is well made." Lady Latimer glanced at Violet's notebook. "If Mrs. Montague will permit, I will write down the address, and also a short note instructing the shoemaker to speak with you. I assure you that without such a note, she will deny any knowledge of Lady Latimer's shoes."

"She?" Griselda showed her surprise. "There aren't many women in that trade."

Violet handed Lady Latimer her notebook and pencil. Accepting them, Lady Latimer nodded. "Indeed. Which, I suspect, is how she came to stumble on the means of creating the shoes—she wasn't content simply doing what all the men were."

Three minutes later, Lady Latimer handed the notebook to Penelope, open to the page on which she had written.

While Penelope pored over the name, address, and the letter of instruction, Lady Latimer said, "If you please, Mrs. Adair, should you discover that Miss Hook has, indeed, allowed a pair of shoes to…escape her custody, so to speak, do assure her that, short of that lapse being deliberate on her part, I see no reason to take any action regarding the apparent breach of our exclusivity agreement. Accidents happen. We must allow for that."

Penelope inclined her head. "I will reassure Miss Hook, should such an assurance be warranted. However, there is one further possibility, other than that the shoes derived from Miss Hook's establishment."

Lady Latimer frowned, uncomprehending.

It was Griselda who explained. "Lady Latimer's shoes have been all the rage for nearly a year. Some other enterprising shoemaker might finally have succeeded in duplicating the effect."

Lady Latimer's brows rose. "I suppose that is a possibility. I've heard of any number of ladies who have had their shoemakers slaving, trying to mimic our shoes."

"So Miss Hook is not the only possible source, merely the only one we yet know of." Penelope rose and held out her hand. "Thank you." Clasping Lady Latimer's fingers, Penelope inclined her head to the four Latimer girls. "Ladies."

The girls all smiled, a trifle weakly, but they were polite and respectful as Penelope, Violet, and Griselda took their leave, with the address of the shoemaker responsible for creating Lady Latimer's shoes safely tucked away in Violet's reticule.

CHAPTER 8

There was no chance in heaven, much less on earth, that Penelope, Violet, and Griselda could possibly wait until the next day before visiting the establishment of Myrtle Hook.

As it happened, Miss Hook's shop was located in New Road in Camden Town, not all that far from Griselda's house in St. John's Wood. Given they were headed in that general direction, the ladies paused in Albemarle Street to take up Megan, who Griselda had left playing with Oliver in his nursery, watched over by Hettie.

But when Hettie came down the stairs, Megan on one hip and Oliver balanced on the other, both children's faces lit at the sight of their mothers, and Penelope, reaching for Oliver, was struck by an idea.

When, minutes later, the carriage rumbled north, it carried Penelope, Violet, and Griselda, and also Megan, Hettie, and Oliver.

The children were delighted with the outing; sitting on their mothers' laps, they pressed their faces to the windows and watched the houses, carriages, horses, and people, and pointed and laughed.

Pushing her spectacles up again—Oliver had a habit of pulling them down so he could stare directly into her eyes—Penelope was curious to see how her latest idea would play out. The excursion was entirely safe; there could be no danger in a shop open to the public on a busy street—and regardless, her three guards were present, Phelps and Conner having been joined by James, who acted as footman. And not only were she and Griselda spending extra time with their children, Penelope had also noted that said children proved a potent distraction for other adults, especially women.

Both Oliver and Megan could be counted on to smile and chortle and generally act sweetly; if some female needed to be won over or distracted, the children were the perfect accomplices.

They reached New Road and located the shop. Hook's Shoe Emporium appeared quietly prosperous.

"As it should," Penelope remarked to Violet and Griselda as they gathered on the pavement. "I can only imagine how much Lady Latimer is paying for those shoes."

"If they successfully work as Cinderella shoes, then I'm sure her ladyship considers them to be well worth the price," Griselda said.

Recalling all she'd heard about the desperation in the marriage mart, Penelope inclined her head. "There is that."

It was now late afternoon; although workers had started to stream home, all the shops were open and busy. James led the way. A bell tinkled as he opened the emporium's door. Entering, he held the door for their party, then after shutting the door, he stood to attention beside it, waiting, as a footman should, to carry any parcels back to the carriage.

His presence was a subtle indication that purchases were anticipated.

Griselda had been the last to enter the shop. Halting just inside the door, she took visual stock. The emporium was laid out much as her milliner's shop, with a counter toward the rear, running across the width of the shop and cutting off the public space from the doorway that led into the back room and the stairs that gave access to the upper floor. The space between the counter and the front door was both display area and salon; racks, shelves, and glass cases lined the area, with shoes and boots of all sizes and styles artfully arranged to best entice, while the central space was given over to an arrangement of chairs, stools, and footstools.

Penelope had taken Oliver to look at some small boys' shoes. Megan had spotted a ladies' shoe sporting a fringe, and Hettie had taken her to get a closer look. Violet was strolling down the room, surveying the shoes as she went.

Penelope, seconded by Violet, had suggested that, as owner of a millinery shop, Griselda should be the one to speak with Myrtle Hook. Hoping she could do her friends' confidence justice, Griselda drew in a breath and advanced on the counter.

One of the young shop girls had left her station to attend to Violet. The remaining girl, a neatly turned out slip of a thing, ventured a small smile. "Can I help you, ma'am?"

Griselda returned the smile. "Indeed, I hope you can. I'm here to see Miss Hook. Please inform her that I have a message from...her most valuable private customer."

The girl blinked. For an instant, she studied Griselda, confirming that she was both assured and in earnest, then, a frown tangling her fine brows, the girl nodded and stepped back. "I'll ask. If you'll wait here, ma'am?'

Griselda assented with a nod and watched the girl disappear behind the curtain that screened the entrance to the back room.

The girl returned within a minute. With a "Miss Hook will be with you momentarily," the girl left the counter to tend to Penelope and Oliver, who was somewhat inarticulately demanding to try on some boots.

Leaning on the counter, Griselda watched the performance and couldn't help but grin.

Two minutes later, the curtain was thrust aside and an older woman, a decade or so older than Griselda, stumped out. Myrtle Hook was a heavy woman with a ruddy complexion and wispy red hair, but her eyes were shrewd in a face that bore the stamp of determination, softened by a level of satisfaction. Griselda got the impression that Myrtle Hook had worked hard for what she'd wanted and was now relatively content with her lot.

While Griselda had been studying Myrtle, the shoemaker had been returning the favor. As quick to pick up the telltale signs of class among her customers as Griselda was, after a glance at Penelope, Violet, Hettie, and the children, and James standing to attention by the door, Myrtle was, understandably, a trifle puzzled.

Griselda smiled. "Yes, we are all together." Myrtle would have heard the shop bell ring only once. Glancing at the others, Griselda said, "While I suspect we are interested in your wares, our primary reason for calling is due to a problem your most valuable customer has encountered that, entirely incidentally, necessitates our looking into the details of the special shoes you make."

Suspicion filled Myrtle Hook's eyes. Griselda met her resistance with a gentle smile. "I'm a milliner, Miss Hook. While our professions might be complementary, they are not sufficiently similar that I would have any use for your secrets. As for my friends, they are not connected with trade of any sort, as I'm sure you can tell." Griselda had been holding Violet's notebook below the counter, out of sight.

Raising it, she opened it to the page containing Lady Latimer's note. "Your special customer gave us this letter to serve as introduction. It makes her wishes plain."

Griselda offered Myrtle Hook the notebook. Retrieving a pair of wire-rimmed glasses from the capacious front pocket of the leather apron she wore, the shoemaker took the book and read. Reaching the end of the note, Myrtle humphed. Then she raised her gaze to Griselda's face and opened her lips—

The bell tinkled again. Both Myrtle and Griselda glanced toward the door and saw a lady with two girls, both clearly her daughters, come sweeping in.

Myrtle's gaze fastened on Penelope's town carriage drawn up outside the shop. Conner, too, was standing on the pavement beside the door, attempting to look unobtrusive but, although not wearing livery, he, James, Phelps, and the carriage screamed of the quality of customers patronizing Myrtle's emporium. Myrtle grinned. "The longer you and your friends remain, the better the day for me."

As if to prove the point, the door opened again and two more ladies came in. From the way they looked around, it was plain they had not previously been in the shop.

Myrtle grunted. "It might be as well if you and your friends come through to my office."

Retrieving the notebook, Griselda nodded. "The children can remain here with the nursemaid, if you like?"

Myrtle considered the toddlers for an instant. "No. You'd better bring them with you. My girls and the customers don't need the distraction."

Griselda glided about the shop, gathering the others. Myrtle flipped back the end of the counter and beckoned them through. The others followed Myrtle past the curtain. Griselda brought up the rear, setting the counter to rights, then slipping past the curtain to join the others in the small cubbyhole that served as Myrtle's office.

It was crowded with all of them in there. Myrtle rummaged in a tin and produced two hard biscuits. She gave one to Oliver and one to Megan; Hettie had balanced both children on the top of an upturned crate in one corner. Thanking Myrtle on behalf of the children, Hettie crouched before the crate and watched over the pair while they ate.

Returning to the chair before the desk pushed against the end wall, Myrtle sat. Griselda had already slipped into the visitor's chair. Violet and Penelope had elected to stand against the wall at her back.

Myrtle considered the three of them, trying to read their faces, then she focused on Griselda. "So what's this about?"

Griselda chose her words with care. "A few nights ago, a lady wearing Lady Latimer's shoes was seen fleeing the scene of a murder. Lady Latimer and her daughters were in the same house at the time, attending a ball. However, there are reasons to suspect that the lady who fled wasn't Lady Latimer or any of her daughters. Which leads to the question of whether any other lady could have, somehow, gained access to a pair of Lady Latimer's shoes."

It took Myrtle a moment to follow the argument, then she scowled. "If you're saying that I sold someone else—"

"No. We're not even suggesting that, much less saying it." Griselda's tone pulled Myrtle up short. "But this is murder in the ton, the police are investigating, and it's all quite serious, so, rather than involve the authorities directly, Lady Latimer has asked us to look into all the possible ways that some other lady might have come to have a pair of these shoes."

"For instance," Violet said, "you might have been burgled and lost a pair of the shoes through no fault of your own."

"Or one of your workers might have been tempted and sold on a pair without your knowledge." Penelope met Myrtle's gaze. "Lady Latimer wanted us to assure you that any such accident outside your control would not be seen by her as a violation of your agreement."

Myrtle studied Penelope for a moment, then blew out a breath. "All right. I understand—at least why you're asking. But all I can tell you is that we haven't lost any of our pairs of those shoes. Her ladyship and I—we were that careful when we set up the system, the ordering, the way we send the shoes to her, and so on. None have gone missing. And as for any of my workers stealing a pair, that's nonsense. They're all relatives of sorts, so that would be like stealing from themselves. And on top of all that, we run a very tight process on those shoes. There are never more than two pairs being made at any time, so it's impossible for any to go missing without us noticing." Turning to her desk, Myrtle pulled out a slim ledger. "This is the Latimer account. Those shoes are difficult to make, the materials are expensive, and the construction is time-consuming, so they end very costly. Against that, her ladyship pays me well. But because of the cost, we keep everything written down, you see." Myrtle showed them a page of the ledger. "Every hour, every skein of thread, every last crystal."

Violet had stepped forward to peer at the ledger. Straightening, she said, "With that degree of oversight, you would know instantly if anything went missing."

"Exactly. That's what I've been trying to say." Myrtle closed the ledger. "If some other lady was wearing shoes like the ones we make, they didn't come from here."

"Hmm." Penelope digested that; she had hoped that Myrtle's shop would prove to be the source of the lady-on-the-terrace's shoes. She frowned. "If those shoes didn't come from here, then we're looking for some other shoemaker." She refocused on Myrtle. "You haven't heard of any competitor, perchance?"

Myrtle snorted. "They've all been sweating in their shops trying to copy my shoes, but, so far, I haven't heard of any succeeding—and I'm sure they would crow if they did." She paused, then pulled a face. "I'm sure that, at some point, someone will succeed, but as far as I know, no one has yet."

Penelope considered, then asked, "Would it be possible for us—the three of us—to see how you make the shoes? If we knew the details, there might be some way to check if anyone else has started duplicating them. I take it that there are critical points in the construction that are not common. Anything *un*common would give us a possible avenue to follow."

Myrtle's resistance showed in her face, but, no doubt recalling Lady Latimer's instructions that she was to give the three ladies who called on her every possible assistance, she debated, then, eyes narrowing, said, "As none of you are shoemakers…if you will each swear on your mother's grave that you will never divulge anything of what I show you to anyone so that it becomes common knowledge or is passed on to some other shoemaker, then, yes. I'll show you."

Griselda and Violet immediately put their hands over their hearts and swore the required oath.

Penelope frowned. "My mother's not dead."

"Your father, then," Griselda said.

Frown evaporating, Penelope complied, rattling off her father's title in the process, which made Myrtle's eyes grow round.

But Myrtle duly nodded and heaved her bulk out of her chair. "Leave the little ones here—they'll be safer."

Hettie was happy to remain with the children.

Griselda, Violet, and Penelope all rather eagerly followed Myrtle from the room.

She preceded them down a short corridor, opened the door at its end, and led them through. The room beyond was a workshop, with a long, wide central table plus benches all around the walls. Several girls and women, and two lads, were working at various stations, some hammering, stretching, and shaping shoes, some cutting out soles, others carving heels on lathes. Penelope was fascinated but didn't dare dally as Myrtle led them to one side of the room.

"This is where we make those shoes." Myrtle stopped before the bench along the side wall. At one end, by a narrow window, a girl sat on a stool embroidering midnight-blue satin with heavy gold thread, while in the middle of the bench, an older woman was fixing satin of the palest pink heavily embroidered with silver thread to a plain ballroom pump.

Myrtle pointed to the blue satin. "That's for her ladyship, for her second daughter's engagement ball. And that"—Myrtle pointed to the pale pink—"is for the youngest daughter, for her come-out ball."

Griselda was peering at the gold embroidery. "That's awfully heavy."

"Yes, but it's necessary." When Griselda looked at her questioningly, Myrtle paused, clearly wrestling with her reluctance, then grudgingly volunteered, "Without a heavy surround of what is essentially metal, the crystals won't stay on."

Penelope and Violet shifted nearer to look at the embroidery on the pink shoe.

After a moment of inspection, Penelope said, "So one of the critical points in the process is to do the right sort of embroidery."

Myrtle nodded. "It has to be thick enough, and it has to be high-quality metal thread. Most shoemakers never use real gold or silver thread—they use all sorts of substitutes that look like gold or silver but are much cheaper, reasoning that, on shoes, no one can tell the difference. And in general, they're right. But for *these* shoes, the thread has to be high-content base metal, and there has to be enough of it surrounding each crystal or the crystals won't stick."

"So," Penelope said, "we could trace the users of high-content gold and silver threads—" She broke off as Griselda and Myrtle shook their heads.

"I use high-content gold and silver threads," Griselda explained. "All milliners do, most often on gloves."

"And jewelers and dressmakers, too," Myrtle said. "Not on everything, obviously, but it's common enough on goods for the nobs."

Penelope grimaced.

Myrtle looked at Griselda. "The glue is also not a common shoemaker's glue. I got it from my grandmother—she was a milliner. She worked up her own recipe and used her glue to stick everything on anything. That said, not even that glue will work to hold crystals on shoes for any length of time, not unless you also have the right metal thread embroidery, and the right crystals."

Griselda looked up and down the bench. "Where are the crystals?"

Myrtle waved them back and opened a cupboard under the bench. A heavy iron safe sat on the floor; it had been mortared in place. Myrtle spun the dial, then opened the door and reached in. She pulled out a covered tray, set it on the bench, and lifted the lid.

Fire blazed out of the black-lined tray. Even in the dull light of the workshop, the crystals all but exploded with light.

Penelope blinked. Several times. "No wonder they were so easily seen, even in moonlight."

"In any light, no matter how weak." Myrtle picked up a handful of crystals and let them fall from her palm in a living river of coruscating light. "They're high-lead-content crystal, specially cut to maximize brilliance, which is why they work so well on the shoes."

Penelope all but held her breath as she asked, "Are they rare?"

Myrtle started to nod, then stopped. "Not rare so much as expensive. They're imported from Slovakia, but because of the cost, they're not used that much, at least not that I know of."

Griselda was shaking her head. "I haven't seen them used anywhere—and I would have noticed."

Penelope shut her lips on the thoughts churning through her head. She glanced at Griselda and saw realization abruptly bloom in her eyes.

Violet, too, was deep in thought. Myrtle closed the tray and bent to put it back in the safe. As she did, Violet asked, "Are there other types of crystals that would work?"

Busy closing the safe, Myrtle shook her head. "Only this brand. No others have both the lead content and the brilliant cut."

Before any of them asked anything more and inadvertently jarred Myrtle from her helpful mood, Penelope smiled as the shoemaker straightened. "Thank you for showing us. I believe we've seen all we need to see." She turned and started for the door to the shop. "You mentioned that other shoemakers have been trying to copy these shoes.

Tell me—have you heard or seen anything that would lead you to suppose that anyone has guessed that it's you"—Penelope gestured at the workshop—"and here, that makes them?"

Myrtle had followed Penelope; Griselda and Violet had fallen in behind.

"No," Myrtle said. "And I assure you that if any of the others in the guild had guessed that those shoes came from here, we *would* have been burgled. No doubt about that." Joining Penelope by the door, Myrtle met her gaze. "As you might expect, given the huge sums other ladies are offering for such shoes, the competition has been fierce, but as yet, no one else has discovered the secret of making crystal-covered shoes."

Penelope smiled and led the way from the workshop.

* * *

"**R**egardless of what Myrtle believes," Penelope said, "I will wager any sum you like that some other shoemaker has finally found a way to duplicate her shoes." She paused, then amended with a shrug, "It's that, or her ledger system failed, and one of her employees has succeeded in smuggling out a pair or in making a separate pair that Myrtle doesn't know about. We only need one loose pair, after all."

They were back in the carriage and rolling around the northern border of Regent's Park on their way to Griselda's house. Hettie and the now-drowsy children were on the seat alongside Penelope, while Griselda and Violet occupied the seat opposite.

Griselda regarded Penelope with amused affection. "You seem to have accepted that the lady on the terrace wasn't any of the Latimers, even though we've yet to check their alibis and Cynthia's, at least, has a rather large gap in it."

Frowning slightly, Penelope rubbed her nose. "I know. I'm not sure why, but by the sum of all things—all my impressions and everything I've heard—I just can't see any of the Latimer girls, and definitely not Cynthia, shoving a cannonball at their Aunt Marjorie. And it couldn't have been Lady Latimer—such an action would have torn her apart. She's torn now, but that would have destroyed her. And I *know* none of that is logical, but there you are."

When neither Violet nor Griselda argued but just smiled at her in unvoiced agreement, Penelope leaned her head back against the squabs and asked, "So where do we stand? What about these crystals?"

"Given they're imported," Violet said, "and expensive and not much used, we might be able to trace whoever is using them via the suppliers."

Griselda wrinkled her nose. "I was tempted to ask Myrtle who her supplier was, but not only would that have put her in an invidious position—she'd given up all her other secrets, and that's the one that's most critical of all, yet she had been instructed to tell us all, regardless of whether that might ruin her business...as I said, invidious. But aside from that, she most likely knows of only one supplier—the one she uses." Griselda glanced at Violet. "With such things, there's usually any number of importers—well, at least a handful and very likely more—who will have contacts in Slovakia and be able to bring in the crystals."

"There's a difference," Violet said, "between being able to and actually doing. We only need to check with the firms who are *currently* importing those particular crystals."

"True." Tipping her head back, Griselda thought, then said, "I wonder if we can get a list of the firms importing the crystals."

"I rather suspect," Violet replied, "that we might need to ask for firms importing goods from Slovakia—it's not a major trading nation, after all."

"No, but..." Griselda shrugged lightly. "I really have no idea how many firms we might find on such a list."

"Heathcote might know—or, at least, Mr. Slocum might be able to find out for me." Violet, too, shrugged. "I can ask and see what they turn up. It might give us a place to start."

Griselda nodded. "And I can inquire from my contacts—the brokers who can usually find me anything I need for my hats and gloves." With rising enthusiasm, she went on, "And then perhaps we can compare our lists—yours of firms importing goods from Slovakia, and mine of those companies known to supply crystals and such for the appropriate trades."

Griselda and Violet exchanged smiles. "Yes, let's," Violet said. "That sounds like a viable path forward."

The carriage slowed and turned into the familiar surrounds of Greenbury Street. Realizing Penelope had been strangely silent, both Violet and Griselda looked at her.

She was staring absentmindedly out of the window, but as the carriage slowed outside Griselda's house, Penelope turned her head and met their gazes. "There's something we've overlooked." She frowned. "Let's postulate that some other lady has, indeed, found some enterprising shoemaker who has succeeded in duplicating Lady Latimer's shoes. If so, why haven't I—or Myrtle, Lady Latimer, or anyone in the ton—heard of it? This lady wore the shoes to the Fairchilds' ball, but made no effort at all to show them off, even before she followed Lady Galbraith outside." Penelope shook her head. "That makes no sense..." Her frown deepened. "Unless..."

The carriage had rocked to a halt; James appeared and opened the door.

Penelope sat staring, unseeing, at the opposite side of the carriage as James helped Hettie and the children down to the pavement, then handed Violet and Griselda down.

At last, Penelope stirred and followed the others out of the carriage.

The instant James had shut the door and Penelope had resettled her skirts, both Griselda and Violet demanded, "Unless what?"

Suddenly entirely sober, Penelope met their gazes. "It just occurred to me. If you were a shoemaker who had finally succeeded in duplicating Lady Latimer's shoes—and having worked to do so suggests that said shoemaker is aware of the ton's intense interest in those shoes, and that in turn means he would almost certainly have heard of the feud—then *who* in all the ton is this shoemaker most likely to contact to sell his version of Lady Latimer's shoes?"

Both Griselda's and Violet's expressions grew as sober and as serious as Penelope's.

All three looked at each other, but none of them put the obvious answer to that question into words.

Penelope nodded. "Just so." She raised her brows. "I wonder how we can meaningfully inquire at the Galbraiths' house."

* * *

*L*ate that night, Hartley Galbraith climbed through an open window into the conservatory at the rear of Latimer House. The house slumbered; there were no lights burning anywhere, not even in the conservatory.

Especially not in the conservatory.

He and Cynthia didn't need light; they could find each other through any darkness, or so it seemed.

She appeared, an angelic phantom gliding out of the shadows to greet him. With a soft smile, she walked into his arms, her arms rising to wind about his neck as she stretched up, and he bent his head, and their lips met.

The kiss...embodied the promise that had kept him going through the days and nights since his mother had been killed. The comfort, the support—all Cynthia so unrestrainedly offered.

He deepened the kiss, wanting more, wanting to touch, to taste, to sample the scintillating passion that, wonder of wonders, had so steadily grown between them. She murmured through the kiss and pressed closer; in wordless communion, she urged him on. Joined with him in waltzing this waltz of the senses that neither had ever shared with anyone else.

And for moments, those moments, they stepped away from the here and now, from the horror and sorrow and tensions of their lives, and they danced.

For each other, with each other.

Their lips fused, and their tongues tangled, stroked, and caressed in a duel of delight. Her fingers speared through his hair and gripped his skull as he drew her flush against him, molding her lithe body to his, easing his hardness with her supple curves, the fullness of her breasts cushioning the contours of his chest, the soft tautness of her belly cradling his erection.

They both wanted so much more.

Both knew they couldn't have it, not yet.

Not while the here and now hovered so close, and so strongly, so insistently, tugged at their hearts.

Now was not the time.

Dragging in a breath, he steeled himself and drew back from the kiss. She matched his resolve, and his reluctance, as she lowered her heels to the floor and looked into his face.

Studied it in the weak light.

He had no idea what she could see, but he grimaced. "I really don't like this." His arms still wrapped around her—unwilling to lose her warmth—he glanced about them. "Meeting here like this." Returning his gaze to her face, he went on, "It's bad enough that we have to meet clandestinely, but meeting here is even worse. I feel as if I'm trespassing in some unforgivable way on your parents' goodwill."

They hadn't previously used the conservatory for their assignations, but after their last meeting in the church porch, Hartley had swallowed his dislike of trysting in her parents' house; better she remain safe indoors than have her court the risks of the streets at night, even with her maid and the undergardener, who was little more than a boy.

Cynthia arched a brow. "You're here at my invitation, but if we're to speak of not liking things...I have to tell you that we—Mama especially, but me and my sisters, too—have started encountering more definite whispers and suspicious looks."

Hartley swore beneath his breath. Lowering his arms, he grasped one of Cynthia's hands and drew her to a wrought-iron seat set beneath one wall of glass panes. She sat, and still holding her hand, he sat beside her. "Tell me the truth—how bad is it?"

They'd moved into an area washed by moonlight; the stronger illumination allowed Cynthia to see just how drawn, how haggard, Hartley was. She swallowed the more colorful description that had leapt to her tongue, and instead said, "It's not yet bad enough that we can't simply ignore it. We're none of us wilting flowers, as you know. For the moment, we're managing." She paused, then added, "But what we can't know is how long the uncertainty will last, and how much society's reactions will escalate before the murderer is caught. And in pursuit of that—the murderer being caught—I persuaded Mama, and the others, too, that calling in Mrs. Adair would be a sensible thing to do. Mama went to see her this morning, and Mrs. Adair and her friends called on us in the afternoon."

Cynthia paused, remembering. "She strikes me as being rather acute, and her friends aren't just hangers-on, either. I got the impression that we were being assessed by three different pairs of eyes and ears." Cynthia continued, describing the interview and the concession her mother had finally been persuaded to make. "So Mrs. Adair and her cronies are hunting for some evidence that some other lady has, somehow, obtained a pair of Lady Latimer's shoes—namely the pair that we saw on the lady fleeing the terrace."

Silence ensued as the words conjured up the vision in both their minds. Cynthia shivered and leaned against Hartley. He put his arm around her and drew her closer.

"So," she said, glancing at his face and seeing the lines shock and grief had drawn there, "how are your family—the girls, your father? How is the household faring?"

Hartley met her eyes, his own heavy and tired. "Not as well as I'd hoped. The pater has rallied, but he's still not up to much. Geraldine, at least, came downstairs this morning. I think she would have improved further, but we had several visitors, and she and I felt we had to be present to support Papa." Hartley paused, then said, "The first through the door were Lady Gresham and Mrs. Foley. As you know, they're connections of sorts, so we couldn't turn them away, although to give him his due, poor Millwell tried. He didn't get far—you know Agatha Gresham. She bullied her way past poor Millwell and demoralized him so thoroughly that he let three other groups in before I realized and put a stop to it. By then, Papa was gray, and Geraldine was in tears and struggling not to break down entirely."

Cynthia hissed in almost ferocious disapproval. "Don't these people have any feelings?"

"What they had," Hartley said bitterly, "was rampant curiosity of the worst kind. All of them in one way or another alluded to the feud, and inquired in circuitous ways about what we imagined the Latimers felt over Mama's death..." Frustration strangled Hartley for an instant, then he ground out, "Agatha even had the gall to ask Papa if he thought your mother had done it."

"Good God."

"Indeed. Papa...that nearly sank him, you know. But what's even worse is that those damned well-wishers have planted seeds in both Papa's and Geraldine's minds, and now they don't know what to feel, much less what to think." Hartley met Cynthia's gaze. "This evening, after dinner, which none of the girls came down for, I went up to see how they did. Monica is still lying in her bed and not speaking—she just stares at the wall. But I found Geraldine with Primrose—they were talking about the murder and whether it could possibly be one of your family who had done it."

Hartley held Cynthia's gaze for an instant, then softly swore and looked away. "They don't *want* to even think it, much less believe it, but they simply don't know...what to think. What to believe." He sighed. "It's eating at them—I can see it."

He looked into Cynthia's face. "It's building—the suspicion, the distrust."

Cynthia held his gaze, then blew out a breath. "I wasn't going to tell you—you have troubles enough—but...quite aside from the suspicion of others, which, as I said, we can currently ignore, Mama, my sisters, and I have been worrying about exactly that. About what your family will think—whether they will suspect one of us of that terrible deed—" Cynthia's voice quavered, and she stopped and looked away. Then she drew in a deep breath and, with more determination, went on. "We—Mama, Papa, and the four of us—discussed coming across the square. Simply walking across and knocking on your door and asking if your family will see us. Mama and Papa feel so strongly that they should be there to support your father through this. They are his oldest friends, and they feel they can't help." She glanced at Hartley. "But it would be impossible to visit—to simply call—without someone seeing and spreading the word. And as Mama pointed out, the ton would immediately be abuzz with people saying that we, the Latimers, were taking advantage of your mother's death to ignore what had patently been her wishes to cut all ties, and that therefore, doesn't it stand to reason that one of us... Well, you know how it goes. Even though Aunt Marjorie has gone, the feud, it seems, lives on."

After a moment, Cynthia continued, "Both our families are coming under increasing strain, not just from society but also from within, from our own worries and uncertainties about what each other might have done, or might think."

"It's a festering sore." Hartley's tone was grim.

"We can see it building, can already see that it's causing damage to your family and mine—all too soon it's going to become intolerable." Cynthia glanced at Hartley, searched his face, then faced forward. After several moments, she said, "Festering sores need to be lanced."

Hartley looked at Cynthia's face, at her profile; her jaw had set in a manner he knew well. "I'm not arguing, but what can we do?"

After a moment, she said, "Consider this. If we don't end this feud, now and forever, the only way you and I are going to be able to get married is if we run off to the Americas. It'll have to be that, for I warn you, I have no ambition whatsoever to feature in any Romeo-and-Juliet-style tragedy."

Hartley choked. "I should hope not!"

"Indeed. So if we want to marry, then we need to do something to...lance this boil that the feud has become." Shifting within his arm, Cynthia faced him. "Neither you nor I care that much for society or its opinion. We care about each other, and we care about our families, both of them."

Hartley nodded. "As I said before, no argument."

He waited, watching her face as she thought; she had always been the one to do the planning, while he, as usual, held himself ready to execute whatever scheme she devised.

But when a minute ticked by and she still didn't speak, his confidence wavered. If she couldn't think of a way...

Ten seconds later, he quietly asked, "*Is* there anything we can do?"

Determination hardened her features, then she met his eyes. "I'm not sure yet. Let me think."

CHAPTER 9

*A*s early as was acceptable the next morning, Barnaby and Stokes climbed the steps to the Galbraiths' front door, primed with the information Penelope, Violet, and Griselda had gained the previous day. On being admitted to the house, they requested an interview with Lord Galbraith. As they had yet to question his lordship and he had sent word to the Yard that he was now willing to speak with them, they had seized on that as their excuse for calling.

From the black wrapping on the door knocker to the drawn curtains and the weight of sorrow that hung in the air, the house was sunk in mourning. The butler, somewhat recovered from the last time they'd encountered him, showed them into the library.

Lord Galbraith rose slowly from the chair behind the desk. "Mr. Adair. Inspector Stokes." Lord Galbraith shook hands, then waved them to the chairs before the desk and sank back heavily into his own. "I apologize for not being able to speak with you previously. My son tells me you will have questions. If you will put them, I will do my poor best to answer."

"Thank you, my lord." Stokes glanced at Barnaby and made a production of getting out his notebook.

Capturing his lordship's gaze, Barnaby smiled reassuringly. "Hartley's no longer here?"

His lordship snorted, the sound laden with gruff affection. "Oh, he's still staying here—one thing I can say about my son is that he's a rock and he'll stick through any drama. I insisted he go out—get some air, have lunch at his club, talk with his friends. He's been holding the fort here singlehanded ever since..." His lordship drew in a quick, tight breath but then doggedly went on. "He needed a break from this house and the drain of having to take care of us all."

Barnaby inclined his head and wondered if the need to relieve Hartley had been a factor in drawing Lord Galbraith out of overwhelming grief. Being needed by others was often cited as a reason for not giving in to tragedy, for girding one's loins and forging on with life.

Stokes, having produced his notebook, cleared his throat and asked, "If I may, my lord, if you could once again tell me when it was that you last saw Lady Galbraith?" Stokes had asked the same question on the evening of the murder, but Lord Galbraith's answer had been vague and disjointed.

Lord Galbraith's features hardened into a mask. "It was in the ballroom. I can't recall what I told you before, but I remember the moment quite clearly. It wasn't that long after we'd arrived. I had joined a group of gentlemen—we were standing closer to the windows, most of the way down the ballroom. Marjorie had been with the girls, not far from the main doors—closer to the other end of the room. But then I glimpsed her moving through the crowd. I didn't know where she was going or why, but I did think it strange that she'd left the girls so early."

"In which direction was she going?' Stokes asked.

"Toward the end of the ballroom opposite the main doors." Lord Galbraith frowned. "She seemed very intent on something, as if she was following someone—I didn't see whom." His lordship paused, then, his expression growing even more rigid, said, "That was the last time I saw her."

Looking down at his notebook, Stokes merely inclined his head.

Beside him, Barnaby shifted, drawing his lordship's attention. "Did you know of anyone who wished your wife ill?"

Lord Galbraith grimaced. "No." He paused, then, as if feeling his way, said, "I have heard…whispers. Suggestions that, frankly, I cannot countenance. This ridiculous feud that Marjorie instigated…if anyone had been driven to murder over those wretched shoes it would have been Marjorie, and it would have been Hester Latimer lying dead somewhere, not my wife."

Barnaby and Stokes exchanged glances. Neither said anything as Lord Galbraith plainly wrestled with competing claims of devotion. Eventually, his gaze on his desk, on his large hands clasped on its edge, he said, "My wife was as she was. In many ways, she was a joy, and I loved her dearly. But in the matter of these shoes, she'd grown obsessed and quite irrational." Glancing up, his lordship met Stokes's eyes, then looked at Barnaby. "I know Humphrey and Hester Latimer, and all their children. By that I do not mean that I know them as acquaintances, but that I truly know them—I know the sort of people they are. No matter what anyone tries to suggest, I cannot imagine that any of the Latimers were in any way involved in Marjorie's death."

Lord Galbraith switched his gaze to Stokes. "Beyond that, Inspector, I most regrettably cannot help you. I have no notion why Marjorie went out to the terrace, much less whom she met, or who caused her death."

Stokes inclined his head. "Thank you, my lord." He glanced at Barnaby, then said, "We wondered if any of the young ladies had recovered enough for us to speak with them. About whether they have any idea why your wife left the ballroom or, perhaps, who she was speaking with before she did."

Lord Galbraith sighed. "I would like nothing better than to have you ask such questions, Inspector—anything to gain clarity in this dark time—but, sadly, none of my daughters have felt strong enough to come down today." His lordship's gaze sharpened. "Geraldine, the eldest, did come down yesterday, but she was so distressed by the tactlessness of several callers that she hasn't made the attempt today, and until she descends, the other two are unlikely to." Lord Galbraith sighed. "Forcing the issue will, I can assure you, end in nothing but storms of hysterical tears, which will get no one anywhere. For my daughters' testimonies, Inspector, we will need to wait."

Stokes nodded more briskly. "Very well. In that case, do you have any objection to us questioning your staff?"

"It's possible," Barnaby said, "that they might have noticed something unusual, perhaps someone asking for a meeting with Lady Galbraith, or even someone loitering outside."

"We need to cover all possible angles, including that the murderer was not a guest at the ball but had somehow arranged to meet Lady Galbraith there." Stokes thought that an unlikely scenario, but it served to have Lord Galbraith give his assent to having his staff questioned. Summoning Millwell, he gave orders to that effect.

Rising, Stokes and Barnaby took their leave of his lordship and left him to mourn in peace.

The last sight they had of him, he was slumped in his chair, his chin on his chest, staring at nothing.

Shutting the library door, Millwell faced them. "Do you wish to speak with us in turn, or will all at once do?" They elected to address the assembled staff in the servants' hall.

The housekeeper fussed over Barnaby and Stokes in her parlor, and the cook provided them with cups of tea and a plate of quite excellent ginger biscuits while Millwell summoned his troops. When the staff was gathered about the servants' hall's long central table, Stokes and Barnaby joined them. Standing at the head of the table, Stokes explained his and Barnaby's role in the investigation into Lady Galbraith's murder, then Stokes put the usual questions: Had they noticed anything unusual in her ladyship's behavior over recent times? Had they witnessed anything out of the ordinary pertaining to her ladyship?

No one had.

"Lastly," Stokes said, "does anyone know of any approach made to anyone in the household by a shoemaker, or anyone involved in the sale or making of shoes?"

Standing just behind Stokes, Barnaby watched the staff, most of whom were in plain sight. One of the maids toward the end of the table shifted, drawing his attention. Her face showed startled surprise—

"Yes." Millwell spoke clearly and definitely; Barnaby looked at him. "There was a young man," Millwell went on, "but that was several months ago—a little before Christmas, when most of the family were no longer in town."

Notebook in hand, Stokes gestured with his pencil for Millwell to continue.

With a faint shrug, Millwell complied. "A young man came to the back door and asked to speak with her ladyship, if you can believe it." Millwell's tone suggested that he'd considered the request highly impertinent. "However, as Lady Galbraith had already departed for the country, denying the fellow was a simple matter. He seemed rather cast down." Millwell paused, then went on, "On consideration, he seemed a decent enough sort, so I suggested he might write to her ladyship if he were that keen to offer her his wares."

"Did he mention any wares in particular?" Barnaby asked.

Millwell widened his eyes. "Just shoes. He told me he was a shoemaker and wanted to inquire whether her ladyship might be interested in his shoes."

Stokes asked the obvious questions, but other than that, the young man had seemed the typical type for a tradesman of that ilk, that he'd been polite and, although assured, reasonably humble and not pushy or aggressive at all, and that he'd been somewhere in his twenties, Millwell could tell them nothing more of the caller, and no one else had seen him.

Shifting his weight, Barnaby asked, "Can anyone tell us whether, after this young shoemaker called at the house, Lady Galbraith or her daughters bought any new shoes, either from their usual shoemaker or anyone else?"

A prim, spare woman garbed in dull black with her hair drawn tightly back from her face stepped forward. "I am...was her ladyship's dresser. She didn't mention anything about any new shoemaker, and I know she didn't have any new shoes made for her—not since last Season." The woman glanced at several other maids among the staff, then looked back at Stokes. "As for the young ladies, they were to visit her ladyship's shoemaker next week to be fitted for new shoes for this Season."

After jotting the information into his notebook, Stokes directed a glance made up of equal parts of triumph and grimness at Barnaby, then nodded to the staff. "Thank you. That's all we need."

The staff started filing out of the hall. Remembering the startled maid, Barnaby looked for her, but she must have been among the first to have slipped out of the door at the far end of the room.

Stuffing his notebook back into his pocket, Stokes caught Barnaby's eye. "Ready?"

Barnaby nodded and followed Stokes out of the servants' hall. Millwell diverted to the library to answer a summons, leaving them in the front hall. Stokes would have shown himself out, but Barnaby planted his feet and, when Stokes arched a brow, quietly said, "So there was another shoemaker with shoes to sell. One who specifically approached Lady Galbraith."

Stokes nodded. "But he didn't speak with Lady Galbraith, and she and her daughters haven't bought new shoes."

Barnaby held up a finger, asking Stokes to wait.

Less than a minute later, Millwell bustled back; he hurried to open the door. "I'm sorry, sir, Inspector. Will there be anything else?"

Barnaby smiled his easy-going smile. "I was just wondering, Millwell, whether any members of the family were at home when the young shoemaker called."

Millwell nodded. "Mr. Hartley—well, he wasn't really *here*, not staying at this house, and he wasn't here right at that moment, but he was in town and he called just after the shoemaker had gone off. Mr. Hartley stopped by to check that Miss Monica would be ready to leave for the country with him the next morning."

"So Miss Monica Galbraith was here at the time, as well?" Stokes asked.

Millwell hesitated, then said, "Miss Monica had just returned from staying with friends, and she and Mr. Hartley were due to go down to the country the following morning. But Miss Monica wasn't in the house at the time the shoemaker called. I remember quite clearly because when Mr. Hartley asked to see her, we couldn't find her anywhere. We'd thought she was in her room, but she wasn't. As you might imagine, that caused some alarm, but before we could send men out to search, Miss Monica walked in the front door. She was surprised—she hadn't known Mr. Hartley would call. He was worried, but Miss Monica assured him that she'd only gone into the park to take the air."

Barnaby considered, then inclined his head. "Thank you, Millwell. I believe that's all."

On gaining the pavement, Barnaby caught Stokes's eye. "What are the odds that Monica ran after the young shoemaker?"

Stokes met Barnaby's gaze and didn't reply.

* * *

*I*n the early afternoon, Violet and Griselda peered out of the windows of Griselda's carriage and studied the façade of Olson's Emporium. The shop was one of a row of smaller warehouse-shops lining the north side of the small cobbled court above the Queen Hithe Stairs, on the north bank of the Thames in the shadow of Southwark Bridge.

At Montague's suggestion and with his encouragement, Violet had started her day by asking Montague's head clerk, Mr. Slocum, whether he could provide details of all the firms currently selling goods imported from Slovakia. The request had engaged the interest of not just Slocum but the other senior clerk, Mr. Pringle, plus the junior clerk, Mr. Slater, and the office boy, Reggie. Between them, they had surprisingly quickly assembled what they had assured Violet was a complete and exhaustive list.

They had managed that by ten o'clock, and Griselda had arrived shortly thereafter with her own long list of suppliers of lead crystals to the ornamented trades—the shoemakers, milliners, glove-makers, jewelers, seamstresses, modistes, and the like—extracted from her contacts in the millinery business.

By combining the lists, they had winnowed their targets to five. Five firms known to sell Slovakian-sourced lead crystals of the sort used by milliners, jewelers, and so on—and also by anyone successfully making Lady Latimer's shoes.

The first firm they had called on had proved to the one supplying the crystals to Myrtle Hook. Buoyed by the confirmation that their strategy should work, Griselda and Violet had taken the disappointment that Miss Hook was the only shoemaker currently buying those crystals from that supplier in their stride. With high hopes and a degree of eagerness, they had climbed back into the carriage and rattled around to the next supplier on their list.

But three more disappointments had taken their toll.

As the carriage rocked to a halt, Griselda looked at Violet. "This is our last chance."

Violet returned her look, then her chin firmed. "We'd better try it, then." Shifting forward, she reached for the carriage door.

Despite its outer drabness, Olson's Emporium appeared prosperous; the space inside was filled literally to the rafters with rolls of cloth of every description, from silks and satins, figured and plain, to velvets, damasks, and chintzes, and richly embroidered felts. Elsewhere, bales and sacks of various wools and stuffings sat opened, inviting one to sample, while row upon row of racks of drawers holding buttons, hooks, fasteners of all types, feathers, lace, and every possible decoration for clothing ever imagined beckoned. The colors and contrasts of all the different goods made for a vibrant, visually distracting scene.

Griselda murmured to Violet, "The children would love this place."

Violet's lips quirked. "If you let them loose on those drawers, I suspect this place wouldn't love them."

"No, indeed." Grinning at the thought, Griselda walked to the long wooden counter that ran along one end of the store.

A bright-eyed shop girl came hurrying to ask, "Can I help you, ma'am?"

Violet and Griselda had refined their approach over the previous four inquiries.

"I'm a milliner," Griselda said, setting her gloves and reticule on the counter as if ready to do business. "And a colleague—a shoemaker—told me of a certain crystal she thought might be useful in my creations. One from Slovakia that has a high lead content, and that's been cut to emphasize its brilliance."

"Oh, I know the sort you mean, but..." The girl looked doubtful. "They're terribly expensive, ma'am, and we don't get much call for them. There's plenty of other crystals that will look as good and that are only a fraction of the cost."

Griselda allowed her smile to deepen. "Perhaps, but there are times when only a certain crystal will do. If you could show me what you have in that type?"

The girl appeared to inwardly sigh. "I'll have to call Mr. Olson. Like I said, those crystals are shocking expensive, and he's the only one allowed to show them. I'll just get him, if you'll wait?"

They'd had the same experience in the other four stores. Violet nodded crisply. "We'll wait."

The girl disappeared through a door in the wall behind the counter.

Frowning slightly, Violet glanced at Griselda. "That's the fifth time that's happened—that the shop girl tries to steer us away from the more expensive crystals. Why would they do that? Surely it's better if we spend more."

Griselda's lips curved. "She told you why, in a way. It's because their wages are based on commission. If she sells us cheaper crystals, she'll at least get something, but only Olson handles the expensive goods, so there's no commission for her if we buy those."

"Ah." Violet nodded. "I see."

She composed her expression as the door to the back room opened and a large man, still shrugging on his jacket, appeared. Seeing Griselda and Violet, he smiled. "Ladies. Allow me to assist you. I understand you're interested in our extremely fine crystals from Slovakia."

He stepped aside to allow the shop girl to set a large covered tray, three times the size of Myrtle Hook's and much deeper, on the counter. "Thank you, Elsie. That will be all." With a flourish, Mr. Olson opened the tray.

Light, brilliant white, sharp and intense, flared from the thick bed of crystals inside the boxlike tray.

Reaching in, Griselda picked out one small crystal. Holding it between her thumb and forefinger, she held it up to the light, examining the way the facets had been cut. She looked at Violet and nodded. "These are the right crystals."

"Oh, indeed, ladies." Olson beamed. "If you're looking for something extra special—"

"What we're looking for, sir," Violet calmly stated, "is the direction of the shoemaker who has recently commenced buying these crystals." She took a chance and, her gaze steady, added, "From you. Perhaps over the past six or so months."

Olson retreated; he almost took a step back. But he was too slow to say, "A shoemaker?" to hide his comprehension.

"Yes." Griselda straightened, perfectly certain, now, that in Olson they had found the supplier to the mystery shoemaker. "We want to ask him about his latest design, so if you will oblige us with his name and direction, we won't trouble you further."

Seeing no sale eventuating and nothing in the exchange for him, Olson tried bluster with overtones of coyness. "Ladies—I can't tell you that. Giving out information on my customers? Why, my good name—"

"Will be mud," Griselda interjected, "if my husband finds himself obliged to come here with a warrant to extract the information from you."

Olson's eyes flew wide. "Husband?" Then he all but goggled. "Warrant?"

"Indeed." Violet caught Olson's gaze. "My friend's husband is Inspector Basil Stokes of Scotland Yard. He is presently investigating a murder, and while no one imagines the shoemaker is in any way involved, the authorities are quite certain that someone wearing shoes that shoemaker produced is." She paused to allow Olson to digest that; she had no wish to have him take it into his head that in supplying them with the name of the shoemaker, he would be doing the man a disservice.

And Olson's statement that giving out information on customers wasn't good business was undeniably true, especially in the trades he supplied, all of which had powerful guilds.

Eventually accepting that there was no easy way out for him, Olson looked from Violet to Griselda. "If I give you his name, you'll go off and not send your husband here? And you won't let on to the customer that I gave him up?"

"As your customer is not going to feel threatened in the least," Griselda said, "I doubt that he'll even ask how we found him. Regardless, even should he ask, there's no benefit to us in telling him."

She held Olson's gaze. "Is there?"

Olson mumbled something, but capitulated and fetched his customer accounts. Leafing back through them, he stopped only a few pages in. "Here he is. He came in four days ago for another half-pound of those crystals—which, I have to tell you, is a pricey purchase. He said as how he was expecting many more sales soon, and was laying in stock." Olson hesitated, then drew out the sheet, turned it, and laid it on the counter so Violet and Griselda could read it. "So there—I've given you what you want, but I haven't actually told you his name, have I?"

"No, indeed." Swiftly, Griselda scanned the page, which listed all the purchases of the crystals made by one Danny Gibson, on the account of Gibson and Sons, of Mercer Street. "Mercer Street…that's off Long Acre, isn't it?"

"Aye." Olson reached for the sheet.

Violet put her gloved hand on it and held it in place. "So he, Danny Gibson, bought just a small sample of the crystals almost a year ago, but then he came back late last year and bought more. Then he returned again in February for another substantial amount, before, as you said, buying still more four days ago." Violet paused, then lifted her hand and allowed Olson to whisk the sheet away.

As Olson tucked the sheet back into his stack, Violet looked at Griselda and smiled. Triumphantly.

Then she glanced at Olson. "Thank you, Mr. Olson. You've been most helpful."

Olson didn't look pleased.

Thoroughly delighted, Violet and Griselda turned and swept out of his emporium.

As they climbed back into the carriage, Griselda said, "I can't wait to see Penelope's face when she hears our news."

* * *

Penelope kept telling herself that her suspicion regarding the possible identity of the lady on the terrace was based on a deductive leap for which she had no firm evidence.

And yet…

"Damn!" Realizing she'd gone off in a distracted daze—again—she shook herself, sat straighter, and reapplied her eyes and her brain to the sadly uninspiring ramblings of the ancient Greek scribe the museum, for some incomprehensible reason, felt they needed to convert into English.

Muttering to herself, she soldiered on through another page, trying not to think jealous thoughts about what Violet and Griselda were doing. That morning when the pair had arrived armed with their list of five importers of the crystals, she had wanted so much to go with them, but as she'd agreed the previous evening, after Violet had inquired how much further she had to go with the translation, she had reluctantly remained in Albemarle Street the better to meet her deadline.

"Although why the museum has placed a deadline on a translation of an archaic work is entirely beyond me." Clutching a pencil, she underlined one passage that, although she was perfectly certain it included all the right words in the correct order, made precious little sense.

In the distance, she heard the front doorbell peal. Pencil poised, she wondered if it was wrong to hope that it was one of her sisters, or even her mother come to demand she attend some afternoon tea.

Even though, by and large, she avoided such social engagements.

"Discipline," she muttered, and bent to her task.

The door opened. She glanced up, and tried not to look too hopeful when she saw Mostyn enter. She arched her brows in question.

"A Mr. Galbraith and a Miss Latimer have arrived and are asking to see you, ma'am."

Penelope blinked. "Mr. Galbraith and Miss *Latimer?*" She blinked again. "Great heavens." She thought for a moment, then smiled. "Of course!" Setting down her pencil, she pushed back her chair and rose. Not even Violet would expect her to continue with the translation rather than see what her unexpected guests had to say. "Where have you put them? The drawing room?"

"Yes, ma'am." Grinning himself, Mostyn followed her from the room.

"I wonder which Miss Latimer it is." In the front hall, Penelope paused to check her hair in the mirror and straighten her gown. She hesitated, then said to her reflection, "Cynthia. My money would be on it being Cynthia...and I can't believe I didn't see that Hartley's intended simply *had to be* a Latimer."

Turning to the drawing room door, she nodded to Mostyn. He opened the door and she swept through.

Immediately, her eyes went to the lady sitting on one sofa—and yes, it was Cynthia Latimer who rose to her feet. She was holding her reticule and, judging by her expression, was almost pugnaciously determined.

Hartley had been standing beside the sofa; he turned to face Penelope as she glided forward. "Mrs. Adair. We haven't been introduced, but I believe you were present at the Fairchilds' on the night…"

"Indeed." With a crisp nod, Penelope gave Hartley her hand. As he took it and half bowed, Penelope shifted her gaze to Cynthia. "Miss Latimer." Retrieving her hand from Hartley's clasp, Penelope extended it to Cynthia.

Touching fingers, Cynthia bobbed a polite curtsy. "Mrs. Adair." Cynthia slanted a swift glance at Hartley. "We hope you will excuse the interruption to your day, but we felt that it was time we came forward, if nothing else to clarify who was with Hartley in the garden and to verify all that he reported we saw."

Already considering the ramifications, Penelope waved the pair to the sofa; sinking onto the sofa opposite, she seized the moment to take in the way Hartley sat Cynthia, the way he hovered protectively before sitting alongside her. Not touching, but close enough to easily take her hand.

Cynthia, however, did not appear the sort of young lady to cling to any gentleman's arm; there was strength in her posture, and a certain steeliness of will in the set of her lips and chin and in the directness of her gaze that Penelope recognized.

"I take it," she said, "that you are Hartley's intended?" When Cynthia nodded almost defiantly, Penelope smiled. "And in one stroke, that explains a great deal." Her gaze on the pair, she said, "I might wish that you had told us earlier, but I can understand why you did not. Given your families do not yet know—"

"Then revealing our secret on top of Aunt Marjorie's murder, with the added complication that we both saw it, and of what it was we saw…" Cynthia met Penelope's gaze. "The very subject we'd been discussing in the folly was how best to reveal our attachment to our families." She paused, then went on, her gaze unwavering, "It was our hope that our betrothal would act as a catalyst to bring an end to the feud, as people call it. That was the reason we were out in the garden, and then on our way back we saw…" Cynthia gestured resignedly. "We were shocked—and confused, as I'm sure you will appreciate. It seemed best at the time to keep our counsel, but"—Cynthia drew a determined breath—"it didn't take long to see that the identity of Aunt Marjorie's murderer needs to be proved sooner rather than later. Courtesy of the feud, with every hour that passes, the pressure on both our families is increasing, compounding the heartbreak of the murder. We"—she glanced at Hartley—"have decided that we need to do whatever we can to assist the police in solving this case as soon as they possibly can." Cynthia concluded, "So we've come to tell you all, to give you, and your husband, and through him the police, the best possible chance to find the murderer quickly."

Penelope nodded approvingly. "That is, indeed, the correct course to take. And the next step along that road is to tell me what you saw that night."

Hartley stirred. "I've already told you the details. Cynthia was beside me." Reaching across, he grasped one of her hands. "She saw no more than I did."

Turning to him, shifting her hand within his clasp, Cynthia squeezed his fingers. "I know you want to protect me, that you would prefer I remain distanced from everything to do with the investigation, but"—lifting his hand, she lightly shook it—"this is too important to us, to both our families, for me to sit quietly by. Not if I can help." Cynthia paused, her gaze locked with Hartley's; when next she spoke, her voice rang with conviction. "Aunt Marjorie was your mother. We must learn the truth about who killed her, because without it, you and I will have the devil of a time marrying, much less forging the life we wish. We will not be able to bring our families together again, not unless we have this resolved and can lay the matter to rest. And to do that, I have to tell Mrs. Adair, at least, all that I know. All that I saw." Cynthia drew breath, and with a faint smile, her gaze still locked with Hartley's, said, "And you, my dear, have to let me."

Penelope held silent, avidly watching the exchange; when, lips thinning, Hartley fractionally inclined his head and Cynthia turned back to her, she felt like applauding. Instead, she said to Cynthia, "You were walking back from the folly by the lake. I've recently walked the same path, so I know it. You were walking alongside Hartley, and you came around a curve and up a slight rise, and then, quite suddenly, you could see…"

Her gaze growing distant, Cynthia nodded. "I could see the path below the side terrace and the end wall of the terrace below the balustrade." She paused, then without prompting went on, "I couldn't see the balusters, not even the bottom of them, but I could see Aunt

Marjorie on the path."

"Which way was she facing?" Penelope asked. It was clear that Cynthia was reporting from a clear visual memory.

"To our left. Toward the bottom of the terrace steps."

"Then what happened?" Penelope asked.

Hartley stirred, but Cynthia tightened her grip on his hand, and Penelope flicked him a frowning glance, and he subsided.

"Aunt Marjorie turned," Cynthia said, "away from us to look up at the terrace. I assumed someone was up there, and she'd heard them and turned to see who they were, or to speak with them."

Penelope moistened her lips. "Then…?"

Cynthia blinked. "It happened in an instant. She was standing there, looking up at the terrace, and in the next second, the ball struck her and she fell."

Constructing her own mental picture from Cynthia's description, Penelope frowned. "How much time elapsed between Lady Galbraith looking up at the terrace—not while she was turning but once she was looking up—and the ball striking her? Did she speak with whoever was up there?"

"No." Cynthia shook her head, the response quite definite. "She looked up and the ball struck her—it happened immediately."

"Instantaneously," Hartley confirmed. His expression grim, his gaze, too, had grown distant as he relived those moments in the Fairchilds' garden.

Pausing only briefly to define her best tack, Penelope quietly directed, "If you can, please think about the ball falling toward Lady Galbraith. Could you tell whether it dropped straight down or fell at an angle?" The question was a test. Given where the pair had stood, Penelope felt certain they wouldn't have been able to discern the difference, but she was curious to see if either Cynthia or Hartley were the suggestible sort; if they answered truthfully and resisted her lead, she would feel justified in placing more reliance on their memories.

Both were frowning, patently studying the images no doubt seared into their minds.

Eventually, still frowning, Cynthia said, "I couldn't say. The ball dropped from above—that's all I saw."

"Yes." Hartley's tone was even more definite. "The ball fell from above, but whether straight down or from an angle—and it could only have been a slight angle—that, we couldn't see." Refocusing on Penelope, he said, "We were too far away, and the perspective was wrong."

Hiding her satisfaction, Penelope nodded. "Very well." She looked at Cynthia. "Tell me what happened next."

Cynthia returned to her mental vision. "We stood frozen with shock for an instant. We simply stared at Aunt Marjorie lying there on the path. Then both of us looked up—I remember that quite clearly— we both raised our gazes at the same time and looked to see who had dropped the ball. We'd forgotten the branch was in the way. We couldn't see. We'd been holding hands. I remember we both suddenly gripped tight, and together we rushed forward."

Pausing, Cynthia stared at the vision only she and Hartley could see. After a moment, she went on, "We had to take several steps before we were clear of the trees and could see the terrace. The moonlight wasn't strong, but we would have been able to see if someone had been standing there. But all we saw—and I saw this through the balusters—was the flick of skirts, the back hem of a lady's gown, and the back of her shoes as she stepped up into the corridor. She was running."

Cynthia studied her vision for a moment more, then she blinked and refocused on Penelope. "That's all I saw. She—whoever she was—was gone in an instant. By the time we reached Aunt Marjorie, the lady would have had time to reach the ballroom or to seek refuge somewhere else in the house."

Penelope had her next question ready, but before she could voice it, Cynthia drew a deep breath and went on, "The one thing I do know is that whoever that lady was, she wasn't one of my sisters, much less my mother."

The degree of certitude Cynthia had infused into her tone was impressive. Curious, Penelope asked, "You weren't in the ballroom at the time, and we haven't yet checked their alibis, so how can you be so very sure?"

Cynthia met her gaze. "Because, quite frankly, I seriously doubt that any of my sisters, and certainly not Mama, could have reacted so swiftly. Even if they had done such a thing, immediately they had done it, they would have been horrified. Aghast. Stricken and unable to move." Cynthia paused, then more reflectively went on, "I suppose what I'm saying is that none of us—the Latimers—wished Aunt Marjorie dead, so even if you imagine some sort of fleeting rage, it's hard to see any of my sisters or my mother reacting and fleeing so very swiftly."

"There was less than a minute, I suspect," Hartley said, "between the time the ball fell and the time we saw the lady disappearing."

Penelope thought, then said, "I'm going to suggest an alternative scenario. I want you to consider it, and then tell me whether, in your opinion, it might be possible." She paused to order the facts in her mind, then commenced, "Let's say that Lady Galbraith left the ballroom and headed for the side terrace—at this point, we do not know if there was someone with her or if she was alone. Regardless, one of your sisters or your mama saw Lady Galbraith leaving the ballroom." Penelope pushed her glasses higher on her nose. "For argument's sake, let's say that her ladyship was with someone, and the sight made one of the Latimer ladies suspicious enough to follow, but, of course, she—the follower—hung well back.

"Our Latimer lady reaches the door to the side terrace in time to see someone—we don't know who—drop the ball on Lady Galbraith. The perpetrator then goes quickly down the steps and leaves via the gardens. We know that, from where you stood, they could have done that and you wouldn't have seen them—the trees along the path you were on block that view. Our Latimer lady rushes onto the terrace to the balustrade, looks over, and sees Lady Galbraith dead on the path. The Latimer lady panics and flees inside, and hers are the shoes you glimpsed." Penelope studied Cynthia's and Hartley's faces. After a moment, she asked, "Could it have happened like that?"

It was Hartley who first shook his head; he now seemed as immersed in the mental vision as Cynthia. "I don't think so. There wasn't enough time for her to come to the balustrade, look over, take it in, and then reach the door again before we saw her."

Cynthia frowned. "There's that, and I agree, but in addition…" She refocused on Penelope. "Hartley sent me inside almost immediately. I returned to our group—the whole family was standing chatting to others but we were all in the same area of the ballroom. I reached the spot less than five minutes after the…murder. Of my family, Georgina and Cecilia were with Fitzforsythe and Brandywell the entire time, and I remember they were laughing at something as I came up. And Millicent was chatting avidly with her friends. They had their heads together and were deep in some subject—I could tell Millicent hadn't a care in the world beyond deciding which gentleman at the ball was the most handsome." Cynthia straightened. "I came up beside Mama." Cynthia met Penelope's gaze and wryly said, "I'm widely known as 'the quiet one,' so standing beside Mama raises no eyebrows and is usually the safest place for me when I wish to avoid attention. So I was right beside Mama as she was talking to her friends about her plans for Millicent's come-out ball." Cynthia held Penelope's gaze. "Mama is reserved and can hide her feelings well, but she's no great actress. I cannot conceive of her having seen Aunt Marjorie murdered, then fleeing and, within minutes, laughing and sharing stories about musicians and decorations. That...really isn't possible."

Penelope returned Cynthia's gaze, then, eminently satisfied, nodded. "Thank you. I now understand why you're so certain the lady you saw fleeing the terrace wasn't one of your family. And despite not having checked their alibis, I accept that your reasoning is sound—the lady you saw wasn't a Latimer." She paused, then said, "All right. Let's leave aside the question of the lady's identity and return to an earlier point." She looked at them both. "Why did Lady Galbraith leave the ballroom and come out to the side terrace? Do either of you have any idea?"

Hartley glanced at Cynthia; resettling her hand in his, he grimaced. "I've been trying to think of the answer." He drew in a deeper, slightly unsteady breath and looked at Penelope. "And I suspect that Mama was following me." He hesitated, then went on. "She was always eager to arrange my life for me—it was one of the reasons I moved into lodgings. Over recent years, she's tried to foist any number of young misses on me, and if anything she's been getting even more insistent... Well, if she'd entertained any suspicion that I was meeting with some lady alone, she would have followed me without hesitation."

Her gaze on Hartley's face, Cynthia said, "I do think she had started to become suspicious." Cynthia swung her gaze to Penelope. "Not that it was me Hartley was seeing, but that he was meeting with some lady clandestinely—"

"And that," Hartley said, "the clandestine nature of our meetings, would have alarmed her and made her even more intent on finding out who I was seeing." Hartley paused, then said, "We had been meeting at my lodgings—for all his faults, or perhaps because of them, Carradale can be exceedingly discreet—but with the balls starting in earnest, it wasn't going to be so easy, which is why we'd arranged to meet in the folly."

After a moment's pause, Hartley stated, his tone flat, "I think the reason Mama came out onto the terrace and then down the steps was because she was following me." Cynthia gripped his hand tighter and shifted closer. Hartley glanced at her, met her gaze, then looked at Penelope. "I think that Mama wanting to know who I was meeting with secretly led to her standing where she was when she was killed."

Penelope heard the underlying emotion in Hartley's tone, saw the veiled guilt in his eyes. Straightening, she crisply stated, "It was certainly not your fault that someone capitalized on her standing there and dropped that ball on her. You cannot hold yourself responsible for that."

Cynthia flashed a grateful look Penelope's way, but had the sense to stay silent.

Penelope approved, both of Cynthia's behavior and also the patently genuine link between the pair. "Now—"

The sound of arrivals in the front hall brought her up short. The front doorbell hadn't pealed, which meant...

The drawing room door opened, and Violet and Griselda came in. From the intrigued looks on their faces, Mostyn had told them who Penelope was interrogating.

Noting their bright eyes and guessing that they'd had some measure of success, with a delighted smile of her own, Penelope rose, along with Hartley and Cynthia. "Allow me to present..." Penelope introduced Violet and Griselda to Hartley Galbraith, then gestured to Cynthia. "You've already met Miss Latimer—who, as it transpires, is Hartley's intended."

Violet and Griselda had assumed as much, but they were quick with their congratulations and good wishes.

Under cover of the talk, Penelope leaned closer to Violet and whispered, "Any luck?"

"Yes," Violet whispered back. "We think we've located the other shoemaker."

"Excellent," Penelope returned. "But keep that for later."

Meeting her eyes, Violet nodded.

In the shuffling as Penelope, Hartley, and Cynthia reclaimed their seats and Violet and Griselda settled alongside Penelope, Violet murmured to Griselda, "Keep mum about our discoveries for the moment."

Griselda faintly inclined her head and turned her attention to the pair on the sofa opposite.

In broad strokes, Penelope described what they'd concluded about why Lady Galbraith had gone outside, what Cynthia had confirmed regarding her and Hartley's seeing the lady fleeing the terrace, and Cynthia's observations on the conduct of her mother and sisters immediately after the murder.

At the end of the recitation, Griselda looked at Cynthia. "Tell me, Miss Latimer, can you see the lady and her shoes vividly in your mind?"

Cynthia nodded. "Yes." She glanced at Hartley. "I suspect it's a sight neither of us will ever forget."

"Perhaps," Griselda said. "But not everyone recalls with the same degree of clarity." She glanced at Penelope, then looked back at Cynthia. "I would like to try a trick that I occasionally use with ladies who want me to recreate some particular bonnet they've seen. They usually give me a vague description and think that's all they've noticed, but by using this trick, we usually discover that they can tell me a great deal more." Without challenge, Griselda held Cynthia's gaze. "Are you willing to try it?"

Cynthia lightly shrugged. "If it might help, then yes, of course."

Griselda nodded. "Very well. All you have to do is close your eyes and bring to mind the image of the lady fleeing the terrace." She paused as Cynthia complied, then asked, "Can you see her?"

"Yes." Eyes closed, Cynthia nodded. "Quite clearly."

"Excellent. Now I want you to look more closely at her shoes. Can you do that?"

Again, Cynthia nodded.

"Now," Griselda said, "you've described the shoes as Lady Latimer's shoes because of the crystals on them. Can you see the crystals?"

A faint frown formed between Cynthia's brows, but she nodded. "Yes, I can see them. They're definitely the same crystals—I can tell by the way they sparkle."

"What color are the shoes?"

Cynthia wrinkled her nose. "I can't really tell—the light's too weak."

"Pale- or dark-hued, then?" Griselda asked.

"Pale—definitely pale." After a moment, Cynthia added, "They might even be white."

"What about the pattern of the crystals?" Griselda asked. "Is that the same as on your Lady Latimer's shoes?"

Cynthia's frown deepened. "I can't really tell. The distance is too great, but...how odd. These shoes have a line of crystals down the back seam of the shoe. Ours don't have that."

"Stay there—keep looking." Griselda exchanged an excited glance with Penelope and Violet, then returned her gaze to Cynthia. "Now look at the shoes themselves. Look at the heel and the cut of the shoe. Are they the same as on the Lady Latimer's shoes Myrtle Hook makes?"

Cynthia's jaw slackened. Her features eased as astonishment took hold. "No. These shoes are different. They have a straighter heel, not the in-swept Louis heel we prefer, and…good heavens!" Opening her eyes, Cynthia met Griselda's gaze. "The shoes that lady wore had a higher, quite different cut to ours." Excited herself, Cynthia gestured, then, frustrated, said, "I don't have the right words to describe them, but I could draw them."

Violet bounced to her feet. "I'll get some paper and a pencil."

As Violet whisked out, Cynthia, her face and eyes alight, looked at Griselda and Penelope. "I got a very clear view of the shoes in the instant when the lady stepped into the house. I didn't realize how well I saw them." She inclined her head to Griselda. "Thank you. I never would have realized if you hadn't had me go back and look again, so to speak."

Griselda beamed.

"Does this mean," Hartley said, "that there's some other source of Lady Latimer's shoes?"

Penelope nodded. "That's what we believe. Once we identify the shoemaker involved, we'll be able to learn who his customers are, and then we'll know who the lady fleeing the terrace was."

Cynthia was still looking faintly stunned. "I can't believe the proof that it wasn't a pair of our shoes has been simply sitting in my memory all this time, and I just hadn't looked closely enough." Turning her head, she exchanged a delighted smile with Hartley.

While he returned the smile and encouragingly squeezed Cynthia's hand, he didn't look quite so relieved; Penelope suspected that Hartley, at least, had seen the difficulty in using what Cynthia had remembered to exonerate her family from all suspicion. They had only Cynthia's word for the critical details; Hartley couldn't recall well enough to confirm her testimony.

But Penelope kept that observation to herself and watched as, supplied by Violet with several sheets of paper and a sharpened pencil, Cynthia quickly sketched the shoe she'd seen.

"I only saw it from the back with just a little of the side view as she stepped up, so I can't draw the toe." Like most young ladies, Cynthia had been trained to draw; her sketch quickly took recognizable shape. Completing it, she rapidly sketched a second shoe seen from the same angle. "This," she said, pointing to the second shoe, "is one of *our* Lady Latimer's shoes. The style is of a typical ballroom pump, cut reasonably low around the ankle and foot, and with a Louis heel. We insisted on the Louis heel because, while it looks delicate, with the point of the heel directly below the middle of the heel, it's nicely stable."

Penelope nodded. "My sisters and I prefer Louis heels for dancing, too."

"But the shoes I saw on the terrace had this sort of heel." Cynthia pointed to her first sketch. "A wider one, with the back of the heel more in line with the back of the shoe—quite unlike a Louis heel. And even more telling, those shoes were cut higher around the ankle and foot. That's quite a different style to *our* Lady Latimer's shoes."

Along with Violet and Griselda, Penelope studied the sketches, then she glanced at her colleagues. "A different style of shoe—a different shoemaker."

Cynthia frowned. "I haven't heard any whispers of a new source of Lady Latimer's shoes, and with the Season commencing, you would think that would be one of the most talked-of topics in the drawing rooms."

"Indeed." Penelope straightened. "But that doesn't mean that such a new source doesn't exit. There may be a good reason for the secrecy, but we"—she glanced at Violet and Griselda—"need to dig deeper on that score."

Penelope rose, bringing everyone else to their feet. With assurances that she, Violet, Griselda, and their husbands were doing and would continue to do all in their power to solve the mystery, and that as soon as possible, she inexorably steered Hartley and Cynthia to the drawing room door.

Pausing before the door, Cynthia glanced at Hartley, then met Penelope's gaze. "I sincerely hope you, your friends, and your husbands discover the answer to this riddle soon. The suspicions and anxieties the situation is breeding within both our families are tearing at them all. Hartley and I had already recognized the need to heal the rift and bring everyone together again—it was bad enough before—but, instead, we've had Aunt Marjorie murdered, and everything's got so much worse." She hesitated, then went on, "Indeed, Aunt

Marjorie's murder is a very real obstacle to everything Hartley and I had hoped, through our marriage, to achieve—the healing of our families."

Sober, Hartley nodded. "We—all of us—were so much happier before. Now...each family has itself, but after all the years of being together, we need each other as well."

Penelope could almost see the weight the pair had willingly taken on their shoulders—could read in their expressions that each took responsibility for their respective families, and also each other's. They were, she realized, alike in bearing that familial devotion. Every bit as serious as they, she inclined her head in reply, then accompanied them into the front hall and watched Mostyn see them out of the front door.

The instant the door shut, she swung about and, frowning, walked quickly back into the drawing room.

Violet and Griselda had shifted to take their usual places, Griselda on the first sofa alongside Penelope's preferred position, with Violet on the sofa opposite.

Reclaiming her spot, Penelope looked from one to the other. "Well? Don't keep me in suspense. What have you discovered?"

They told her. Penelope's eyes gleamed. "Well done! Gibson and Sons in Mercer Street—that's in the theater district."

Griselda nodded. "Yes, and I've heard of the firm before. I believe they're quite old and established, but not, I think, in the ton side of the trade."

Violet was studying Cynthia's sketches. "If we take these, perhaps Danny Gibson can confirm that this is the style of the Lady Latimer's shoes he makes."

"That," Penelope said, "would be my hope, because otherwise we only have Cynthia's word that the lady she and Hartley saw fleeing the terrace was wearing that different style of shoe, rather than the same style she, her sisters, and her mother wear. I'm certain that Hartley didn't notice the shoe well enough to describe it. If asked, he'll support Cynthia, but that's not going to stand up in court, and evidence that only Cynthia saw will not be sufficient to clear the Latimer ladies of suspicion." Penelope paused, then added, "And, indeed, Cynthia and Hartley themselves are still very much potential murderers, no matter what we might believe. There is no unequivocal evidence to clear them, either."

Griselda and Violet grimaced.

Penelope focused on Violet. "I'm starting to feel a sense of urgency over this, as if fate is prodding. Consider—if I hadn't remained at home with my nose in that translation, I wouldn't have been here when Cynthia and Hartley called, and so we wouldn't now know all we do—and we wouldn't, I suspect, have felt any need to go and speak with Danny Gibson until sometime tomorrow."

Griselda glanced at the clock. "We've just got time to reach Mercer Street before the shops shut."

Penelope met Violet's eyes. "The translation's not yet done, but I believe this takes precedence."

Violet widened her eyes. "Oh, indubitably. We tend the living before the dead."

"Indeed." With one of her signature brisk nods, Penelope rose. "I vote we take the carriage around to Mercer Street immediately, and see what Danny Gibson can tell us about this new version of Lady Latimer's shoes."

Griselda gathered her reticule and stood. "Let's go."

Violet folded Cynthia's sketches, tucked them into her reticule, then came to her feet. She glanced at the clock, then followed Penelope and Griselda to the door. "We'd better tell Phelps to hurry if we want to catch Danny Gibson before he leaves for the day."

CHAPTER 10

To visit Mrs. Adair, in order to avoid being seen by others of the ton, Cynthia and Hartley had met in the porch of St. George's and taken a hackney to Albemarle Street. But when they emerged from the Adairs' house, there was no hackney in sight.

Pausing on the front step, Hartley looked up and down the street, then met Cynthia's eyes. "We could go back inside and ask for a footman to be sent to summon a hackney."

Cynthia held his gaze, then her lips firmed. "I'm fast approaching the point where I no longer care. Should anyone see us together, let them make of it what they will."

Hartley studied her eyes, read her resolution, then he offered his arm. "In that case, let's stroll down to Piccadilly. We'll be able to get a hackney there."

Taking his arm, Cynthia went with him down the steps. As they set off strolling along the pavement, openly together, she felt a smile tug at her lips. Gradually, she gave in to the impulse, smiling as a degree of happiness—a small degree, perhaps, but definite nonetheless—warmed her. As they neared the end of the street and the busy thoroughfare of Piccadilly, she leaned closer to Hartley and murmured, "It feels good to be able to be together like this. To simply be us, openly, without obfuscation."

Hartley glanced down and met her eyes. "To stop pretending." He nodded. "I know."

Reaching Piccadilly, they paused and considered the passing carriages, then they exchanged a glance and, in mutual accord, turned and strolled on along the street.

Let anyone seeing them make of it what they would.

The ornate entrance of Burlington Arcade lay just past the end of Bond Street; another shared glance and, both smiling to themselves, Cynthia and Hartley let their feet carry them into the enclosed avenue of shops. The arcade was well known as a precinct hosting shops of the best art and antiquities dealers; at that hour, with most of the ton heading home to prepare for their evening entertainments, the arcade was quiet. Only a few other shoppers were idly strolling, peering into this window or that, and most of those looked to be collectors or scholars, not the sort to concern themselves with social gossip.

Ambling past windows stacked with curiosities from Egypt and the Orient, or packed with ancient tomes and scientific devices, Cynthia thought back over the events of the last days—over all that had happened after she and Hartley had met in the folly at Fairchild House. She glanced up at Hartley. "I'm so glad we took the bit between our teeth and went to see Mrs. Adair. If we hadn't, I never would have recalled all I'd seen of those shoes." She paused, then, looking ahead, went on, "I *knew*—in my heart, if you like—that the lady we saw could not possibly have been one of my sisters or my mother, but having the proof of my own eyes to back that up...it's comforting."

Hartley nodded. "The mists that have been obscuring who the murderer is are thinning."

"I believe," Cynthia said, her voice growing stronger, "that we can safely leave identifying the murderer to Mrs. Adair and her colleagues, and Mr. Adair and the police."

"I admit," Hartley said, "that I now feel much more confident that they will, indeed, succeed. And with luck, fairly soon."

"Which brings us"—Cynthia glanced up and met his eyes—"to our next question. How much longer should we wait?"

Hartley knew she meant how much longer should they wait before telling their families of their wish to marry, of the fact that they already considered themselves betrothed and had for years. How many more days should they wait before they made a push to reunite their families? "Our families, both sides, need each other."

Cynthia halted and waited until he did the same and faced her, then she said, "Your family might need my family's support, but my family is aching to be able to give that comfort—it's hurting them that they can't."

Taking her hands, Hartley squeezed her fingers lightly. "And your family's support would mean immeasurably more to all of us than the superficial condolences extended by those others who have called. Augusta Gresham and Mrs. Foley, for example." He shook his head. "Both sides, your family and mine, are not just hurting but bleeding."

Lips firming, Cynthia nodded. "They are—and it's time we put a stop to it. It's time we brought them together again so we can all start healing. So we can all be stronger."

Looking into her eyes, Hartley drew on the strength she always offered him. Taking a breath, he admitted, "My father and my sisters...the funeral's tomorrow. If they can't lean on your family for support, I honestly don't know how any of them are going to get through it—and having half the ton watching is only going to make things so much worse."

"But if the police haven't identified the murderer before then...?" Cynthia raised her brows. Her tone steady, she said, "Having my family supporting yours through the ordeal is going to cause a furor. That said, I'm sure my family would do it without hesitation, if your family wished it."

"Just as I'm certain that my family, all of us, want more than anything to have your family with us, at our sides." He paused, then, features shifting, lowered his voice to say, "Burying one's mother is always hard, but in this case..."

Cynthia squeezed his hands, then, releasing them, wound her arm around his and started them strolling once more.

After a moment, Hartley closed his hand over hers where it rested on his sleeve. "It's time to do it."

Cynthia glanced at him, read the certainty etched in his face, and nodded. "Yes. It is." She'd already reached that conclusion, but the decision had had to be his.

"We can't wait any longer for the police to determine who the murderer is. We know who it isn't—namely, any of your family." Hartley's voice gained in strength, in decisiveness. "Our families need to be together to weather the funeral tomorrow. So we bring them together."

Cynthia had already thought of how to manage it. "It has to be done, accepted, and all in place before the funeral tomorrow afternoon, so I suggest we—you and I—meet in Hanover Square after dinner." Tipping her head closer to Hartley, as they walked on through the arcade, she explained how she thought they should go about bringing their estranged families together again.

* * *

𝒫enelope, Violet, and Griselda hadn't needed to fear missing Danny Gibson; the Gibson family lived over the Mercer Street shop, which they had owned for decades. According to the notice hanging in the window, three generations of Gibsons were currently active in providing shoes, boots, and leather goods to the theatrical trades. Danny Gibson's name appeared to have been penciled in only recently.

A bell tinkled as Penelope led the way inside. The shop was quite different to Myrtle Hook's establishment; here, walls comprised of wooden pigeonholes reached nearly to the ceiling, dividing the shop into long, narrow aisles. Each pigeonhole in every wall was crammed with shoes, gloves, gauntlets, wristbands, leather ties, bags, and every other conceivable leather-based item. The smell of leather was nearly overpowering.

The walls blocked the light from the wide window facing the street, leaving the interior decidedly gloomy, but the glow of lamplight from deeper in the shop drew Penelope down the center aisle. At its end, she stepped into a narrow space before a long wooden counter that extended across the width of the shop.

Perched behind the counter, a rather ancient personage tipped his head down to peer at Penelope over the top of his spectacles; in his hands he held a gauntlet that he'd been stitching.

Penelope smiled and walked forward.

As Violet and Griselda followed her into the light, the old man's eyes widened. Setting aside his work, he got off his stool and faced them. "Can I help you, ma'am?" He nodded deferentially. "Ladies."

"We do hope you can," Penelope said. "We're looking for a shoemaker making a particular style of shoe."

Joining Penelope, Violet had Cynthia's first sketch ready. Taking it, Penelope glanced at it, then turned the sheet so the old cobbler could see. "This is a partial sketch of the style."

Resetting his spectacles, the old man looked, then straightened. "That's similar to a very old style. I used to make shoes like that when I first started."

Penelope allowed her smile to grow conspiratorial. "We had heard that...your grandson, is it? Danny Gibson? We heard that he's making shoes in this style." She widened her eyes. "Perhaps he got the notion from old sketches of yours?"

The old man eyed her with a certain native shrewdness. "Aye. Happen he did. Nothing wrong with that."

"Not at all," Penelope agreed. "But we'd like to speak with Danny, if we may?"

The old man studied her for a long moment, then, slowly, he nodded. "Aye—that might be best." He turned to the screened doorway leading to the rear of the shop. "He's in the workshop. I'll fetch him."

The instant the leather dividing curtain fell back into place, Penelope turned to Griselda. "Damn! He's guessed there's something going on. I hope he doesn't take it into his head to tell Danny to run away and hide."

Griselda considered, then shook her head. "Families like the Gibsons don't work like that. This is their trade—Danny will be expected to stand up for his work, especially if he used his grandfather's designs."

Penelope blinked, then nodded. "I hadn't thought of it like that."

Griselda proved to be correct; three minutes later, the leather curtain was lifted aside and a bright-eyed, rather lanky young man of perhaps twenty summers presented himself. He looked at Penelope, Griselda, and Violet, and gave them all a respectful smile. "Granddad said as you were asking after the new style of shoe I've been making. So how can I help you, ladies?"

Penelope showed him Cynthia's first sketch. "This is the style of shoe we're interested in, but the shoes we want to know more about are the Lady Latimer's version." Danny's gaze had dropped to the sketch, but at Penelope's last words, he looked up and met her eyes. She smiled intently. "The ones covered with the special crystals you buy from Olson's Emporium."

Danny looked from Penelope to Griselda, then at Violet. "Ah...I'm not sure I know—"

"Danny." Penelope waited until he looked back at her. "We already know that you are creating this new style of Lady Latimer's shoes. There's nothing wrong with that. But we need to know the name of the lady or ladies you've supplied with these shoes. It's important."

Danny frowned. "It was supposed to be a secret—an exclusive secret license, just like Lady Latimer has with whoever's making the shoes for her. She—the lady—said I wasn't to tell anyone, or show anyone else the shoes, or the deal couldn't be made. She had to have an exclusive supply, or there could be no guarantee of me selling the shoes to her family for the special exclusive price."

Griselda stepped to the counter. "Danny, I'm a milliner to the ton. I know all about exclusive licenses. We're not here to ask you to break faith with any deal you've made with your client. But we do need information about her."

Violet, too, fronted the counter on Penelope's other side. "Just think—it's not Lady Latimer's identity that's a secret. There's no reason to keep your exclusive customer's name a secret, either. And if you tell us her name, we promise not to tell anyone else about you making this new version of Lady Latimer's shoes."

"Well," Penelope amended, "we won't tell anyone other than the police."

"The police!" Danny goggled at her.

Penelope grimaced. "Sorry." She glanced at Griselda and Violet. "That just slipped out. The downside of having a too-logical brain."

Danny blinked. He glanced at the leather curtain, then, facing them, leaned closer and lowered his voice. "Why do the police want to know about my shoes?"

Penelope pointed to the sketch. "These shoes were worn by a lady the police want to speak with in relation to a murder." She waited until Danny looked up, and caught his gaze. "It's vitally important, Danny. We don't want or need to cause any problems for you. We just need to know who—which ladies—you've supplied with these shoes."

Danny searched her eyes, then he swallowed and straightened. "It's just one. One lady. A young lady. I'd heard about Lady Latimer's shoes—well, who in the trade hasn't? And the exclusive deal that shoemaker has with Lady Latimer must be worth a pretty penny—who wouldn't want a deal like that? So I thought I should try to see if I could make my own version, and eventually, I did. Took me months and months, but I got it right. I asked around quiet-like, and heard that a Lady Galbraith was the lady most interested in getting her own version of Lady Latimer's shoes—she's been asking around lots of shoemakers. So I thought that, if I wanted an exclusive deal, she— Lady Galbraith—was the one to go and see."

He paused, then went on, "Only she wasn't at home. Wasn't in London, apparently. This was early December, you see. So I was walking away, a bit hangdog, from the Galbraiths' house, when this young lady came pelting after me. She asked me about the shoes. She said she was Lady Galbraith's daughter and that if the shoes were as I said, proper Lady Latimer's shoes, that she would show them to her mother and help to arrange an exclusive deal, just like I wanted. I wasn't sure, but *she* was really convinced, and I thought, why not? She was heading off to the country the next morning, but I always have my tape with me, so we did a quick measurement in the park there, and I agreed to make her a pair in white satin, and to hold off offering the shoes to anyone else until she came to get the shoes in February."

He shrugged. "As most of the nobs seem to go off to the country for December and January, it wasn't likely I'd get any other chance to get the sort of exclusive deal I wanted, so I decided I'd do better to be patient and see what this Miss Galbraith could arrange."

"And...?" Penelope prompted.

"She came back in February and tried on the shoes. Like a little princess, she was, twirling and swirling. She was that thrilled with the shoes. She assured me her mother—Lady Galbraith—would definitely be interested in doing an exclusive deal, just like I wanted, but that I had to let her, Miss Galbraith, present the shoes to Lady Galbraith in the best possible way. And to do that, she'd have to wait until about now. Late March, she told me. Meanwhile, she ordered two more pairs, one in pale pink and the other in pale green." Danny pulled a face. "Truth to tell, I've been waiting for her to come in and pick them up. She hasn't paid for any of the pairs and those crystals...they're expensive."

He looked increasingly despondent. "We don't do much on tick here—Granddad's against it. But even though those shoes have costly materials and are hellishly time-consuming to make, I figured the potential return was worth taking a risk on them—and that giving Miss Galbraith the shoes without demanding payment first was worth it to get her to show them to her mama." He grimaced. "I guess she didn't. Or at least, she hasn't yet."

The comment confirmed that Danny had no notion that it was Lady Galbraith who'd been murdered, but his words made Penelope blink as a completely novel perspective on the case unfolded in her mind.

Noting Penelope's sudden abstraction, Griselda said to Danny, "I don't think you'll have any difficulties recouping your costs and establishing a very viable line of business with those shoes."

Recognizing the voice of experience, moreover of one who

supplied the ton, Danny started to look more hopeful. "You think they'll want them?"

"I think," Griselda said, "that if and when you choose to make your shoes generally available, you'll have ladies literally beating a path to your door."

"So not an exclusive deal, then?" Danny inquired.

Griselda considered, then said, "If I were you, I'd talk to your father and grandfather and see what they think. An exclusive deal will be easier to manage with a small workforce, but if you make your shoes in limited numbers and sell to whoever is willing to pay the best price, then I suspect you'll be able to charge a very high price and still find ladies willing to pay it." She held Danny's gaze. "In the end, it's a balance, but I believe you'll do better without an exclusive license."

Danny looked much struck by Griselda's wisdom.

Shaking free of her thoughts, Penelope refocused on the young shoemaker. "The last thing we need from you, Danny, is the name of the Miss Galbraith for whom you made those shoes."

Danny blinked. "She just said Miss Galbraith. Is there more than one?"

Penelope nodded. "There are three. But if you don't know her name, perhaps you could describe her?"

Danny had the eye of a craftsman; he rattled off a description that could only have fitted one Miss Galbraith.

After thanking Danny and departing the shop, then climbing into her carriage, Penelope tipped her head back against the squabs and heaved a troubled sigh. "There are times when I wish my logical mind wouldn't come to such disturbing conclusions."

Now free of the need to reassure poor Danny, both Violet and Griselda were also looking grim.

"Griselda and I haven't yet seen any of the Misses Galbraith," Violet said, "but I assume that Danny's description fits only one."

Griselda said, "The one who would naturally ask for the first pair of shoes to be made in white satin."

Penelope nodded. "Exactly so. And no, I cannot for the life of me understand what it means. I had no inkling that this murder was a case of matricide. And I cannot conceive of what situation could have driven Monica Galbraith to murder her mother."

* * *

*A*fter a short discussion, the ladies detoured to Greenbury Street. They were largely silent as Penelope's carriage rumbled north, each busy with their own thoughts—none of which, Penelope felt certain, were likely to be cheery. Matricide was shocking enough in concept, as an abstraction, but to have to genuinely face it in real life—that was something else again.

They halted at Griselda's house just long enough for Griselda to gather little Megan and her nursemaid, Gloria. Then, in Griselda's carriage, the three followed Penelope and Violet back to Albemarle Street, where they had arranged to dine with their husbands.

Mostyn admitted them into the front hall. As they divested themselves of their coats and bonnets, Penelope inquired after Oliver, only to have Mostyn say, "The little master's in the back parlor with Mr. Adair, Mr. Montague, and the inspector, ma'am." When Penelope, Violet, and Griselda all turned surprised looks on him, Mostyn elaborated, "I understand there have been developments and that they're waiting to speak with you."

Penelope exchanged a wide-eyed look with Griselda and Violet, then turned and made for her garden parlor. Likewise intrigued, Violet followed, and—after taking Megan from Gloria and releasing the maid to join Oliver's nursemaid, Hettie, upstairs—Griselda, with Megan on her hip, brought up the rear.

They walked into the parlor and beheld a scene of unusual domesticity. Montague was sitting on the sofa, leaning forward, his forearms on his knees, a smile wreathing his face as he watched and encouraged Oliver, who was kneeling on the rug before the sofa; assisted by Barnaby and Stokes, both of whom lay sprawled on the rug, Oliver was constructing a multi-towered edifice out of wooden blocks.

Penelope had crept the last little way. The men, talking in their deep, rumbling voices, hadn't heard her, but Oliver's sharp ears picked up her familiar footsteps; he saw her and crowed, "M'ma! See!"

Penelope smiled and felt the darkness that had closed about her lift. Walking forward, eyes only for her son, she beamed with proud affection. "Yes, darling." She crouched on the other side of the structure and dutifully examined it. "What a wonderful building."

Oliver beamed back and raised his arms. "Up!"

Unable to stop smiling, Penelope closed her hands about his sturdy body and, rising, lifted him up. Reaching out, Oliver closed both chubby hands in her upswept hair and held her face steady so he could lay a smacking kiss on her lips—something he'd recently learned he could do. "M'ma home."

"Yes, my son. Mama is, indeed, home." Settling him on her hip, Penelope looked at Barnaby, who was getting to his feet.

Stokes had already scrambled to his and gone to take Megan from Griselda; he was currently throwing his one-year-old daughter into the air and catching her, much to Megan's shrill delight.

Montague, meanwhile, had gone to greet Violet and kiss her check.

Capturing Penelope's gaze, Barnaby leaned forward and placed his lips where his son's had been.

For a moment, Penelope clung to the kiss, savored it.

Straightening, Barnaby smiled. "Welcome home."

Her lips still curved, Penelope started to smile back, but then her thoughts caught up with her and she felt the expression fade. Her eyes on Barnaby's, she hugged Oliver a trifle tighter and said, "We have to speak with Monica Galbraith."

Barnaby frowned. "How did you know?"

Penelope blinked, then frowned back. "Know what?"

The others had all turned; all exchanged glances.

"Let's take this chronologically," Barnaby suggested. "This morning, Stokes and I went to see what we could learn at Galbraith House, while Montague worked to learn what he could of any rumors of another exclusive license being offered for a different version of Lady Latimer's shoes, and Violet and Griselda went off to search for any clues from the crystal suppliers."

Sitting on the sofa, waving the others to the various chairs, Penelope settled Oliver in her lap. "You and Stokes first. I think we've discovered what you ought to have learned by a different route, but tell us anyway."

Between them, Barnaby and Stokes outlined their findings. "So," Stokes concluded, his expression turning grim, "we now know that a young shoemaker called at the Galbraiths' house intending to make some offer regarding shoes, but Lady Galbraith and most of the family were not in residence at the time, except for the youngest daughter, Monica Galbraith, who *may* have had the opportunity to speak with the shoemaker, but as yet we don't have any evidence that she did."

Penelope nodded. "We have such evidence, but as Barnaby said, we should take this step by step." She looked at Montague. "From what we learned an hour or so ago, you shouldn't have found anything—no rumors, no whispers of a second source of Lady Latimer's shoes."

Sober, Montague nodded. "There was no hint anywhere about a second supplier of those shoes."

Penelope looked at Griselda and Violet. "You two and your hunt through the crystal suppliers comes next."

Violet detailed their search, and Griselda filled in the details of what they'd discovered through Mr. Olson of Olson's Emporium. Griselda bumped Stokes's shoulder. "We had to invoke your authority to make him see the necessity, but he did, in the end, give us the information we were after—that a young shoemaker of the name of Danny Gibson has been buying the right crystals."

"In the expected quantities and over the right time frame," Violet added. "Gibson and Sons is off Long Acre, so we came back to tell Penelope."

"Meanwhile"—Penelope pushed her glasses back up; Oliver had dislodged them again—"I was wrestling with my Greek scribe's outpourings when Hartley Galbraith and his intended came to call. They had decided that it was time they dispensed with their veil of secrecy in pursuit of what I was given to understand is their overriding goal." Meeting the three men's intensely curious gazes, Penelope explained, "The pair intend to reunite their families—and as Hartley's intended is Cynthia Latimer, their reasons are self-explanatory."

"Cynthia *Latimer*?" Stokes looked faintly stunned. "But...that means she saw..."

"Exactly." Penelope nodded. "She was the one who saw the shoes of the lady fleeing the terrace most clearly, but as it happens, Cynthia actually saw far more than she'd realized. Courtesy of Griselda's milliner's tricks, we discovered several notable points about those shoes—they had a different arrangement of the crystals, a different cut, and had a distinctly different heel to those on the original Lady Latimer's shoes, meaning all the shoes made for the Latimer ladies. Cynthia's description, corroborated by the information we subsequently got from Danny Gibson and his grandfather, confirms that the lady fleeing the Fairchild's terrace immediately after Lady Galbraith was killed could not have been one of the Latimer ladies but was, in fact, Monica Galbraith."

Barnaby held up a hand. "Griselda and Violet had joined you by this time? All three of you heard this?"

"Yes." Penelope nodded decisively. "Everything came together in a rush." She paused, clearly casting her mind back. "Before Violet and Griselda came in, I had questioned Hartley and Cynthia on several matters, but in light of our subsequent discoveries, the only point that remains relevant is that both Hartley and Cynthia believe that Lady Galbraith came out to the side terrace and down onto the path because she was following Hartley, wanting to learn who he was meeting with clandestinely."

Barnaby arched a cynical brow. "Motherly concern?"

"I gathered from Hartley that his mother had some notion of managing his marriage, a notion he didn't share." Penelope frowned. Oliver squirmed and she set him down on the rug. Immediately, Megan wriggled off Griselda's lap and joined him. "Where was I?"

"When we came in and Griselda got Cynthia to describe the shoes," Violet supplied.

"Ah, yes. Well," Penelope went on, "Cynthia described a style of Lady Latimer's shoes that matched the single pair Danny Gibson later confirmed he'd completed and passed on. Cynthia doesn't know anything about Danny Gibson, not that he's making a different version of Lady Latimer's shoes, let alone their style, so she must be telling us the truth of what she saw. She saw the shoes Danny Gibson had made, and the person to whom Danny Gibson supplied those shoes—one pair made of white satin—is Monica Galbraith."

Penelope looked at Stokes. "Monica did, indeed, race after Danny when he was turned away from the Galbraiths' house. He knew her only as Miss Galbraith, but he described her accurately. He gave her the shoes in February and, as he understood it, she was going to present them to her mother in the best way to convince Lady Galbraith to give him an exclusive license of the same sort Lady Latimer has with her shoemaker."

Silence fell as they all revised their constructions of what had happened at the Fairchilds' ball.

Stokes stirred. "Answer me this—if Monica Galbraith wore these fantastical shoes to the ball, why is it that no one noticed? I thought the point of the shoes was that they attract attention."

Penelope blinked. She looked at Violet, then Griselda. "I'm not sure…"

"It depends on the length of the gown." Griselda's tone indicated that she knew of what she spoke. "Modistes generally set the hems of gowns worn to dance in at ankle level, but if Monica had her hems set lower—"

"She wouldn't have been dancing," Penelope said. "She wasn't out yet, so no dancing, at least not at an event like the Fairchilds' ball." Griselda nodded. "So she could easily have had her hems almost to the ground. And if she didn't dance, there would be little likelihood of anyone noticing her shoes, not unless she raised her skirts."

"As she did when she fled the terrace and stepped up into the house." Penelope looked at Stokes as if asking for his next question.

Stokes grimaced and looked down at Megan, playing with the blocks alongside Oliver.

Montague sighed. "So we now believe that Monica Galbraith followed Lady Galbraith outside." He looked around the circle of faces. "Do we have any idea why?"

Violet looked at Penelope. "Do you think it might be connected with what Monica told Danny Gibson—that she, Monica, had to pick the right time to present the shoes to her mother? I assume she meant for greatest effect, and she did tell Danny that she would need to wait until late March."

Head tilting, Penelope considered, then said, "We know Lady Galbraith was beyond keen to have her own Lady Latimer's shoes, and yes, I agree it's possible that given the timing—when the family returned to town and the start of the Season—then the Fairchilds' ball might well have seemed the most obvious choice for Monica's big revelation. Everyone who was anyone in the ton could be counted on to be there…but I can't see why Monica didn't tell Lady Galbraith of the shoes before they reached the ball. Why wait until during the ball?"

Barnaby shifted. "Let's assume that, for some reason, Monica couldn't tell her mother about the shoes earlier. Monica then notices Lady Galbraith slipping out of the ballroom and sees an opportunity to speak with her mother alone, and so follows her outside." His features hard, uncompromising, he went on, "Even if Monica's reason for following her mother outside was something quite different, it seems we're certain now that Monica did, indeed, follow Lady Galbraith out onto the terrace, and possibly even down the steps and onto the path." He paused, then said, "What we don't know is what happened next."

After a moment, Stokes said, "But we do know that, within a minute of Lady Galbraith being struck down, Monica fled the terrace, and she has subsequently said nothing at all about that, not even admitting that she had been there."

Penelope grimaced. "In Hartley and Cynthia's opinion, there wasn't sufficient time for someone standing inside the terrace door to have seen someone *else* drop the ball on Lady Galbraith, then to have rushed to the balustrade, looked over, and fled back to the terrace door before Hartley and Cynthia reached the point of being able to see the terrace."

"Time is often difficult to judge in such situations," Barnaby said. "Nevertheless…"

"Nevertheless," Violet said, "we appear to be dealing with a case of matricide." She glanced at Montague. "Again."

Barnaby shook his head. "This isn't a family like the Halsteads." The Halstead case was one in which he, Stokes, Penelope, and Griselda had assisted Montague; it was the case that had brought Violet into Montague's life, and, indeed, all their lives. "The Halstead case was a matricide, but the Halsteads were a distinctly aberrant family. The Galbraiths are entirely normal." He paused, then dipped his head. "Admittedly, Lady Galbraith had her faults, but they lay well within the norm of a ton matron with a large family."

"Which," Stokes said, "brings us back to the critical questions. What happened on the terrace, or on the path below it, between Lady Galbraith and her daughter Monica, and did Monica subsequently kill her mother?"

"Hmm," Griselda murmured. "I'm still tripping over why Monica didn't tell her mother, and her sisters, too, about discovering a new source of Lady Latimer's shoes. In their terms, it was a huge coup." She looked at Penelope. "Monica is the youngest daughter, isn't she?"

"Yes…and perhaps that's relevant." Penelope paused, then said, "I haven't yet inquired about how Lady Galbraith got on with her daughters, but it's certainly true that with all the fuss and excitement of ton balls and the marriage mart, younger daughters do sometimes get short shrift, certainly when it comes to their mothers' attention." Penelope arched her brows. "I can't say I ever felt that way, but then I was never interested in balls and the marriage mart."

"But Monica most likely is," Violet said. "Could she have seen the shoes as her opportunity to shine in her mother's eyes?"

"Very likely," Penelope returned. "And that fits with her waiting to make her revelation on the evening of the Fairchilds' ball. For the purpose of focusing not just her mother's but all of society's attention on her, that ball *was* the perfect moment, the most glittering stage, with the crème de la crème of the ton in attendance. In terms of a grand revelation of the sort Monica would have wanted to make, there could have been no better venue."

After a moment, Stokes sighed. "We're going around and around, circling the one point we still do not know. Let's say that Monica followed her mother out onto the terrace to show her the shoes. What happened next? Did Monica kill her mother? And if so, why?"

Barnaby heaved a sigh. He met Penelope's eyes, then looked at the others. "As far as I can see, the only person who knows the answer to those questions is Monica herself."

Entirely sober, Penelope nodded. "Which is why we need to speak with her."

The door opened and Mostyn came in, Hettie and Gloria at his heels. "Dinner is served, ma'am."

Penelope glanced at the others, then looked at Mostyn. "As ever, your timing is impeccable, Mostyn."

Relinquishing the children to their nurses to be carried to the nursery and put to bed, the adults rose and, setting aside the disturbing case for later consideration, followed Mostyn to the dining room.

CHAPTER 11

*A*fter dinner that evening, Hartley saw his father settled in his favorite armchair by the library hearth with a large glass of brandy within easy reach, then Hartley excused himself and went into the front hall, opened the front door, and stepped outside.

Quietly closing the door, he looked across the darkened park at the house opposite and one door up. In the poor light, he couldn't be sure, but he thought he glimpsed a curtain shift in one of the upstairs windows.

He paused for an instant. What he and Cynthia were about to embark on was blazoned on the forefront of his brain, snaring every last iota of his attention. Oddly enough, he didn't feel nervous so much as impatient; they'd been wanting to take this step, had been discussing it for more than a year. Jaw firming, he stepped off the porch and went to meet his fate.

It was past time.

The evening had closed in, unusually dark and almost menacing with heavy black clouds louring, impenetrable and weighty. The scent of rain was pervasive, carried on the chill breeze that snaked through the park, twining through the still-bare branches and setting them creaking.

Hartley strode through the park. At this hour, there was no one else about; this wasn't a neighborhood in which vagrants curling up under a bush to see out the night were common. As far as he could tell, in that moment he was the only person abroad in that little pocket of London. Reaching the huge old oak that stood at the center of the park, he halted beneath the cage of its outer branches.

A minute later, Cynthia appeared; letting herself out of the side gate of her family's house, she came to join him. Wrapped in her cloak, with an additional shawl to combat the chill in the air, she walked to meet him with her head high.

She had never, to his eyes, appeared more serenely assured. More confident of herself, and of him. Of them and their way forward.

He was sure, too, but he had never had quite the same clarity of purpose, the same never-wavering resolution that she possessed. Hers was a strength he was man enough, wise enough, to appreciate. And to value.

As she neared, he smiled, in appreciation, in welcome.

In lingering wonder.

She returned the gesture with much the same emotions shining in her eyes.

Barely slowing, she walked into his arms.

Of their own volition, his arms closed around her. When she raised her face to his and offered her lips, he accepted the invitation, bent his head and kissed her.

There, in the middle of the square, for all their world to see.

Even if no one was looking.

It was the statement that counted, a declaration of their intent, and as they surrendered to the kiss and let it deepen, both accepted and rejoiced.

And gave themselves over, once again, committed once again to their direction, their avowed purpose.

And to what the journey to their goal required them to do.

There was no backing away, no retreat. Not in either of them.

Cynthia sensed that, knew that, as his lips moved on hers, as his tongue claimed her mouth and she returned the caress with her own brand of ardor. Her fingers locked in the silk of his hair, her breasts crushed to the hard planes of his chest, she met him and matched him and held fast within the tumult of their swirling passions. Her hips tight against his thighs, his erection cradled against her taut belly, she held to the kiss, to him, to the promise of what would be.

But there were deeds they had to accomplish that night before they could claim the haven of each other's embrace.

When Hartley drew back from the kiss, she did, too.

When he raised his head and looked into her face, she was waiting to meet his eyes.

He searched her face, her eyes, then asked, "Are you ready?"

Easing back, she nodded. "I am." He took her hand and she twined her fingers with his. "We can't wait any longer."

He nodded. His gaze rose to her home, silhouetted against the night sky. His face hardened. "We were so much happier before."

Cynthia's lips twisted as she followed his gaze. "Before Mama found those wretched shoes."

Hartley hesitated, then sighed. "No—that wasn't the real source of the problem. My mama was. If she hadn't grown so obsessed with those shoes… They were just shoes, but she wouldn't listen to reason. In pursuit of what she wanted, she wantonly wrecked not just her relationship with Aunt Hester, but all our relationships, too."

He met Cynthia's gaze. "All over a particular style of shoe—but, even more, because she couldn't have something she'd set her heart on." He hesitated, then said, "It's important we see it for what it was. If we don't, it'll be harder to put things right."

He looked into Cynthia's upturned face, into the shadowed pools of her eyes. She had always anchored him. From somewhere between them, within them, he found the strength to face what he felt he had to. Lowering his voice, he said, "I would never have wished her dead, but now that she is, I—we—have to accept that her death has removed the largest obstacle in our path. I didn't kill her, and neither did you. But with her gone, it opens the way for us to bind our families together again."

Cynthia held his gaze steadily. "Just as we had always hoped to do, but your mother's death has also made our goal imperative. It's time we made a start. With the funeral tomorrow afternoon, we haven't got much time to do for the others what they need to have done."

Hartley dragged in a breath, glanced back at his home, then looked at hers. He gripped her hand more tightly. "Are you ready to attempt to turn back the clock?"

Tipping her head, her gaze on her home, Cynthia considered, then shook her head. "No—we're not turning it back. We're not going to even attempt to pretend all the direness never happened. We *are* going to work to—do our damnedest to—push it aside, and to get our lives, which have been derailed, back on track." She met Hartley's eyes. "That's what we're doing. That's what we're going to do."

Lips firming, an answering determination infusing his expression, he nodded.

Hand in hand, they left the oak and walked to the Latimers'

house.

* * *

*B*arnaby, Penelope, and the others had long ago realized that taking a respite from their investigative deliberations and enjoying each other's company over a relaxed dinner allowed their minds to settle, which invariably resulted in greater clarity when they returned to the drawing room and the matter at hand.

That evening, while the others reclaimed their accustomed seats about the drawing room fireplace, Penelope fell to pacing before it. Barnaby, Stokes, and Griselda knew that was not a good sign. What was even more troubling was that they shared her disquiet.

Less experienced in Penelope's ways but nevertheless sensitive to the welling uneasiness, Montague settled on the sofa beside Violet, his arm stretched along the sofa's back. Rather carefully, he offered, "It occurs to me that it's possible, despite all we now know, that Monica Galbraith might, indeed, have seen someone fling the ball down on her mother. If she had followed her mother from the ballroom, as we now surmise she had, but had hung back in the shadows of the corridor, she might have overheard an argument, seen the murderer fling down the ball...and heard enough to realize what had happened. She would have been paralyzed with shock, at least for an instant. She would have wanted to rush forward to the balustrade, might have impulsively stepped over the threshold and onto the terrace, but was too frightened to go any further. She balked, then turned and bolted. That, I think, would account for everything we currently know."

Stokes blinked, then slowly nodded. "Yes, you're right." He glanced at Penelope, who had halted to look at Montague. "What we know to this point does not prove that Monica herself was the killer."

Penelope drew in a breath, then somewhat stiffly nodded. "I agree—but that's not what's weighing, increasingly heavily, on my mind."

Violet tipped her head. "What is?" She had worked with Penelope for some months and had realized that sometimes her friend needed a simple question to focus her thoughts.

The ploy worked. Remaining stationary, her expression turning blank as she looked inward, Penelope eventually said, "Regardless of whether she saw someone else murder her mother or whether she herself was the murderer, can you imagine what Monica—a young lady not yet out, who would have led a very sheltered life—must be feeling and thinking now? Tonight?" Warming to her theme, Penelope glanced at the others. "Try, if you can, to put yourselves in her place. She spends months scheming for her big moment. She craves her mother's attention and everything's in place—she's wearing the shoes, and she's at the major ball of the moment along with all the ton—but she's getting frustrated because, for one reason or another, she hasn't been able to show her mother her new shoes. Not yet. Then she sees her mother slip out of the ballroom. Monica follows, hoping for the few moments of privacy, which are all she needs—a few moments of her mother's time, of her undivided attention."

Penelope paused, then went on, "We don't know what happened next." She looked at Stokes, then Barnaby. "Did you see Monica when you called there today?"

"According to Lord Galbraith," Barnaby reported, "his younger daughters are keeping to their rooms and have not come downstairs since the tragedy."

Penelope grimaced. "I only really saw her that once, in the Fairchilds' drawing room. Thinking back…" Penelope closed her eyes and did.

Softly, Griselda murmured, "Focus on the element in your memory that you want to see. Then look closer."

Her head up, her eyes still closed, Penelope drew in a long, slow breath, then exhaled. "My God—I saw it then, but I didn't realize what it meant." Opening her eyes, she looked at Griselda. "Monica was *already* upset—deeply upset—before Stokes revealed that her mother had been murdered. She was sitting with her head down and her hands clasped in her lap. She was clutching her hands so tightly her knuckles were white. And then when Stokes broke the news, she burst into wrenching sobs. Immediately."

"Because she'd been bottling them up," Violet said.

"Exactly!" Penelope's face filled with certainty. "At the time, I thought maybe Monica had been thinking dark thoughts about her mother for deserting her in the ballroom…but it was something far worse." Penelope paused, then frowned. "But I have to say, even given what I saw, it could all have happened as Montague suggested, and Monica was bowed down by guilt over running away and leaving her mother dying."

"She would have been in a state," Violet said. "She couldn't have returned to the ballroom—someone would have noticed."

Penelope cast an exasperated look at Barnaby. "We collected the alibis of the Latimer ladies, but we never thought to check those of the Galbraiths."

Resigned, Barnaby shrugged.

Montague stirred. When the others looked at him, he grimaced. "I know I made the suggestion, but on thinking further...while I *can* accept that if Monica had seen someone kill her mother, she might have been so shocked that she precipitously fled—she is young and was in a social situation that would have been new and overwhelming—what I *can't* accept is that she then did nothing. For more than an hour. She didn't seek help. She didn't confide in her sisters, or her father, or her brother, all of whom were present." Increasingly certain, Montague met Penelope's gaze and shook his head. "No. However terrible it is to think it, Monica Galbraith must have been responsible for her mother's death. That's the only way to explain her subsequent behavior."

Penelope stared at Montague for several seconds, then made a frustrated sound. "You're right. Which—"

"Brings us back to the fact," Stokes said, "that the only person who knows what happened on the terrace is Monica Galbraith."

Penelope swung about and resumed her pacing. "I'm still having a very hard time believing she killed her mother. Young ladies of her ilk normally balk at squashing a spider."

"Be that as it may," Stokes said, meeting Barnaby's eyes, "we'll speak with her tomorrow and learn the truth."

Violet frowned. "Actually, I don't think you'll be able to speak with Monica tomorrow." When the others looked at her, Violet explained, "Lady Galbraith's funeral is tomorrow. The notice was in this morning's *Gazette*."

"Oh." Penelope halted. Head rising, she stared across the room. Then she whirled to face Barnaby. "I—we"—she waved to include them all—"need to speak with Monica tonight." Urgency filled her tone. "Now! We can't wait."

Barnaby met her gaze and didn't argue.

It was Stokes who somewhat warily asked, "Why now—tonight?"

Penelope swung to face him. "Because tomorrow might be—I greatly fear will be—too late. I was never"—she gestured—"as *young* as Monica Galbraith, but if I'm even half right about the pressures that must be building on her...what if she *was* responsible, in whatever way, for her mother's death? What if somehow something went wrong with her grand scheme to give her mother what she wanted in the form of a version of Lady Latimer's shoes, and instead her mother *died*? Don't ask me how it happened—I don't know. But I do know that Monica was deeply distressed that night, and after three long days and nights to dwell on whatever happened..." Pausing to draw breath, Penelope met Stokes's eyes. "If we wait, I really don't think Monica will be there to see her mother's body lowered into the ground."

"You think she'll take her own life?" Griselda asked.

Penelope looked at her, then simply said, "I'm perfectly certain she'll make the attempt, and what more appropriate time than tonight?"

Silence held them all, then Penelope looked again at Stokes. "We cannot allow this to turn into an even worse tragedy. We need to speak with Monica now."

* * *

𝒫enelope had succeeded in very effectively communicating her trepidation to the others; they were all on edge as they piled into Stokes's and Montague's carriages for the short journey to Hanover Square.

Less than fifteen minutes after making their collective decision, they gathered on the pavement outside the Galbraith residence. Stokes was about to lead their party up the steps when he noticed a group of four people heading their way through the unlit park.

Spotting Stokes and company, the group walked faster.

Following Stokes's gaze, Penelope turned as the group reached the street and the light from the streetlamps fell on them.

"Adair! Inspector!" With one hand locked about the hand of a young lady, Hartley Galbraith strode quickly across the street.

The young lady kept pace by his side, her expression concerned, her gaze swiftly raking their group. "Has something happened?" The young lady directed her question to Penelope.

Stokes realized the young lady had to be Cynthia Latimer—which suggested that the older couple currently crossing the street were most likely her parents. Stokes's first impulse was to reassure everyone that all was in hand...but it wasn't.

Inwardly sighing, he glanced at Penelope.

She barely waited for the acknowledgment to take charge. In her usual no-nonsense fashion, she introduced the older couple to everyone they hadn't previously met.

Stokes found himself having his hand wrung by Lord Latimer.

"Has there been some breakthrough, Inspector?" Lord Latimer was a strong, hearty gentleman; he had a grip like iron.

"Yes, and no," Penelope answered, saving Stokes from having to obfuscate. "But there have been some developments, and we felt it imperative to pursue them immediately." She glanced at Cynthia and her parents. "Indeed, I'm rather glad to see you. It's possible you might be needed."

Hartley's anxiety plainly escalated, but before he could speak, Penelope held up a hand. "We believe we are close to understanding what happened, but we need to go inside. This isn't a conversation for the front steps."

"Yes, of course." Recalled to his manners, Hartley stepped up, opened the door, and waved everyone inside. "Please—come in."

Accepting the invitation, they entered and milled in the front hall.

Penelope turned to Hartley. "We need to speak with Monica."

Hartley blinked. "Monica?"

Barnaby quietly said, "We believe she can shed some light on what occurred."

"Oh." Hartley looked surprised.

But before he could probe further, drawn by the commotion, Lord Galbraith came out of the library. He appeared weighed down, his movements slow; his loss clearly still rode heavily on his shoulders. Then his gaze fell on Lord and Lady Latimer, and he stopped dead.

The three old friends stared at each other.

A moment of tortured silence ensued, then Lord Galbraith said, "Hester? Humphrey?" His voice was weak, then he swallowed and managed, "Thank God you're here."

Lady Latimer swept across the intervening yards. Lord Galbraith opened his arms, and they embraced. Lady Latimer murmured soothing words, and then Lord Latimer joined them.

Penelope watched as the three older people clustered together, sharing their loss, the Latimers clearly providing desperately needed and deeply welcome comfort to Lord Galbraith.

Hartley and Cynthia exchanged a relieved glance, then, drawing in breaths and raising their heads, they crossed the hall to join their elders.

Penelope and the others hung back by the door, allowing Hartley and Cynthia to break their news to Lord Galbraith; clearly, they'd already gained the blessing of Cynthia's parents. As his lordship looked from Hartley and Cynthia to the Latimers, taking in their approval and their hopes, his face slowly suffused with even deeper relief and the first hint of life beyond his sorrow.

It was necessary to give the families time to regroup; Penelope told herself that, yet impatience prodded her like a sharpened spur. She wasn't sure why her trepidation was mounting, why she felt so strongly that they needed to act *now*; all she knew was that she did, and that her amorphous dread was building.

Rustling and light steps on the stairs drew all eyes to the landing above. The voices rising from the hall—Lord Galbraith's much firmer and with quite a different timbre as he congratulated his son and embraced Cynthia with sincere joy—had drawn Geraldine and Primrose from their rooms; they paused on the landing, clearly uncertain.

Lord Galbraith saw them and, smiling, beckoned. "Come down, come down! See who's here."

That was all the encouragement Geraldine and Primrose needed; lifting their hems, they rushed down the last flight and across the tiles. Their expressions dissolving, they flung themselves into Cynthia's and Lady Latimer's arms. Amid a storm of weeping and choked words, the ladies clung, while the three gentlemen patted shoulders and stroked backs and tried to calm and soothe.

Then Cynthia and Hartley told his sisters their news, which provoked a fresh round of tears. From the broken words and disjointed phrases it was clear that all in the group were caught between relief and welling joy on the one hand and lingering grief and sorrow on the other.

A frown in her eyes, Penelope shifted from foot to foot. "This is all very touching," she murmured, "but we need to see Monica."

Griselda was watching the head of the stairs. "She hasn't even come to look."

Montague said, "Perhaps her room is further away, or she might be sleeping."

"Or…" Penelope paused, then, lips setting, she walked across the hall, circling to come up by Hartley's side. She tugged his sleeve.

When he glanced at her, she said, "We need to speak with Monica rather urgently. Can you please send someone to fetch her?"

Hartley glanced around the heads as if only then realizing his youngest sister wasn't there. "Yes, of course." He looked around and spotted the butler, who had come into the hall but hung back. "Millwell—please send someone to ask Miss Monica to join us."

"Indeed, sir." Having overheard the family's latest news, the old butler was teary-eyed. With a bow, he retreated toward the rear of the hall, to where a young footman stood at attention in the shadow of the stairs.

Returning to Barnaby and the others, who had remained closer to the front door, Penelope watched the footman go quickly up the stairs. Straining her ears, after a moment she thought she heard a knock, followed by the footman's voice.

A sudden burst of chatter from the family drowned out further sound from above, but then the footman, looking puzzled, came back down the stairs alone. The elderly butler met him at the bottom of the stairs. The footman said something, his voice too muted for Penelope to hear. Frowning, the butler replied, then the footman turned and, followed by the butler, went quickly back up the stairs.

Penelope glanced at Violet, then both hurried to the stairs. Griselda was right behind them.

Gaining the top of the stairs, Penelope looked around.

"That way." Violet pointed down a corridor.

Penelope hurried forward, Violet at her heels. Entering the short corridor, in the light from the wall sconces, they saw the old butler urging on the footman, who was attempting to break down the door at the corridor's end.

Glancing back, Penelope saw Griselda enter the corridor behind Violet. "Tell Stokes and Barnaby we need them here *now*."

Having glimpsed the activity further down the corridor, Griselda turned and ran back to the stairs.

Penelope and Violet hurried on.

The elderly butler was working himself into a state; when Penelope and Violet reached him, he was wringing his hands, and the tears in his rheumy eyes were threatening to overflow.

The footman bounced back from his third try at shouldering open the door.

Penelope addressed the pair equally. "Has anyone replied from inside?"

The footman glanced at the butler, then said, "No, ma'am. I came up and knocked, and I thought I heard something. But when no one answered, I knocked again and called, then I tried the door and"—he waved at the panel—"it's locked. It never normally is."

A stir along the corridor heralded Stokes, followed by Barnaby and Griselda.

"Monica's door is locked," Penelope said. "And she might be in there."

Grim-faced, Stokes nodded and waved them all aside. He positioned himself before the door, then raised one large boot and kicked hard at the panel just below the lock.

The frame splintered on the inside and the door swung free.

Penelope whisked inside. Violet and Griselda followed.

The room wasn't that large. It contained a tester bed with a frilly pale blue bedspread. Although the bedspread was rumpled, the bed was empty.

A lamp turned very low had been left alight on a small desk beside the fireplace. As Griselda went to turn up the wick, Penelope heard a muffled *thump-thump* from the corner beyond the wardrobe. Crossing the room, she called, "Bring the lamp."

As Griselda complied and the light strengthened, Penelope walked past the end of the wardrobe and found herself looking down into the tear-stained face of a young maid, trussed and gagged and left propped in the corner.

"Mmm-*mmm*!" The maid thrashed helplessly, squinting in the sudden glare.

Penelope crouched and reached for the gag. "It's all right."

The maid was still weeping.

Violet crouched on the maid's other side and started working on the rope binding the girl's hands.

A strip of cotton flounce, the gag had been tied tightly; it took a minute and more for Penelope to ease the knot apart and pull the material from the girl's face. As it fell away, the maid gasped, then choked.

"Here." Griselda held out a glass of water.

Penelope took it and helped the maid to sip. "We need to know where your mistress is."

Still sipping, the maid nodded, then she raised her head, swallowed, and hoarsely said, "You have to go after her—quickly. She's gone down to the river—she said she was going to throw herself in."

"Why?" Penelope asked.

The maid hesitated, obviously unsure.

Violet glanced at the others, then took one of the maid's freed hands in hers and simply said, "It's important that you tell us so we can save your mistress—we can't help her if we don't know."

The maid stared at Violet for a second more, then she turned to Penelope. "Miss Monica thinks she killed her mother, but that can't be right—she loved the old lady, even if her ladyship didn't pay much attention to her. Like a puppy, Miss Monica was, just wanting and waiting for a smile—there's never been even the smallest bit of nastiness in Miss Monica, and I'll swear that all the way to my grave."

The maid drew breath and went on, "Then she found those shoes, and she made her big plan to show them off to her ladyship, all to make her mother happy—so excited she was when she went off to that big ball..." The maid's expression grew grim. "But then she came back, and her ladyship was dead, and Miss Monica fell apart. She was a wreck. I thought she'd come around, but she only got worse. This evening...I didn't see it coming. She knocked me out. When I woke up, she'd already gagged me and tied my hands and was tying my feet."

Struggling to sit up from her slump, the maid gripped Penelope's sleeve. "She spoke like someone who believed there was no hope. She said she had to do what was right because she'd killed her mother...but she didn't! She couldn't have—not her. Not in a million years."

Penelope patted the maid's hand as she detached it from her sleeve. "I don't believe she murdered her mother, either."

"Unfortunately," Barnaby said, "it appears that Monica believes she murdered her mother."

Barnaby was standing by the fireplace with Stokes; when Penelope looked his way, he held up the note he'd found on the mantelpiece. "Her explanation for what she intends to do, but no hint of how or why she did the deed." He glanced again at the neat schoolgirl script. "All she says is that she didn't mean to do it, and she's sorry."

Penelope's face set. "We can ask her all our questions when we find her." Turning back to the maid, she caught the girl's eyes. "How long ago did Miss Monica leave?"

The maid glanced at the mantelpiece; Stokes stepped out of the way so she could see the clock. The maid paled. "Oh, God—it's been a good twenty minutes. She'll be more than halfway there."

"I need you to think as if you were Miss Monica." Penelope's commanding tones overrode—quashed—the maid's rising hysteria. "If she's going to the river to throw herself in, how would she go? In a hackney? To where?"

The maid opened her mouth, paused, then nodded to herself. "Walking—she has to be walking." She met Penelope's eyes. "That's why I said halfway there—she can't have taken a hackney because just this afternoon, she gave me all her pin money and told me to give it to that young shoemaker, the one who made her the shoes. She said it was only fair. But I know it was all of it—and she was dressed to walk. She had her half-boots on, and she put on her bonnet, too."

"Good," Penelope said. "So where along the river would she go? Is there any particular place she would make for?"

The maid blinked. "The Privy Gardens. The family used to go there when the girls were little. She used to love going there."

Stokes stirred. "What route would she take?"

"Down Saville Street and through Albany." The maid spoke with certainty. "She won't go down Piccadilly—we never went that way. She'll go past St. James's Square and down onto the Parade Grounds, then around and across Whitehall to the gardens." The maid looked at Stokes. "They border the river."

Stokes nodded. "I know them." He turned to the door. "Now let's see if we can get there in time." He led the way from the room.

Barnaby waved the three ladies ahead of him; leaving the footman and the butler to tend to the maid, they all went quickly downstairs to where Monica's family was waiting with Montague in the front hall.

As they stepped onto the tiles, Stokes flicked a glance at Penelope.

She caught it. Before anyone could voice the questions burning their tongues, she crisply stated, "Monica has left the house. She believes she killed her mother, which seems highly unlikely, but we don't have time to go into that now." Sternly, she eyed the family. "And we don't have time for any vapors or hysterics, either—we need to go after Monica and get her back. We can sort everything out later, but you all need to help. We don't have much time."

She'd succeeded in capturing everyone's attention. No one spoke, much less argued. Appeased, she rolled on, giving a brief outline of where they thought Monica had gone and what route they believed she would take.

Recovering from the shock most rapidly, Hartley and Cynthia confirmed that the Privy Gardens via St. James's Square was, indeed, the most likely destination and route Monica would have chosen.

"Good." Penelope met Hartley's eyes. "You and Cynthia are in charge of the family search party. Take carriages or hackneys to St. James's Square and start from there—on foot, because in a carriage you might easily miss her. You need to hurry, because we know she's well ahead of you, but she might have paused or stopped to think anywhere along the way. She might be sitting on a bench somewhere. We need her found and brought back here—do you understand?"

Hartley wanted to go straight to the river; it was there in his face, but he was the only one who could keep the family members focused. Clearly swallowing his reluctance, he nodded. "Yes. All right."

"Stay in small groups," Stokes advised. "At least two together at all times, and stay within sight of each other."

"How far should we go?" Cynthia asked.

"Keep searching thoroughly all the way to the Privy Gardens," Stokes said.

"We," Penelope stated, "will go straight there. We'll be the last line between Monica and the river." She paused, then waved at everyone. "We don't have time to discuss anything more. We have to act immediately if we're to save Monica."

CHAPTER 12

We have to act immediately if we're to save Monica.

Deep inside, Penelope had known that was true—not just a prediction but a certainty. She didn't breathe freely until she and the others had taken up positions in the Privy Gardens alongside the river. If Monica had already thrown herself into the murky waters, there was nothing they could do; they had to pray that they'd managed to get ahead of her and plan and act accordingly.

Along that stretch, the river ran south to north; the rectangular gardens, one longer side fronting the river, lay on the western bank. The southern half of the gardens stretched unbroken from Whitehall Road to the low stone wall above the embankment against which the Thames moodily lapped, but the northern half of the gardens, abutting the old Banquet Hall of Whitehall Palace, contained a row of narrow buildings between the gardens and the river. Because there were passageways between the buildings that could be used to reach the riverbank, Penelope, Barnaby, and the others had had to spread out to ensure Monica couldn't slip past them.

If she succeeded in throwing herself into the Thames, she would be lost. The tide was high, the river darkly murmurous, and the currents along that stretch were strong.

"We have to stop her before she gets close enough," Penelope muttered to herself. With her back to the river, she stood still as a statue beneath a tree and scanned the sector of the gardens that had fallen to her to patrol. It was the section farthest south. Barnaby stood some way to her right, with Griselda beyond, followed by Stokes, Violet, and Montague.

Desperate to ensure they reached the river before Monica, they'd tumbled out of their carriages in Whitehall. Stokes had spotted a constable and had been about to hail him when Penelope had caught his arm and fiercely whispered, "Don't!" When Stokes had blinked at her, she'd said, "We can't treat Monica as if she's a criminal, not until we've proven that she is. And I'm absolutely not sure she is."

The latter statement had sounded ludicrous coming out of her mouth, of all mouths, yet it had been the unvarnished truth. Her incapacity to make sense of the murder, combined with the strong premonition that something dire was about to befall, left her deeply uneasy. Unexpectedly, unprecedentedly disturbed.

Logical incapacity and premonitions was the province of others, not her.

Folding her arms, she frowned into the night. It wasn't the blackest night she'd ever been out in, but the leaden clouds had thickened and seemed to press ever lower over the spires of the nearby cathedral, a denser shape among the shadows identifiable more by its bulk than by any discernible features. If there was a moon, they couldn't see it; what little light there was came from the distant streetlamps, pools of soft, diffused light that didn't reach as far as the trees.

At least the trees were still largely bare; if they'd been in full leaf, spotting anyone before they got too close to the river to intercept would have been all but impossible.

Although she had donned her pelisse to call on the Galbraiths, the rising wind slid chill fingers past the folds. Dragging in a breath, she steeled herself against the cold and raised her head—

A slight figure wrapped in a cloak came trudging into the park.

Monica—Penelope was sure it was she—walked slowly but steadily nearer. Her gaze on the ground, she seemed completely immersed in her inner world and unaware of anything around her.

She's already let go. Penelope didn't know where the thought came from, but she heard the words clearly in her mind.

Monica was following the southernmost path leading through the gardens to the river. Penelope was standing just off that path, ten yards before the embankment wall.

Glancing to her right, Penelope saw that Barnaby had spotted Monica and was silently drawing nearer; she held up her hand palm out, and when he halted, head tilting quizzically, she waved him around and behind her. With a nod, he changed directions, circling to take up station behind her, closer to the river, the better to ensure Monica didn't slip past.

Looking back at Monica, still half the garden away, Penelope glimpsed Stokes moving swiftly toward the street, keeping to the lawns so Monica wouldn't hear him. He must have seen Penelope's direction to Barnaby and had elected to circle around Monica and come up on Penelope's other side to block access to the next stretch of bank.

Refocusing on Monica, Penelope suddenly realized that, given she had no idea what was going on in Monica's mind, she had no idea what she herself was going to say. What she should say—what would best serve?

She'd never dealt with a suicidal young lady before.

She couldn't even think of any of her acquaintance who had.

She waited until the last possible moment to step smartly out from under the tree directly into Monica's path.

Head still down, Monica didn't at first see her—then she did. Jerking her head up, Monica recoiled and halted.

And stared.

Penelope looked calmly back at her. She had thought Monica was the same height as she, but, in fact, Monica was at least two inches taller.

Monica finally placed her, blinked, then frowned. "What are you doing here?" Understandably, her tone held a great deal of confusion.

Yet even then, Monica didn't glance around, didn't register the oddity of Penelope being there alone, almost as if she thought Penelope an apparition that had popped into existence on the path before her.

"Actually," Penelope said, taking her time and keeping her voice level, "that was the question I wanted to ask you." She tilted her head, let curiosity show, and asked as if she didn't know the answer, "Where are you going?"

She'd decided that the best way to handle Monica was to keep her talking and on the path until her family arrived; they couldn't be that far away.

Several seconds ticked by.

Penelope started to wonder if Monica would answer, but then the blankness that had laid siege to the girl's features fractured into an expression of such painful intensity—such shattering remorse—that Penelope suddenly couldn't breathe.

Monica looked past Penelope to the river and, in a fragile voice all the more terrible for still holding echoes of the child she had been, replied, "I'm going where I'm supposed to go." She gestured to the river, then looked at Penelope. "Isn't that what I'm supposed to do? Go, and save my family any more horror? It's the least I can do. They've all suffered enough because of what I did."

Caught—all but paralyzed—by the sheer depth of pain radiating from Monica, Penelope managed to shake her head. "No. They don't want you to do that—they love you."

Some emotion akin to frustration crossed Monica's face. Impatiently, she shook her head. "You don't understand—I killed Mama. No one can love me after that."

Penelope forced herself to keep her eyes on Monica's face and not yield to the impulse to look away and allow the girl her pain. "Actually, I think it's you who don't understand. Killing someone by accident isn't murder." An accident was the only option that fitted all the facts, the intangible as well as the tangible. Holding Monica's tortured gaze, Penelope demanded, "Did you mean to kill her?"

"No!" Monica recoiled. "*Of course* I didn't mean to—*I loved her!*"

The pain thrumming through the statement underscored its veracity.

Penelope nodded. "That's what I thought. And if you didn't mean to kill her, you can't have murdered her."

Monica stared at her.

As Monica searched her face, Penelope started to hope—

"No." Slowly, Monica started to shake her head. "You're just trying to confuse me. If I stay, they'll put me in prison and there'll be a trial..."

Penelope tried to think of what to say—

Monica lunged for the river.

She broke past Penelope and raced for the wall.

Whirling, Penelope raced after her.

Grabbing up her skirts and cloak, Monica leapt for the top of the wall.

Penelope leapt up, too.

Landing on the wall beside Monica, she fisted her hands in Monica's cloak and the layers beneath and desperately held on as the pair of them teetered.

After seconds of crazed see-sawing, panting, Monica stopped

trying to break free. Turning on Penelope, she glared. "Let me go!"

"No!" Penelope glared back. "If you go over, I'll go, too. I have a small son—is that fair?" She threw every last card she had on the table and belligerently held Monica's gaze.

She didn't want the girl to look down and see Barnaby. While she'd seized Monica, Barnaby had grabbed her. He had a strong grip about her knees; she wasn't going anywhere. But he'd moved silently and was below Monica's line of sight as long as Monica kept her gaze on Penelope's face.

Then Monica looked past Penelope and tensed anew.

Realizing what Monica was seeing, Penelope rapped out, "Stop! Stay back!"

Distantly, she heard Stokes swear.

But he must have obeyed because, after a tense second, Monica swung her gaze back to Penelope's face. In the faint moonlight bathing the scene, she looked at Penelope as if Penelope was demented. "Why are you doing this?"

Penelope hadn't thought she'd known, but the answer was there. "Because I'm a youngest daughter, too." The revelation almost made her blink, but she took the brakes off her tongue and let it run on. "I know what it's like to be overlooked, to be the last in line for attention." In her case, she'd encouraged that at every turn. "I know what it's like to want to please your mother, to have her look at you with pride rather than merely comparing you to your older sisters and finding you less." Despite Penelope's unconventional pursuits, her own mother had never stinted in her praise. Had never, ever, been less than wholehearted in her support.

She was putting the pieces together—all the little snippets she'd heard about Lady Galbraith and her relationship with her daughters—at lightning speed, but it seemed to be working; she seemed to be reaching Monica.

But Monica was still stronger and heavier than she was; Penelope didn't know whether she could hold her if she jumped. Tightening her grip on Monica's cloak, she stated in her most definitive tone, in her most authoritative voice, "You cannot do this. If you take your life over this, your family will blame themselves." She held Monica's gaze. "Can't you see? You won't be saving them— you'll be condemning them."

And where the hell were they—her family?

Penelope had done all she could. She'd run out of words.

And Monica still stood on the wall, uncertain. Undecided.

Then crisp footsteps sounded, along with the rustle of an evening gown. Penelope didn't take her eyes from Monica's, but Monica glanced at the newcomer—and confusion filled her face.

The lady, whoever she was, halted several paces back from the wall.

Monica blinked. Then, in a small, lost voice, she said, "Aunt Hester?"

"Yes, baby girl."

Penelope risked a sideways glance and saw Lady Latimer standing there; her face, as always, was set in reserved and uncommunicative lines, but her gaze held a wealth of understanding, and when she spoke, her tone held conviction and pleading.

"We've come to take you home. All of us came." Her eyes glimmering with unshed tears, Lady Latimer waved toward the figures in the park behind her, all gradually drawing nearer. "We don't want to lose you, baby girl. Please don't do this. There's no need—I swear it."

Monica hesitated, then she raised her gaze and scanned those other figures. Something in her stance, in the way she still held herself ready to jump, reached them, and all halted and waited.

Penelope eased out the breath she'd been holding and softly said, "They've all been out combing the streets, searching for you. Everyone wants you home, safe. There's no danger, truly."

Monica looked at Penelope and met her eyes.

Sensing the uncertainty that still lingered, Penelope said, "Do you remember Inspector Stokes? He was at the Fairchilds' that night." Seeing Monica's eyes flare, Penelope quickly demanded, "Stokes."

"If whatever happened was an accident, then there is no murder." Stokes's deep voice rang with judgelike certainty.

Monica blinked. Then she glanced at Lady Latimer.

Who managed a smile. "There—you see? There truly is no need for any sacrifice on your part." Walking closer, Lady Latimer held up a hand. "Come along, baby girl. Let's go home and you can tell us what happened, and between us all we'll see everything right. We'll all stand by you, sweetheart—you're family, and that's what families do."

Lady Latimer's voice quavered over the last phrase, but still Monica hesitated, her eyes wide, as if the unfolding events were so far from what she'd imagined that she didn't feel able to trust her senses. Not yet.

Hester Latimer drew breath, and when next she spoke, her voice was stronger. "Cynthia and Hartley are getting married, so we truly will be one family again. And we want you with us, because you're a part of us." Holding Monica's gaze, Lady Latimer reached up and, grasping one of Monica's hands, drew Monica down from the low wall.

Penelope released her death grip on Monica's cloak as the girl stepped off the wall and, with a sob, collapsed into Lady Latimer's arms.

Hester Latimer gathered her in. "There, there, sweetheart." Dipping her head, she placed a kiss on Monica's forehead. "Everything will work out, you'll see."

Still standing on the wall, Penelope turned away from the river, watching as, now the danger was past, all the other Galbraiths and Latimers gathered around her ladyship and Monica, soothing and comforting and behaving as families should.

Glancing down at Barnaby, who had shifted to sit on the wall beside her, Penelope patted his shoulder. "You can let go, now." He still held her legs in a viselike armlock.

Barnaby turned his head to look up at her. For a long moment, he held her gaze, then said, "Just as well my hair is fair, or else it would already be showing gray."

Penelope looked into his eyes. "I didn't want to do it—I had to."

After a moment, he nodded. "I know. She moved so fast—I couldn't reach her in time."

Penelope understood that, in the fraught instant when he'd had to make a choice, he'd chosen her.

She smiled and leaned down to whisper against his lips, "I know you're proud of me—and I love you, too."

She kissed him briefly, then unwound his anchoring arm and stepped down from the wall. He rose as she did, his hand reaching for, then closing about, one of hers.

Together, they walked to where Stokes, Griselda, Violet, and Montague waited, watching with relief and approval as the lost chick was reunited with her brood.

Stokes glanced at Penelope as she halted alongside him. "That was close." He looked back at the Galbraiths and Latimers. "We still need to hear her story, and that sooner rather than later. As you mentioned, the funeral's tomorrow."

Penelope nodded. "Indeed, but let's give them a few minutes to find themselves again. Now we've solved the riddle of the mysterious lady who fled the Fairchilds' terrace wearing Lady Latimer's shoes, and we have her safe, we can, if we wish, take all night."

* * *

*F*orty minutes later, they re-gathered in the drawing room of Galbraith House.

Lady Latimer sat at the end of one sofa, with Monica beside her. Millicent Latimer, fetched from her home across the square to support her dearest friend, sat on Monica's other side, Monica's hand clutched firmly in hers. Because of the feud, the girls hadn't spoken for the past year, but after several minutes of teary reunion in the front hall, Millicent had firmly taken Monica's hand, marched into the drawing room, and they'd sat side by side, transparently prepared to face any inquisition.

Together.

Settling with Griselda and Violet on the sofa opposite, Penelope noted Millicent's trenchant support of Monica with an approving eye. Regardless of what was to come, with such friends, Monica would do.

Montague came to stand behind the sofa, behind Violet, while Barnaby and Stokes took up positions before the hearth.

Lord Latimer and Lord Galbraith occupied the armchairs flanking the fireplace. Geraldine and Primrose sat on straight-backed chairs facing the hearth, while alongside the pair, Cynthia accepted the chair Hartley set for her. Hartley stood behind the chair, and finally, everyone gave their attention to Stokes.

Stokes let his gaze travel the faces turned his way. It was nearly midnight, but after the last hours of tension, everyone was wide awake and as ready to learn the truth as they'd ever be. He looked at Monica. Her head bowed, she sat staring at her lap. Despite everyone's assurances and the support of her family and friends, Monica remained uncertain, not just of her future but, Stokes sensed, of her right to be heard, of her worth, of her standing.

Her face, finally fully revealed in the light of the front hall, had struck even him; the sheer misery and pain…so much—too much—for someone so young to be carrying.

Before Cynthia and Hartley had followed Monica, Millicent, and the others into the drawing room, they'd drawn Stokes aside and told him that Monica was much frailer than she normally was; although

Hartley had spoken to her several times since their mother's death, Monica had always been in bed when he'd seen her—he was deeply shocked by how gaunt and wan she was. Having witnessed Lord Galbraith's reaction to his first sight of his youngest daughter's state, Stokes had assumed as much. Now, in the gentlest voice he could muster, he said, "Perhaps it will be easiest for you, Monica, if Mrs. Adair leads you through the questions we need you to answer for us."

Monica glanced at him, then looked at Penelope, sitting directly opposite.

As mildly as she could, Penelope raised her brows in question. In light of the rapport she had shared with Monica on the low wall above the murky waters of the Thames, Stokes had suggested that she was better placed than he to lead the questioning.

After a moment, Monica moistened her lips and nodded. "Yes. All right."

Her voice was a hoarse whisper.

"We need to understand what occurred as completely as possible," Penelope said. "So perhaps you could start by telling us how you came to learn about Danny Gibson and his version of Lady Latimer's shoes."

She had chosen that as the place to start because the events were distanced from Lady Galbraith's demise but were, she suspected, critical to all that had subsequently happened.

Monica nodded and in a quiet, raspy voice said, "I'd just returned home after staying with friends. My maid, Susie, and I had finished unpacking and repacking for the next day—I was to go with Hartley to our home in Sussex. Susie went off downstairs, and I went to the window—we'd opened it to air out the room. I was reaching to close the sash when I heard a young man speak—he was talking to Millwell at the back door." Monica met Penelope's eyes. "My room looks out that way." When Penelope nodded, Monica went on, "I heard the young man say that he'd made some special shoes that he thought Mama might be interested in…"

They listened as the tale unfolded as they already knew it to be, yet, rendered in Monica's own words, the events came alive.

"I was so excited and thrilled!" Even now, Monica's weary eyes lit, reflecting the emotion she'd experienced when she'd brought her pair of Lady Latimer's shoes home. "They were perfect, and I couldn't stop thinking about how pleased Mama would be."

Monica stalled at that point, all joy fading as she realized that hadn't come to pass.

Understanding that she couldn't allow Monica to dwell too much on things, not if they wanted to hear the whole story that night, Penelope gently prompted, "But you didn't tell your mother immediately. Why was that?"

She appreciated the reason Stokes had asked her to put the questions, but interrogating such a fragile person was unquestionably a challenge, and she wasn't known for her delicacy.

Drawing in a deeper breath, Monica replied, "I wanted it to be a grand occasion. Mama had pushed to get us such shoes for so long—she'd wanted them with such a *passion*—that I couldn't just go to her and say: Look what I found." Monica paused, her gaze distant as she examined the recent past, then her lips twisted. "And I wanted her to...to acknowledge me. She didn't usually pay attention to me, not beyond making sure I was dressed appropriately and that I was where I was supposed to be, doing something of which she approved. She was always too busy fussing over Geraldine or Primrose, and, of course, Hartley was her first concern. With the four of us...well, I was always last in line and she rarely had time left over for me. Even though it was my come-out year, she'd barely started thinking about my come-out ball." Monica drew in a huge breath, then looked at Penelope. "So I wanted the shoes to focus her on me—just for once, I wanted her complete and undivided attention."

Penelope nodded encouragingly, her gaze steady on Monica's face, but from the corner of her eye, she'd caught the stricken looks on Geraldine's and Primrose's faces, the hardening of Hartley's features, and the look Monica's older sisters had turned in their chairs to share with Hartley. Penelope doubted Monica had ever voiced her feelings of being fourth-best to her siblings, yet the picture her words were painting was one they recognized.

Monica dragged in a tight breath and went on, "The Fairchilds' ball seemed the perfect opportunity for revealing the shoes. I thought of how to do it, imagined how it would go—I didn't want the shoes to be obvious right away but, instead, to be able to show them off, so I had the hem of my new gown made lower so that the gown hid the shoes as long as I stood straight. I wasn't going to be dancing anyway. So on that evening, everything was in place—I'd planned to go down to the drawing room before dinner and make a grand entrance and show Mama the shoes then, before we left for the ball...I knew just how she would react. I rehearsed it like a play. I could imagine her looking at me—really looking and seeing me. I could hear her saying how proud she was of me—" Monica broke off, swallowed, then drew a shaky breath and said, "But Mama accepted a last-minute dinner invitation. She was gone from the house before I knew about it. So there was no meeting in the drawing room, and Geraldine, Primrose, and I met up with Mama in the foyer of Fairchild House."

Her gaze growing distant once more, Monica went on, "I'd worn the shoes anyway. I thought I would be able to find a moment with her—engineer one if I had to—because, after all, the Fairchilds' ball was still the most perfect venue in which to reveal the shoes to all the ton. But when Mama joined us in the foyer, she was distracted with greeting her friends and checking that Geraldine and Primrose had their dance cards, and with everyone milling about, there was no chance for me to speak with her. So I waited."

Monica lifted her head. "We went into the ballroom and did the rounds, greeting people. I waited until that was all over and we settled at one side of the ballroom, then I tried to draw Mama aside—just enough to be able to speak with her, to make her focus on me while I showed her the shoes for the first time—but she wouldn't come." Monica glanced at Hartley. "Hartley had escorted Geraldine, Primrose, and me in the carriage, and waited with us in the foyer until Mama and Papa arrived, but he parted from us when we entered the ballroom." Monica looked at Penelope. "Mama saw Hartley moving through the crowd. She brushed me aside, told me to just wait with the others, and she set off, following Hartley." Monica drew breath, then continued, "I didn't wait—I followed her. I hoped she might step out of the ballroom and then I could speak with her—all I needed was five minutes of her time. She got stopped by some of her friends, but she must have seen Hartley go out of the ballroom, because as soon as she could, she excused herself and slipped out of the ballroom, too."

"Which door?" Penelope quietly asked.

"The one at the end of the ballroom, closer to the windows." Monica moistened her lips. "I followed her. I thought at last I would be able to have the moment I wanted…I saw her turn down a corridor and went after her. At the end of the corridor, she stepped out onto a terrace—I thought for a moment that I was wrong about her following Hartley and that she might be meeting someone…I hung back in the corridor. Mama went to the balustrade and looked out over the gardens. She seemed to be searching for something, then she turned and went down the terrace steps.

"I rushed to the terrace door, but quietly. When I stepped outside, I could hear her walking on the gravel, a few steps this way, a few steps that. I was puzzled, but there wasn't anyone else about. This seemed like the opportunity I'd been waiting for, so I seized the moment and walked to the steps and went down. She heard me and glanced across." Monica's face clouded. "She frowned. Angrily. I...faltered, but then I asked what she was doing there. She said she was looking for Hartley and that I was to turn around and go inside again—back to the ballroom—immediately. I left the steps and walked to her—just a few steps along the path. She glared at me. And then...she lost her temper.

"She hissed at me to turn around and go back inside *immediately*, that she didn't have time for me and"—Monica dragged in a shuddering breath; her grip on Millicent's hand tightened—"that she didn't know what silliness I'd taken into my head to dare follow her outside, but she didn't want to hear a word of it. She waved me back to the steps. She said she didn't want to see me again until I was in the ballroom talking to some eligible young gentleman. I stood there, trying to find words...and then she made that furious sound she sometimes makes, and she reached out, grabbed me by my shoulders, turned me and pushed me back toward the steps. She said: 'Go! *Now*.'"

Monica's voice hitched and broke. Her expression was a medley of disillusionment and pain. "I was so...upset." Her voice had faded to a thready whisper.

Along with everyone else, Penelope leaned forward the better to hear.

"I'd gone to all that trouble to get the shoes she so badly wanted and she wouldn't even let me show her. I was...not just angry, although I was that, but at myself as much as at her for ever believing that I'd get any attention from her, not even when I was wearing my very own pair of Lady Latimer's shoes. I...I lost my temper, too. And I said that aloud—that I was a fool for believing she'd ever look at me, not even when I was wearing Lady Latimer's shoes. And I rushed back up the steps."

Her gaze faraway, Monica stilled, then on a rush of shattering emotion, her voice weak and breaking, she gasped, "Those stupid shoes! I wasn't used to the heel and I'd had my hems lowered—I trod on my hem on the last but top step." Her breathing shallow, she dragged in a breath, horror seeping into her voice. "I half tripped. I flung out my hand to catch myself and I pushed against the ball on the pillar there—the one at the top of the steps." Her voice quavered. "The ball...fell. It rolled off the pillar and just fell..." She gulped, then, her voice shaking, went on, "I'd stumbled a few steps toward the door, but I turned back...and heard the...the horrible *thud*."

Monica closed her eyes tight; her face was etched in indescribable sorrow and stark pain. "I said, 'Mama?' When she didn't answer, I rushed to the balustrade and looked over and saw..."

Monica's voice suspended. She started to shake; tears leaked from beneath her lashes and dripped down her face. With an immense effort, she whispered, "I was so horrified, so frightened, I fled."

With sounds of distress, Lady Latimer and Millicent drew nearer, putting their arms around Monica as she crumpled. Spontaneously, Geraldine and Primrose left their chairs to rush behind the sofa and, leaning over, enfolded their younger sister in their arms, murmuring soothingly as they patted and stroked.

After several moments, Monica drew a shuddering breath and, with tears glistening on her cheeks, looked not at Penelope but at Lord Galbraith. "I didn't mean to do it, but I killed Mama."

With that pronouncement of self-judgment, Monica dissolved into tears.

Raising her head, Penelope discovered that she, too, had to drag in her next breath. Straightening, she sat back, her gaze going to Barnaby; he was watching Monica, his expression reserved, but his gaze held a wealth of compassion. After a moment, Penelope looked at Stokes; he was quietly scribbling in his notebook, as he had been throughout, but then he looked up and exchanged a troubled glance with Griselda.

What a horror this case had turned out to be.

As if despite her tears and the emotional turmoil Monica still sensed Barnaby's regard, she gulped, used the handkerchief someone had pressed into her hand to wipe her eyes and blow her nose, then, heroically composing herself, she looked at Barnaby and Stokes. "Are you going to arrest me? Will I have to stand trial?"

Barnaby glanced at Stokes, who almost imperceptibly shook his head, then Barnaby looked at Monica and met her anguished gaze. "As I understand it, you have committed no crime. You have nothing to answer for. Your mother died by accident. You couldn't have foreseen it, and you could not have prevented it. You are not to blame."

Monica's eyes widened. "But I knocked that ball onto her!"

"Did you intend to?" Barnaby asked.

"No! Of course not. I had no idea it would fall..."

Barnaby nodded. "Exactly. Not only did you not intend to harm your mother, but you had every reason to believe that the ball was attached to the pillar and wouldn't have moved, no matter how hard you pushed against it." Barnaby paused to let his words sink in—for Monica to hear them clearly and start to accept. Believing would take longer. Understanding that, when comprehension started to dawn in her eyes, he said, "We all *do* understand, and I know this won't be easy, but you cannot go through life blaming yourself for what was an unprecedented and entirely unforeseeable chain of events."

Monica stared at him for a long moment, then she bowed her head and wept.

Feeling very much that his and the others' presences were no longer required, Barnaby met Penelope's gaze and arched a brow. She nodded and glanced at Stokes, then she, Griselda, and Violet quietly rose.

Stokes, Montague, and Barnaby followed their ladies from the room.

"That," Stokes said, as they gathered in the front hall, "was not what I was anticipating, but it is unquestionably the truth. It fits all the facts. Both about that night and about those shoes."

Accepting coats, cloaks, and bonnets from Millwell and the footman, the others nodded.

The drawing room door opened, and Hartley Galbraith stepped out. Shutting the door behind him, he inclined his head to them all. "I can't thank you enough. Without the assistance of all of you, we would never have got to the bottom of this. We would have lost Monica on top of everything else...and then no one would have known what to think."

"It was a conundrum unlike any other." Penelope pulled on her gloves. She glanced at Stokes. "But once the police make their announcement—"

"Actually"—Hartley turned to address Stokes—"that was one point I wanted to clarify. What, exactly, will happen next?"

Settling his greatcoat on his broad shoulders, Stokes said, "As far as the police are concerned, this case is closed. I'll report to the chief commissioner in the morning, and he'll issue a statement that the Yard has completed the investigation and that we are entirely satisfied that Lady Galbraith's death came about through an unfortunate and unforeseeable accident."

Hartley nodded. "Thank you. But, you see, the funeral is tomorrow afternoon. I was wondering..." Hartley clearly didn't like to voice his request—that, or he didn't know what words to use.

Barnaby and Penelope understood. Barnaby offered, "Perhaps, Stokes, we can get a statement in tomorrow morning's news sheets." Hauling out his watch, Barnaby consulted it. "We still have a few hours before the presses run."

Given Barnaby's contacts and the welling public interest in the case, getting the editors to include a last-minute announcement wouldn't be difficult.

Comprehending, Stokes nodded. "Yes, we can do that." He glanced at Hartley. "I can see that it will help if the mourners know the situation before they gather."

Hartley's relief was palpable. "Thank you."

He wrung Stokes's, Barnaby's, and Montague's hands.

When he turned to Penelope, she patted his arm. "A word of advice. If I were you, I would delay putting your own notice in the Gazette for at least a week. No sense raising unnecessary hares."

"No, indeed." Hartley shook her hand and found a smile. "Thank you so much for your help. My family—our families—will always be in your debt."

Penelope smiled and stepped back. After thanking Griselda and Violet, Hartley showed the group to the door.

As they went down the steps to their waiting carriages, Penelope felt her customary satisfaction over having solved a difficult case well, but this time the sense of fulfillment went deeper.

Opening the door of his carriage, Stokes glanced at the others. "While the mystery of Lady Galbraith's murder-that-proved-not-to-be-a-murder might be solved, we're not finished for the evening yet. Given you volunteered me to compose a piece for tomorrow morning's news sheets, I deem it only fair that you all help me write it."

The others laughed softly, smiled, and obligingly climbed into the carriages for the short drive back to Albemarle Street.

CHAPTER 13

*T*hey all helped Stokes compose his statement. Sitting relaxed in the drawing room, with the ladies as well as the gentlemen sipping Barnaby's excellent brandy, they bandied about suggestions and phrases, and Violet wrote down their selected words.

In the end, all agreed that to be convincing and conclusive some detail was required, such as the information that Lady Galbraith had been killed by a finial accidentally dislodged from the balustrade of the terrace beneath which she'd been standing.

"The police are satisfied that there was no malice or intent involved"—Violet read from her notes—"and have concluded that the incident was an unforeseeable accident." She looked at the others. "Will that do, do you think?"

Swirling the brandy in her glass, Penelope looked at Stokes. "It occurs to me that one last little touch of verisimilitude is warranted. To advance the official position one step beyond simply being satisfied." When Stokes arched his brows, inviting her suggestion, she continued, "For instance, something like a warning to all householders to check that the finials atop their balcony and terrace balustrades are securely attached and not likely to create a hazard for anyone below."

"An excellent idea," Montague said. "An oblique underscoring that the ball falling was an accident."

The others agreed. They toyed with the wording, and when they were satisfied, Barnaby wrote several short notes requesting that the statement be run in the news sheets alongside the notice of the funeral—a placement that would ensure that the statement did, indeed, achieve its purpose—then he dispatched copies of the statement Violet had penned along with the notes to the various news sheets' offices.

Checking his fob watch as he returned to the drawing room, Barnaby stated, "More than an hour to go—they'll have it in plenty of time."

"Good," Stokes said. "So we're finally done."

"And we got to the solution in a bare three days," Penelope said. "That must be a record."

"Regardless," Barnaby said, reclaiming his glass, "in this case, time was very much of the essence, and that we got to the gardens in time to save Monica is a credit to us all." He raised his glass. "Here's to us."

"To us!" the others echoed, and drank.

His gaze on Penelope, Barnaby drained his glass.

Griselda stirred. "We should go—it's long past midnight."

Wrapped in the satisfaction of a communal job well done, they adjourned to the front hall. While word was ferried upstairs to the nursery, Violet and Montague took their leave. Penelope, Barnaby, Stokes, and Griselda stood in the doorway and waved them off.

They turned inside as Gloria and Hettie came down the stairs, a sleeping Megan sprawled in Gloria's arms.

Griselda and Stokes said their good-byes, then Griselda took her sleeping child and settled her in her arms. Stokes ushered his family down the steps and helped Griselda into the carriage. Before following her, Stokes looked back at Barnaby and Penelope, smiled one of his rare smiles, then saluted them and climbed in.

Penelope leaned against Barnaby as they waved their friends away, then she sighed and looked up at his face. "This is one case I'm very glad to see the end of."

Barnaby looked down into her dark eyes and saw all the nuances of emotion the day had challenged them to face. He smiled and, with the back of one crooked finger, brushed her cheek. "It's been a hellishly long day. Let's go and check on Oliver, and then get some sleep."

Unspoken between them lay the understanding that this case had one more scene yet to play.

Penelope nodded and slipped her hand into his, and they retreated into the hall and let Mostyn close the door.

* * *

*A*s their carriage rolled northward, Griselda looked down into her sleeping daughter's face. After a moment, she dropped a gentle kiss on Megan's baby-soft brow. "I swear that no matter how many children we are blessed with, I will never take you, or any of your siblings, for granted."

Stokes heard the quiet vow and silently echoed it. Gloria had elected to ride home on the box with their coachman, with whom she was walking out, leaving Griselda and Stokes to the privacy of the carriage. After a moment of considering, of looking back and re-examining his view of Lady Galbraith and her family, he murmured, "That's what she did in the end, wasn't it? Her daughters, even Hartley—they were more a means to an end, and what they wanted, what they needed and desired, wasn't important to her."

Griselda nodded, then softly said, "Obsession. I think that's what it does. You believe that only one thing—that thing, whatever it is—is important, that only it has any significance, and you forget about, ignore, or dismiss everything else."

Several moments passed, then Stokes looked at his sleeping daughter, nestled in her mother's—in his wife's—arms. If he had an obsession, it would be them, but if, as some believed, life was a succession of lessons sent by Fate to inform...then he would take due note and consider himself warned. Taking the people you loved for granted...if she hadn't done that, Lady Galbraith wouldn't have died.

Reaching for Griselda's hand, Stokes twined his fingers with hers; feeling her grip lightly in return, feeling the soft, warm weight of Megan resting against their linked hands, he leaned his head back against the squabs, closed his eyes, and gave himself over to fully appreciating the contentment and satisfaction he'd already secured.

* * *

*A*s Montague and Violet's carriage rattled deeper into the City, Violet looked out at the familiar façades draped in shadows and only just discernible in the glow cast by the street lamps. Although shocked and saddened by all they'd learned, she felt a gentle happiness inside, a contentment that she'd played an active part in getting to the answers in time to prevent Monica from embracing what she'd believed to be her fate. As Penelope had put it, in time to stop their "murder case" from turning into an even greater tragedy.

Violet felt confident that, in the accounting ledger of her life, that contribution would feature as a definite credit.

Her satisfaction welled as they rocked toward their home.

Seated beside Violet, his hand clasping one of hers, Montague swayed as the carriage rounded a corner. Violet's shoulder pressed against his arm, a simple touch that spoke of their closeness.

It was a closeness he'd come to treasure; he couldn't understand how he had lived so long without it. Without that connection to another, most especially to one who held his heart.

But now the connection was there, he had come to realize that it brought responsibilities. The responsibility to protect it, along with a conjoined responsibility to do all he could to protect, support, and nurture Violet in the converse of the way in which she nurtured him.

During this investigation, he'd suppressed his initial resistance to Violet participating on the grounds that her happiness was his principal and overriding goal in life, and if investigating alongside Penelope and Griselda made Violet happy, then so be it; he would cope.

He had not only coped, but in the end, he'd felt proud of her contribution.

And while those moments in the Privy Gardens had been harrowing, and the instant when Penelope had leapt to the wall remained etched in his mind, he had a shrewd notion that, even if Penelope hadn't consciously thought of it at the time, she had placed her trust in Barnaby to keep her safe, and he had.

That was how a relationship where both partners walked in potential danger worked.

With unquestioning trust and unwavering commitment.

That was what he wanted with Violet—that sort of trust, that depth of commitment.

And through this case, his business-self—Montague, man-of-business to the ton—had gained a valuable perspective, too. He knew of the children of the noble families he served, but usually only by name, and so he tended to think of them as inanimate objects, as entities to be noted in accounts, trusts, and wills, rather than as people with emotions and desires, with passions and lives of their own.

He would, he vowed, pay greater attention to their personalities in the future, along with any relevant family dynamics, and inquire as appropriate so that he would be better placed to advise his clients, both parents and offspring. When Fate handed one lessons, a wise man gave thanks and absorbed them.

"What are you thinking of?"

He glanced at Violet to find her regarding him quizzically. He hesitated for an instant, then said, "I was thinking that children are an integral part of any family, yet too often in business we overlook the impact decisions made might have on them."

She considered him, her smile as always serene and soothing, then her brows rose. "Do you have a ledger with the names and ages of the children of your clients?"

He blinked. "Not as such. The names and birthdates would appear somewhere, I would think..." He frowned. "I'm really not sure."

"Perhaps," Violet said, "that's something we should consider—making up a ledger containing the names, birthdates, and current ages of the children of your major clients, so you can easily check that you have the full picture of the family at any point before you give advice."

Gently squeezing her hand, Montague nodded. "That would be a great help."

Violet smiled. "I'll start tomorrow." She looked out of the window as the carriage slowed. "And now we're home."

After descending to the pavement and helping Violet down, then turning to the gold-lettered door beyond which lay his offices and, on the floor above, the apartment he and Violet shared, Montague discovered he felt quietly confident as well as satisfied.

His and Violet's relationship was deepening and expanding, one step—one investigation—at a time.

Smiling himself, he opened the door and followed Violet inside.

* * *

"Is she sleeping?" Hartley straightened from the wall outside Monica's bedroom as Cynthia quietly closed the door.

Joining him, she whispered back, "The sleeping draft's finally taken hold." Slipping her hand into his, Cynthia urged him along the corridor. Glancing back at the door at its end, she murmured, "Primrose is sitting with her. Geraldine will take over later, then I'll spell her until Millicent arrives to be here when Monica awakes."

They'd discovered that Monica hadn't been taking the sleeping drafts the doctor had prescribed, but Susie, Monica's maid, had saved the powders so they hadn't had to send for the doctor again. Hadn't had to subject Monica to any further inquisition.

It had still taken Lady Latimer's firm intervention to convince Monica that she should take the draft and rest.

"I think," Cynthia said, walking slowly down the corridor by Hartley's side, "that it will take some time before Monica accepts that this truly is an end to it."

Hartley drew in a breath, and realized that the simple action was easier than it had been for days. "It'll be a long time before any of us truly puts this behind us." He paused, then went on, "I spoke with Geraldine earlier, before she went to bed. Given I haven't been spending much time with them, I hadn't realized that Mama had a particular focus in steering the girls through the marriage mart, but Geraldine confirmed that that was, indeed, the case. That Mama was more interested in them marrying gentlemen who would advance Mama's and the family's social position than in them finding partners they wished to marry, much less that there should be any actual attachment on either side."

Catching Cynthia's gaze, shadowed in the unlit corridor, he grimaced. "She would never have accepted us marrying."

Cynthia held his gaze. "We wouldn't have let her stop us."

"No. But her attitude would have created even more stress and difficulty." Hartley squeezed Cynthia's hand. "Far from linking our families again, our announcement and eventual marriage might well have forced them even further apart. I hadn't comprehended what Mama's true goal really was."

They'd halted before another door. Cynthia studied Hartley's face, then gripped his hand more tightly, reached past him and opened the door, and towed him into the room beyond—his bedroom.

She waited until Hartley, his gaze on her, closed the door behind them, then she stepped into his arms. Twining hers about his neck, leaning back against his hands as they rose to splay across her back, she captured his gaze. "It's over. It's done. Fate intervened, an accident occurred, and now it falls to us to chart our way forward. Tomorrow, we'll bring our families together, and together we'll survive the ordeal of the funeral. After that, it'll be up to us all, but most especially you and me, to determine how our families fare. To aid and assist, and ensure that each member has whatever help they need to go forward and make the most of their lives."

Hartley looked into her face for several moments, then nodded and simply said, "Yes."

That was all Cynthia needed to hear. Stretching up, she set her lips to Hartley's, and with a sigh that was borne more in the release of the tension that had had him in its grip over the last days, he responded. His lips closed over hers with the ease of familiarity, with masculine confidence laced with the intoxicating first stirrings of passion.

The other members of her family had retreated across the square; other than Primrose, watching over Monica, the rest of his family were abed. About them, the house was silent and still.

Faint moonlight gilded them as she stepped closer, pressed closer, and his fingers flexed on her back.

The kiss deepened. They supped and rejoiced, tongues tangling, lips melding. Desire flared as the embers of passion, so often for them in recent times left stoked and smoldering, were finally given air and erupted into flame.

Into flames that incited and enticed.

Breaking the kiss only to tip her head to the side and with his lips trace her jaw, before sliding his lips along the taut column of her throat, eliciting a crystalline shiver, Hartley murmured, "Should we go to one of the guest rooms?"

On the words, he closed his hands about her breasts.

On a stifled gasp, one tight with burgeoning need, Cynthia replied, "Geraldine will guess where to find me."

That was all the information—all the confirmation—he required.

They'd become lovers the year before, during the unexpected, year-long wait brought about by the feud, but in recent times, with him back in this house, their passions—their need for each other—had of necessity taken second place to his family's need of him.

Now, tonight, they finally felt free to indulge their senses again.

To glory in the give and take, in the bestowing and receiving of caresses that grew increasingly heated, increasingly intimate, increasingly laden with a passionate hunger that swelled and drove them wild.

Drove them to shed their clothes with abandon, to seize the heady delight of the moment, to drink in the joy of two passionate hearts united with no insurmountable barriers remaining between them and their goal.

Both shivered and closed their eyes, the better to appreciate the unadulterated, senses-stealing thrill of that moment when naked skin met naked skin.

And then the deeper jolt to both senses and emotions when they joined.

They paused, eyes opening to look into the other's, to drown in the passionate yearning. Swollen lips parted, their breaths mingling, they grasped the moment to wordlessly communicate. This was who they were, as they were in this fused togetherness, this place where there were no barriers, no screens, no possibility of veils or guile.

They were as one in every sense—of word, of deed, of thought. As one as their hearts thudded in a heavy, synchronous beat.

As one as, lids falling, they moved in concert, and the storm of their passions closed around them and the pinnacle of their desire rose swiftly before them.

And they gave themselves up to the driving rhythm, to the relentless glory, to the cataclysm of their senses and the wondrous oblivion that lay beyond.

To the unfettered fusion of not only their bodies, not only their hearts, but of their lives—now and in the years to come.

* * *

Penelope lay on her back in the big bed she shared with Barnaby and, with her limbs all but boneless, held him as he lay slumped, sated and spent, upon her.

Her body still thrummed with the fading glow of ecstasy. Breathing rarely seemed important at this point; her wits were still scrambled, her senses still waltzing to the symphony of pleasure he and she had wrought.

And if there had been a honed edge to their lovemaking, born of that moment by the river when she'd trusted in him, in his abilities and in his unwavering protectiveness, and had leapt and reached for Monica, there had also been a bone-deep recognition that all had held steadfast and true—and that together they had triumphed; they'd seen the fraught minutes through and were now sailing amid the calm of peaceful waters once more.

Contentment, deep and indisputable, lay heavy upon her.

Along with him. Wracked by their passions, he was heavy, too.

Not that she cared. She secretly delighted in these moments that were the outcome of his surrender to their passions.

But eventually, he stirred. Lifting from her, he collapsed in the bed alongside her. After a moment, he reached for her, tucking her against his side. She turned to him and snuggled beneath the arm he draped over her.

From under heavy lids, through the screen of his lashes, Barnaby studied Penelope's face. Although the lamps were unlit, he could see her features reasonably clearly in the glow cast by the moonlight streaming in through the windows flanking the head of the bed.

As was their habit before retiring, they'd checked on Oliver. As usual, their son had been sleeping soundly—the sleep of the innocent; every time Barnaby saw his son slumbering so blissfully in his cot, he comprehended what that phrase truly meant.

With the vise that, earlier in the evening, had locked unforgivably about his heart finally exorcised, and the memory largely erased courtesy of their passions—courtesy of the way she gave herself to him so unstintingly every time—he was, at last, at peace.

Shifting, he turned onto his back, raising his arm to allow her to wriggle closer against his side and, as she often did, to pillow her head on his chest.

Settling with one hand resting over his heart, she sighed.

Closing his arms about her, he felt all tension leach from her limbs, yet sensed she remained awake. Dipping his head, he looked into her face.

As he'd suspected, his devastatingly logical wife of the exceedingly busy mind was thinking.

Several heartbeats later, she glanced up and met his gaze. Held it for a moment, then asked, "Do you ever think that, sometimes, a victim simply reaps what they've sown?"

He could guess what path her mind had taken, but by now he knew his role. She wouldn't sleep until she'd examined and accounted for every nuance of their recent case, philosophical and social as well as factual. He arched his brows. "How so?"

"Well, for instance, in this case, the entire sequence of events that culminated in Lady Galbraith being struck dead grew out of just one thing—out of one decision she herself made and subsequently adhered to despite all the evidence that it was a bad decision, and that she should alter her course. She had warnings aplenty, but she refused to retreat. It was almost as if she rushed headlong to her death."

Penelope paused, then went on, "Marjorie Galbraith was obsessed, but her obsession wasn't merely to acquire Lady Latimer's shoes. That was a symptom, but that wasn't what her obsession was actually about—and I'm fairly certain that both Lady Latimer and

Lord Galbraith understood that."

Barnaby frowned. "If she wasn't truly set on getting those shoes—"

"Oh, but she was. She wanted those shoes, but the reason why she wanted them? *That* was her obsession."

Somewhat wryly, he admitted, "I thought I understood it, but now you're going to have to explain."

Her lips curved; shifting her head, she dropped a kiss on his chest. "Lady Galbraith's obsession arose out of the nature of her longstanding friendship with Lady Latimer. Lady Galbraith was the bright, vivacious one, and Lady Latimer was the quiet, reserved one. Marjorie was outgoing, while Hester was retiring. Marjorie grew to expect that, of the pair of them, she would be the one who would always socially shine, that her social star would always eclipse Hester's, and that she—Marjorie—would be the more socially prominent. To Marjorie, that was probably a very important element in their friendship—she needed that prop. It was most likely vital to the way she saw herself.

"Marjorie would always have been touchy about who was more socially prominent, her or Hester, but given Hester's character, I'm sure that wouldn't have mattered to Hester, and she would always have been happy to, socially speaking, play second fiddle to Marjorie, so everything went along smoothly. Until recently, when Lady Latimer's shoes gave Hester, and more specifically her daughters, a telling advantage in the crowded marriage mart. That altered the social balance between Marjorie and Hester—in Marjorie's eyes, in the wrong direction. Aided by Lady Latimer's shoes, Hester's daughters formed highly eligible alliances. Marjorie's daughters had yet to receive an offer. Marjorie needed to restore the social balance between herself and Hester, and that, to her mind, meant securing her family's advancement over and above what the Latimers had achieved.

"*That* was her obsession—regaining her relative social prominence over Hester Latimer. Getting access to the shoes was one part of her strategy, but managing Hartley's marriage was an even more urgent avenue, and second to that came Geraldine and Primrose. Monica didn't impinge on Marjorie's mind at all because Monica is as yet too young to marry—Monica offered no immediate prospect of advancing the family socially, so she simply didn't matter to Marjorie. That's what Monica felt and reacted to—the lack of even figuring in her mother's thoughts."

Penelope paused, then went on, "In essence, this was all about Marjorie Galbraith herself, and her need to be socially dominant with respect to Hester Latimer. Without that dominance, Marjorie probably felt threatened and, almost certainly, in an odd way, cheated. Her being second to Hester wasn't the way things had ever been—to Marjorie, Hester's social success with finding the shoes and settling her daughters simply wasn't right. And if you need proof that what's happened has been all about Marjorie and not actually about her daughters, I got the clear impression that none of Marjorie's other children—not Hartley, who had moved out of home, or Geraldine and Primrose—felt content and happy over the way Marjorie had treated them, certainly over the last year or so. They didn't complain—and once Marjorie was dead, how could they?—but they would have sensed that she saw them as pawns in her bid to one-up Lady Latimer. Given their closeness to Hester Latimer, that wouldn't have been a pleasant feeling."

After another brief pause to order her thoughts, Penelope continued, "Marjorie's initial and most obvious way forward was to try to wrest the secret of the shoes from Hester. She pushed and pushed—and when it came to the point of rupturing a bond that, as we've seen, went very deep and was supportive to both families, Marjorie had no qualms over sacrificing the others to her cause. But creating and then enforcing the rift between the families—even when it must have been plain that all the other members of both families mourned the loss and were hurt by it—was a truly selfish act. And, if you consider it, much that subsequently happened occurred because of that."

Penelope's voice grew crisper, more hard-edged as she expounded on her theme. "It was the rift that forced Hartley and Cynthia to keep their attachment and eventual betrothal a secret. It was the rift that forced them—the two most driven to protect their families—to plot and plan to secretly meet and discuss how to heal, overcome, or counter it. It was Marjorie's fixation on directing Hartley's marriage that had her following him outside. Her obsessive focus on social advancement had already caused her to dismiss Monica from her thoughts, to withhold attention from her youngest daughter at the very time when Monica, about to make her come-out, needed maternal support the most. That led Monica, when the chance offered, to seize on the one sure route guaranteed to gain her mother's attention—getting a pair of Lady Latimer's shoes. But not knowing or caring what Monica had to show her, Marjorie dismissed her youngest daughter yet again and sent Monica off with a flea in her ear...." Penelope paused, then went on, "If she hadn't done that, if Marjorie Galbraith had behaved toward her daughters and her son in a supportive rather than an exploitative way, she wouldn't be dead."

Transfixed by Penelope's ability to dissect the motives and emotions that drove others, especially those living within the hothouse of the ton, Barnaby had been following her argument; he took a moment to digest the implications, and discovered that he didn't disagree. "As you said"—he murmured the words against the soft silk of her hair—"she reaped what she sowed."

After a moment more of dwelling on that, chest swelling, he drew a deeper breath and glanced at Penelope's face. "Now that Lady Galbraith is gone, perhaps the Galbraiths can bring themselves about."

"And the Latimers." Penelope looked up at him. "It's sad that it had to come to this—for Lady Galbraith to have to die to allow the families to combine again—but she took that position herself. It was of her own making."

Barnaby nodded. "I sensed that Cynthia and Hartley are the future there."

"Indubitably." Penelope's lips curved, then she settled once more in his arms. "They're committed, not just to each other but to bringing their families peace again. And despite a year and more of discord driven by one person, the link between the two families runs so very deep, really is so strong, that I don't believe the happenings of this time have materially damaged what years of togetherness had forged."

"Hmm." Barnaby thought of his own family, and of Penelope's. They were both younger children of large broods; neither he nor she could truly imagine not having the ready and freely given support of all their kin.

As their limbs grew heavier and sleep beckoned, he settled his arms more comfortably about her, then lightly rubbed his jaw against her hair. "So...our latest mystery is solved, two families have been reunited, two lovers are now free to marry, and a young girl has been hauled back from the brink of taking her own life due to misplaced guilt. All in all, an excellent result." Looking down, he met Penelope's dark eyes. He hesitated, then softly said, "I'm exceedingly proud of you for following your instincts, of having the conviction to speak even when what your instincts were urging didn't seem logical." He felt his lips lift in an irrepressible, entirely understanding smile. "I appreciate that, for you, that was exceedingly difficult, yet I've noticed that when it comes to matters of life and death, and especially of family, your instincts are invariably sound."

She heard the compliment for what it was, for the understanding and encouragement it contained. Her answering smile warmed his soul.

"Why, thank you, kind sir." Delighted with the accolade and knowing that he, wise man that he was, intended it in a much wider context, Penelope stretched up and touched her lips to his.

A warm, gentle kiss, a giving and a sharing, an acknowledgment of all that together they were.

Drawing back, she met his eyes, then sighed and snuggled down again. "I in no way regret deserting my translation to follow up the question of Lady Latimer's shoes, but tomorrow I'm going to have to write an exceedingly apologetic letter to the museum's head librarian. My translation is going to be woefully late."

Lifting the hand she'd laid over his heart, Barnaby placed a kiss in her palm, then set her hand back as it had been. "Just tell him that your time was unexpectedly taken up by what even he would agree to be a very good cause."

Penelope softly snorted. Sleepily, she advised him, "Librarians don't think like that. To them, the wisdom of ancient scholars stands far above the mundane matters of modern life."

Closing his eyes, Barnaby smiled. There had been a time in her younger days when she herself might have clung to that maxim, but her heart was too big and her understanding too expansive to allow her to turn her back on her fellows, especially those in need of her particular and peculiar expertise.

And that, he had accepted, was how it should be.

Which was why he foresaw a long life ahead of them, investigating whatever came their way.

Side by side. Hand in hand.

Together.

EPILOGUE

*T*he funeral of Marjorie, Lady Galbraith, was held at St. George's in Hanover Square. The subsequent burial and committal service was held at the new cemetery at Kensal Green.

With Barnaby, Violet, and Griselda, Penelope attended the church service as well as the burial. She was quite clear in her own mind that her purpose in doing so was to support the living rather than mourn, much less honor, the dead. As she murmured to Barnaby as they took their seats in the upper gallery of the church, "I'm finding it difficult to muster any sympathy for a lady who so signally failed to extend that sentiment to her nearest and dearest." After a moment, she added, "And who was so silly as to not value the best things in life."

Barnaby's lips twitched, but he didn't reply.

The coffin was already in place before the altar. From her perch in the gallery, Penelope observed those congregating in the nave below. Stokes's announcement had appeared in all the major news sheets that morning; from the myriad snippets of conversation floating up from the crowd—along the lines of "I say, did you see…?" and "It was an accident after all"—most of those in attendance had caught up with the news.

The arrival of the Latimers together with the Galbraiths, Lord and Lady Latimer walking slowly up the aisle on either side of Lord Galbraith, caused what in any other situation would have been a sensation. But as the members of both families followed their elders up the aisle, Hartley, pale and drawn, with Cynthia on his arm, followed by Georgina and Lord Fitzforsythe supporting Geraldine, Cecilia and Brandywell supporting Primrose, with Millicent and

Monica, arms twined, heads bowed together, quietly bringing up the rear, the incipient speculation transmogrified into approving murmurs.

Alert to the nuances, Penelope spent much of the short service reading the expressions, and where possible the lips, of those she knew to be the biggest gossipmongers among the crowd. There had been a decent turnout, and those who actually knew the family greatly outnumbered those who had merely come to gawp and say they had attended the funeral of a three-day celebrity.

Eventually satisfied that the overall impression later conveyed to the wider ton would be one of a reconciliation to be approved of and quietly applauded—and of a service that was otherwise unremarkable and in understated good taste—Penelope relaxed and allowed herself to be swept up in the singing of the hymns.

Later, after they had traveled in their carriage in slow procession to Kensal Green, she stood with the others on the fringes of the mourners and watched the final laying to rest of Marjorie, Lady Galbraith. The crowd was smaller, perhaps a hundred strong; Penelope recognized several faces from the Fairchilds' ball, Lady Howatch among them.

Monica, the veil she'd worn in the church put back for the final farewell, looked utterly wretched but had thus far borne up. Millicent stood beside her, her arm wound in Monica's; Monica leaned on Millicent, who stood staunchly beside her throughout, occasionally dipping her head to murmur something soothing. Or perhaps distracting. Deeming Monica in capable hands, Penelope considered the rest of the Galbraiths. As in the church, all were supported by their Latimer counterparts.

Then the coffin was lowered, the last prayer said, and the benediction offered.

At the minister's invitation, Lord Galbraith, moving stiffly, bent and cast the first sod. Then, with a quiet word and a wave, he invited Lady Latimer to the graveside.

Garbed in unrelieved black, her veil put back, Hester Latimer stepped forward and cast her own sod. In that moment, her customary mask was not in place; her sorrow and sadness were there for all to see as she farewelled her childhood friend. None could doubt the sincerity of what, in that instant, was revealed, and in the face of one who was usually so rigidly reserved, the naked emotion was all the more powerful.

What followed as Galbraiths, then Latimers, stepped forward in turn, was deeply moving.

Behind her glasses, Penelope blinked several times; she noticed Lady Howatch wielding a lace-trimmed handkerchief.

And then it was done. It was time for the living to get on with their lives, and for the dead to be left in peace.

Lady Latimer's bosom swelled as she drew in a deep breath, then, raising her head, she turned to her family—not just her own but the Galbraiths as well—and like the matriarch she was, she gathered them up, gently chivvied them into line, and with her husband on Lord Galbraith's other side, she took his lordship's arm and led them all from the grave.

Penelope watched for a moment longer, and saw Hester Latimer raise her head and glance back, casting her eye over her brood—all of them—in a manner Penelope recognized from having seen her own mother so often do the same.

Barnaby turned to her and raised his brows.

Penelope met his eyes and smiled. "The Galbraiths and the Latimers are going to be all right."

Barnaby glanced at the families in question, then he smiled, set his hand over hers where it rested on his sleeve, and with Violet and Griselda, they started walking back to their carriage.

* * *

Eight days later, Penelope was sitting in her garden parlor, curled up in one corner of the sofa, slippers off and feet tucked under her skirts while she devoured that morning's *Gazette*, catching up with the latest news.

On the floor before the sofa, Griselda and Violet were playing with Oliver and Megan. Earlier, Violet had admitted to having felt queasy for the last several mornings, which had raised hopes, but it was too early yet to tell. The possibility of another baby to add to their group had delighted them, but they'd agreed to keep their raptures in check for the moment, and that their husbands didn't yet need to know.

With Violet's help, and after an emergency outing to Montrose Place to seek Jeremy Carling's advice on several convoluted passages, Penelope had finally finished her translation and dispatched it to the museum. She'd been glad to see the last of it; it had been one of the most boring tracts she'd ever read.

Reaching the announcements section in the *Gazette*, her eyes alighted on the notice she'd hoped to find. "Aha! Here it is."

Both Violet and Griselda looked up expectantly.

Penelope duly read, "Lord and Lady Latimer, of Hanover Square and Beechly Park, Surrey, are pleased to announce the betrothal of their daughter, Cynthia Alice, to Mr. Hartley William Galbraith, the son of Lord Galbraith and the late Lady Galbraith, of Hanover Square and Colmey Grange, Sussex. Due to recent bereavement, neither family is presently receiving."

"Good." Griselda nodded approvingly. "I'm glad they didn't wait."

"Indeed." Violet handed Megan the block she was stretching for. "Those families have had their lives suspended for quite long enough."

Folding the paper and setting it aside, Penelope said, "Neither Cynthia nor Hartley struck me as the sort to let life pass them by, but I'm glad their elders are supporting them in that. Both families need to move forward, and it's reassuring to see that they are."

Oliver got to his feet and toddled over to the sofa, a block in one chubby hand. Casting himself at Penelope, he held out the block. "M'ma, play."

Penelope grinned, took the block, and bent to place a kiss amid Oliver's golden curls.

Impatient, he tugged her sleeve. "M'ma, play *now!*"

Both Griselda and Violet burst out laughing.

"He may have Barnaby's curls," Griselda said.

"But he has your temperament," Violet finished.

Penelope's eyes were all for her demanding son. She beamed at him. "Yes, my darling, now that Mama's work is all done, it is definitely time to play."

With that, she slid off the sofa and joined the others on the Aubusson rug for a rowdy hour of simple fun.

Later, when both children were sated and lolling dozily in their mothers' laps while, sitting amid the strewn blocks, the three ladies leaned contentedly against the sofa and chairs, Violet looked at the others—not in envy but in expectation—and murmured, "The greatest pleasures in life are, indeed, free, and most often found with family."

"Mmm." Penelope gently combed her fingers through Oliver's curls. "Truer words, Violet dear, would be hard to find, but I feel compelled to clarify that family in that context isn't only about blood. Family, in that sense, is what you make it."

Griselda and Violet murmured agreement, then Hettie and Gloria arrived to take the children upstairs for their luncheon, and the ladies rose, shook out their skirts, re-gathered their dignities, and sat down to plan the rest of their day.

* * *

The wedding of Cynthia Latimer and Hartley Galbraith was celebrated quietly just over a month later. Penelope, Griselda, and Violet were thrilled to have received gilt-edged invitations; they duly took their seats in the nave of St. George's and watched with interest and appreciation as Cynthia and Hartley succeeded in formally linking their families.

"Of course," Penelope whispered, "the link was already there, but as the minister just stated, it's now a link that no man—or woman—can put asunder."

Despite the subdued nature of the event, an undercurrent of happiness welled, carried in Cynthia and Hartley's shared glances, in the joy and the hope that lit their faces and was reflected in their siblings' and parents' eyes. Regardless of the recent past, it was a joyous occasion, and that joy burgeoned and overflowed, and, combining with hopeful expectations for the future, swept away the wraiths of sorrow lingering from the previous time the two families had gathered in that church.

And when the time came and the music from the organ swelled into the triumphal march, the assembled friends and connections all rose, cheering, clapping, smiling with sincere pleasure and encouragement, and calling out greetings and good wishes as the beaming couple, now man and wife, walked back up the aisle.

As Penelope, Griselda, and Violet—all smiling delightedly, too—gathered their shawls and reticules and prepared to follow, Penelope whispered, "Did you see?"

When, brows rising in question, the other two looked at her, she grinned. "All the ladies in the bridal party are wearing Lady Latimer's shoes."

* * *

Several months later, Penelope sat at the breakfast table, munching a slice of toast slathered with her favorite gooseberry preserves, while she mentally reviewed the recent announcements from the Latimer and

Galbraith families.

Geraldine was now engaged to Major General Quigley, a senior man in the army, and was no doubt busily arranging her wedding, which was to be held later in the year—a month after Cecilia Latimer and Herbert Brandywell's nuptials. Primrose and the highly eligible Mr. Hammond had announced their betrothal, which had been quickly followed by the news that Millicent Latimer and Rupert, the Duke of Salford's son, had fallen rather dramatically in love, but as both were relatively young, their parents had suggested—and everyone was expecting—a long engagement.

And in the last week, Penelope had heard via her very efficient grapevine that Monica Galbraith and the Earl of Exeter's son, a close friend of the Duke of Salford's son, were inseparable, and the Exeters had invited both the Galbraiths and the Latimers for an extended visit at their castle.

Thinking of how Marjorie Galbraith would have wallowed in such excitement and social interest, Penelope humphed and muttered to herself, "If she'd only done the right thing, she wouldn't be just happy, she would be in alt."

Unsurprisingly, the latter two announcements in particular had enshrined the reputation of Lady Latimer's shoes as Cinderella talismans. To Penelope's mind, in light of her own, somewhat unexpected interest in the shoes, that was all to the good.

Seated at the other end of the table, sipping his coffee, Barnaby had been immersed in reading *The Times* and the other major morning news sheets; suddenly, he gave a surprised laugh. Setting down his cup, he stared at the page he'd been perusing. "Huh!"

Folding the news sheet open to the relevant page, he leaned forward and, smiling, tossed the paper down the table to Penelope. "I don't suppose you know anything about that?"

Picking up the news sheet, Penelope focused on an announcement prominently placed and outlined in black. In clear and concise language, it stated that the exclusive agreements held by the Latimer and Galbraith families for the supply of the ladies' ballroom shoes known as Lady Latimer's shoes had been made over to the Foundling House of London. All ladies wishing to acquire such shoes were directed to make inquiries at either Hook's Emporium in New Road, Camden Town, or at Gibson and Sons in Mercer Street, Long Acre. Prospective purchasers were advised that a portion of the sale price would be paid to an account managed by Montague and Son of

Chapel Court in the City for the upkeep of premises and the furthering of lessons for the foundlings of London.

The announcement concluded with a subtly worded exhortation to all ladies, young and old, to buy.

Reaching the end of the notice, Penelope grinned. "Violet outdid herself."

Barnaby had been checking the other news sheets. "The same notice is in all the others, too."

"Excellent." Penelope had sent the notices herself. "I couldn't be sure they would all run on the same day."

After studying another copy of the notice, Barnaby looked down the table and caught her eye. "This is really very neat."

Penelope's grin widened into a beaming smile. "I thought so. And I have to say, along with the other directors of the Foundling House, I am really very pleased with the way everything's turned out."

For alerts as new books are released, plus information on upcoming books, sign up for Stephanie's Private Email Newsletter, either on her website, or at: http://eepurl.com/gLgPj

Or if you're a member of Goodreads, join the discussion of Stephanie's books at the Fans of Stephanie Laurens group.

You can email Stephanie at stephanie@stephanielaurens.com

Or find her on Facebook at
http://www.facebook.com/AuthorStephanieLaurens

You can find detailed information on all Stephanie's published books, including covers, descriptions and excerpts, on her website at
http://www.stephanielaurens.com

If you enjoyed THE CURIOUS CASE OF LADY LATIMER'S SHOES, you might enjoy other titles in THE CASEBOOK OF BARNABY ADAIR NOVELS:

WHERE THE HEART LEADS
VOLUME 1: Full Length Novel

THE PECULIAR CASE OF LORD FINSBURY'S
DIAMONDS
VOLUME 1.5: Short Novel

THE MASTERFUL MR. MONTAGUE
VOLUME 2: Full Length Novel

LOVING ROSE: THE REDEMPTION OF
MALCOLM SINCLAIR
VOLUME 3: Full Length Novel
Coming July 29, 2014.

COMING on JULY 29, 2014
**The next fascinating installment in the Casebook of Barnaby
Adair**

LOVING ROSE: THE REDEMPTION OF MALCOLM
SINCLAIR
Volume 3 in the Casebook of Barnaby Adair Series

Miraculously spared from death, Malcolm Sinclair erases the notorious man he once was. Reinventing himself as Thomas Glendower, he strives to make amends for his past, yet he never imagines penance might come via a secretive lady he discovers living in his secluded manor.

Rose has a plausible explanation for why she and her children are residing in Thomas's house, but she quickly realizes that he's far too intelligent to fool. Revealing the truth is impossibly dangerous, yet day by day he wins her trust, and then her heart.

But then her enemy closes in, and Rose turns to Thomas as the only man who can protect her and the children. And when she asks for his help, Thomas finally understands his true purpose, and with unwavering commitment, he seeks redemption the only way he can—through living the reality of loving Rose.

A pre-Victorian tale of romance and mystery in the classic historical romance style.
Full length novel of 100,000 words.

Short Excerpt from LOVING ROSE: THE REDEMPTION OF MALCOLM SINCLAIR:

CHAPTER 1

March 1838
Lilstock Priory, Somerset

Thomas rode out through the gates with the sun glistening on the frosted grass and sparkling in the dewdrops decorating the still bare branches.

His horse was a pale gray he'd bought some months previously, when traveling with Roland on one of his visits to the abbey. Their route had taken them through Bridgewater, and he'd found the dappled gray there. The gelding was mature, strong, very much up to his weight, but also steady, a necessity given his physical limitations; he could no longer be certain of applying sufficient force with his knees to manage the horse in stressful situations.

Silver—the novices had named him—was beyond getting stressed. If he didn't like something, he simply stopped, which, in the circumstances, was entirely acceptable to Thomas, who harbored no wish whatever to be thrown.

His bones already had enough fractures for five lifetimes.

As he rode down the road toward Bridgewater, he instinctively assessed his aches and pains. He would always have them, but, in general, they had sunk to a level he could ignore. That, or his senses had grown dulled, his nerves inured to the constant abrading.

He'd ridden daily over the last month in preparation for this journey, building up his strength and reassuring himself that he could, indeed, ride for the four or five days required to reach his destination. The first crest in the road drew near, and a sense of leaving something precious behind tugged. Insistently.

Drawing rein on the rise, he wheeled Silver and looked back.

The priory sat, gray stone walls sunk into the green of the headland grasses, with the blue sky and the pewter of the Channel beyond. He looked, and remembered all the hours he'd spent, with Roland, with Geoffrey, with all the other monks who had accepted him without question or judgment.

They, more than he, had given him this chance—to go forth and complete his penance, and so find ultimate peace.

Courtesy of Drayton, he had money in his pocket, and in his saddlebags he had everything he would need to reach his chosen abode and settle in.

He was finally doing it, taking the first step along the road to find his fate.

In effect, surrendering himself to Fate, freely giving himself up to whatever lay in wait.

Thomas stared at the walls of the priory for a moment more, then, turning Silver, he rode on.

* * *

$\mathcal{H}$is way lay via Taunton, a place of memories, and of people who might, despite the disfigurement of his injuries, recognize him; he rode straight through and on, spending the night at the small village of Waterloo Cross before rising with the sun and continuing west.

Late in the afternoon on the fourth day after he'd ridden out from the priory, he arrived at Breage Manor. He'd ridden through Helston and out along the road to Penzance, then had turned south along the lane that led toward the cliffs. The entrance to the drive was unremarkable; a simple gravel avenue, it wended between stunted trees, then across a short stretch of rising open ground to end before the front door.

He'd bought the property years ago, entirely on a whim. It had appealed to him, and for once in his life he'd given into impulse and purchased it—a simple, but sound gentleman's residence in the depths of Cornwall. In all his forty-two years, it was the only house he'd personally owned, the only place he could imagine calling home.

A solid, but unimaginative rectangular block constructed of local bricks in muted shades of red, ochre, and yellow, the house consisted of two stories plus dormers beneath a lead roof. The windows of the main rooms looked south, over the cliffs to the sea.

As he walked Silver up the drive, Thomas scanned the house, and found it the same as his memories had painted it. He hadn't been back in years—many more than the five years he'd spent in the priory. The Gattings, the couple he'd installed as caretaker and housekeeper, had clearly continued to look after the house as if it were their own. The glass in the windows gleamed, the front steps were swept, and even from a distance the brass knocker gleamed.

Thomas halted Silver at the point where the track to the stable met the drive, but then, in deference to the old couple who he hadn't informed of his impending arrival, he urged Silver nearer to the front steps and dismounted. Despite the damage to the left side of his face and his other injuries, the Gattings would recognize him, but he didn't need to shock them by walking unheralded through the back door.

Or clomping, as the case would be.

Retrieving his cane from the saddle-holder that the stable-master at the priory had fashioned for it, then releasing Silver's reins, Thomas watched as the big gray ambled a few steps off the drive and bent his head to crop the rough grass. Satisfied the horse wouldn't stray much further, Thomas headed for the front door.

Gaining the small front porch, he was aware of tiredness dragging at his limbs—hardly surprising given the distance he'd ridden combined with the additional physical effort of having to cope with his injuries. But he was finally there—the only place he considered home—and now he could rest, at least until Fate found him.

The bell chain hung beside the door; grasping it, he tugged.

Deep in the house, he heard the bell jangling. Straightening, stiffening his spine, adjusting his grip on the silver handle of his cane, he prepared to meet Gatting again.

Footsteps approached the door, swift and light. Before he had time to do more than register the oddity, the door opened.

A woman stood in the doorway; she regarded him steadily. "Yes? Can I help you?"

He'd never seen her before. Thomas blinked, then frowned. "Who are you?" *Who the devil are you* were the words that had leapt to his tongue, but his years in the priory had taught him to watch his words.

Her chin lifted a notch. She was tallish for a woman, only half a head shorter than he, and she definitely wasn't young enough—or demure enough—to be any sort of maid. "I rather think that's my question."

"Actually, no—it's mine. I'm Thomas Glendower, and I own this house."

She blinked at him. Her gaze didn't waver but her grip on the edge of the door tightened. After several seconds of utter silence, she cleared her throat, then said, "As I'm afraid I don't know you, I will need to see some proof of your identity before I allow you into the house."

He hadn't stopped frowning. He tried to look past her, into the shadows of the front hall. "Where are the Gattings? The couple I left here as caretakers?"

"They retired—two years ago now. I'd been assisting them for two years before that, so I took over when they left." Suspicion—which, he realized, had been there from the outset—deepened in her eyes. "If you really were Mr. Glendower, you would know that. It was all arranged properly with...your agent in London—he would have informed you of the change."

She'd been smart enough not to give him the name. As she started to edge the door shut, he replied, with more than a touch of acerbity, "If you mean Drayton, he would not have thought the change of sufficient importance to bother me with." With a brief wave, he indicated his damaged self. "For the last five years, I've been otherwise occupied."

At least that served to stop her from shutting the door in his face. Instead, she studied him, a frown blooming in her eyes; her lips—quite nice lips, as it happened—slowly firmed into a thin line. "I'm afraid, sir, that, regardless, I will need some proof of your identity before I can allow you into this house."

Try to see things from the other person's point of view. He was still having a hard enough time doing that with men; she was a woman—he wasn't going to succeed. Thomas stared at her—and she stared back. She wasn't going to budge. So...he set his mind to the task, and it solved it easily enough. "Do you dust in the library?"

She blinked. "Yes."

"The desk in there—it sits before a window that faces the side garden."

"It does, but anyone could have looked in and seen that."

"True, but if you dust the desk, you will know that the center drawer is locked." He held up a hand to stop her from telling him that that was often the case with such desks. "If you go to the desk and put your back to that drawer, then look to your right, you will see a set of bookshelves, and on the shelf at"—he ran his gaze measuringly over her—"about your chin height, on the nearer corner you will see a carriage clock. In the front face of the base of that clock is a small rectangular panel. Press on it lightly and it will spring open. Inside the hidden space, you will find the key to the center drawer of the desk. Open the drawer, and you will see a black-leather-covered notebook. Inside, on the first leaf, you will find my name, along with the date— 1816. On the following pages are figures that represent the monthly ore tonnages cleared from the two local mining leases I then owned." He paused, then cocked a brow at her. "Will that satisfy you as identification?"

Lips tight, she held his gaze steadily, then, with commendable calm, replied, "If you will wait here, I'll put your identification to the test."

With that, she shut the door.

Thomas sighed, then he heard a bolt slide home and felt affronted.

What did she think? That he might force his way in?

As if to confirm his incapacity, his left leg started to ache; he needed to get his weight off it for at least a few minutes, or the ache would convert to a throb. Going back down the three shallow steps, he let himself down to sit on the porch, stretching his legs out and leaning his cane against his left knee.

He hadn't even learned her name, yet he still felt insulted that she might imagine he was any threat to her. How could she think so? He couldn't even chase her. Even if he tried, all she would have to do would be to toss something in his path, and he would trip and fall on his face.

Some people found disfigurement hard to look upon, but although she'd seen his scars, she'd hardly seemed to notice—she certainly hadn't allowed him any leeway because of his injuries. And, in truth, he didn't look that bad. The left side of his face had been battered, leaving his eyelid drooping, his cheekbone slightly depressed, and a bad scar across his jaw on that side, but the right side of his face had survived with only a few minor scars; that was why he'd been so sure the Gattings would know him on sight.

The rest of his body was a similar patchwork of badly scarred areas, and those relatively unscathed, but all that was concealed by his clothes. His hands had survived well enough, at least after Roland had finished with them, to pass in all normal circumstances. The only obvious outward signs of his injuries were his left leg, stiff from the hip down, and the cane he needed to ensure he kept his balance.

He was trying to see himself through her eyes, and, admittedly, he was still capable sexually, but, really, how could she possibly see him as a threat?

He'd reached that point in his fruitless cogitations when he realized he was the object of someone's gaze. Glancing to the right, he saw two children—a boy of about ten and a girl several years younger—staring at him from around the corner of the house.

As they didn't duck back when he saw them, he deduced that they had a right to be there…and that they might well be the reason for his new housekeeper's caution.

The little girl continued to unabashedly study him, but the boy's gaze shifted to Silver.

Even from this distance and angle, Thomas saw the longing in the boy's face. "You can pat him if you like. He's oldish and used to people. He won't bite or fuss."

The boy looked at Thomas; his eyes, his whole face, lit with pleasure. "Thank you." He stepped out from the house and walked calmly toward Silver, who saw him, but, as Thomas had predicted, the horse made no fuss and allowed the boy to stroke his long neck, which the lad did with all due reverence.

Thomas watched the pair, for, of course, the girl trailed after her brother; from their features, Thomas was fairly certain they were siblings, and related to his new housekeeper. He'd also noticed the clarity of the boy's diction, and realized that it, too, matched that of the woman who had opened the door. Whoever they were, wherever they had come from, it wasn't from around here.

"Nor," Thomas murmured, "from any simple cottage."

There could, of course, be many reasons for that. The role of housekeeper to a gentleman of Mr. Thomas Glendower's standing would be an acceptable post for a lady from a gentry family fallen on hard times.

Hearing footsteps approaching on the other side of the door, rather more slowly this time, Thomas picked up his cane and levered himself back onto his feet. He turned to the door as the woman opened it. She held his black notebook in her hand, opened to the front page.

Rose looked out at the man who had told her what date she would find in the black-leather-covered notebook in her absent employer's locked desk drawer—a drawer she knew had not been opened during all the years she'd been in the house. Hiding her inward sigh, she shut the book and used it to wave him in as she pulled held the door wide. "Welcome home, Mr. Glendower."

His lips twitched, but he merely inclined his head and didn't openly gloat. "Perhaps we can commence anew, Mrs....?"

Her hand falling, Rose lifted her chin. "Sheridan. Mrs. Sheridan. I'm a widow." Looking out to where Homer and Pippin were petting Glendower's horse, she added, "My children and I joined the Gattings here four years ago. I was looking for work, and the Gattings had grown old and needed help."

"Indeed. Having added up the years, I now realize that was likely to have occurred. I haven't visited here for quite some time."

So why had he had to return now? But Rose knew there was no point railing at Fate; there was nothing for it but to allow him in, to allow him to reclaim his property—it was his, after all. She no longer had any doubt of that; quite aside from the date in the book, she would never have found the hidden compartment in the clock if he hadn't told her of it. She'd handled the clock often enough while dusting, and had never had any inkling that it contained a concealed compartment. And the clock had been there for at least the last four years, so how could he have known? No, he was Thomas Glendower, just as he claimed, and she couldn't keep him out of his own house. And the situation might have been much worse.

Stepping back, she held the door open and waited while, leaning heavily on his cane, he negotiated the final step into the house. "Homer—my son—will bring up your bags and stable your horse."

"Thank you." Head rising, he halted before her.

She looked into eyes that were a mixture of browns and greens—and a frisson of awareness slithered down her spine. Her lungs tightened in reaction. Why, she wasn't sure. Regardless, she felt perfectly certain that behind those eyes dwelled a mind that was incisive, observant, and acutely intelligent.

Not a helpful fact, yet she sensed no threat emanating from him, not on any level. She'd grown accustomed to trusting her instincts about men, had learned that those instincts were rarely wrong. And said instincts were informing her that the advent of her until-now-absent employer wasn't the disaster she had at first thought.

Despite the damage done to his face, he appeared personable enough—indeed, the undamaged side of his face was almost angelic in its purity of feature. And regardless of his injuries, and the fact he was clearly restricted in his movements, his strength was still palpable; he might be a damaged archangel, but he still had power.

Mentally castigating herself for such fanciful analogies, she released the door, letting it swing half shut. "If you'll give me a few minutes, sir, I'll make up your room. And I expect you'd like some warm water to wash away the dust."

Thomas inclined his head. Stepping further inside as the door swung behind him, he reached for the black notebook she still held. His fingers brushed hers, and she caught her breath and rapidly released the book.

So…the attraction he'd sensed moments earlier had been real, and not just on his part?

He felt faintly shocked. He hadn't expected…straightening, he raised his head, drew in a deeper breath—and detected the fragile, elusive scent of roses.

The effect that had on him—instantaneous and intense—was even more shocking.

Abruptly clamping a lid on all such reactions—he couldn't afford to frighten her; he needed her to keep house for him, not flee into the night—he tucked the notebook into his coat pocket and quietly said, "I'll be in the library."

One glance at the stairs was enough to convince him that he wouldn't be able to manage them until he'd rested for a while.

"Indeed, sir." His new housekeeper shut the door, and in brisk, no-nonsense fashion informed him, "Dinner will be ready at six o'clock. As I didn't know you would be here—"

"That's quite all right, Mrs. Sheridan." He started limping toward the library. "I've been living with monks for the last five years. I'm sure your cooking will be more than up to the mark."

He didn't look, but was prepared to swear she narrowed her eyes on his back. Ignoring that, and the niggling lure of the mystery she and her children posed, he opened the library door and went in—to reclaim the space, and then wait for Fate to find him.

ENTRIES IN THE CASEBOOK OF BARNABY ADAIR

WHERE THE HEART LEADS
Volume 1: Full Length Novel

THE PECULIAR CASE OF LORD FINSBURY'S DIAMONDS
Volume 1.5: Short Novel

THE MASTERFUL MR. MONTAGUE
Volume 2: Full Length Novel

THE CURIOUS CASE OF LADY LATIMER'S SHOES
Volume 2.5: Mid-length Novel

LOVING ROSE: THE REDEMPTION OF MALCOLM SINCLAIR
Volume 3: Full Length Novel – July 29, 2014.

&

THERE ARE 3 MORE CASES PENDING FOR BARNABY, PENELOPE, AND FRIENDS:

starring the following characters:

Dr. David Sanderson – Ryder's friend, first sighted in *The Taming of Ryder Cavanaugh*

Hugo Adair – Barnaby's cousin, first sighted in *The Curious Case of Lady Latimer's Shoes*

Lord Carradale – Barnaby's acquaintance, first sighted in *The Curious Case of Lady Latimer's Shoes*

ABOUT THE AUTHOR

#1 *New York Times* bestselling author Stephanie Laurens began writing romances as an escape from the dry world of professional science. Her hobby quickly became a career when her first novel was accepted for publication, and with entirely becoming alacrity, she gave up writing about facts in favor of writing fiction.

All Laurens's works to date are historical romances ranging from medieval times to the mid-1800s, and her settings range from Scotland to India. The majority of her works are set in the period of the British Regency. Laurens has published 56 works of historical romance, including 31 *New York Times* bestsellers, and has sold more than 20 million print, audio, and e-books globally. All her works are continuously available in print and e-book formats in English worldwide, and have been translated into many other languages. An international bestseller, among other accolades, Laurens has received the Romance Writers of America® prestigious RITA® Award for Best Romance Novella 2008, for *The Fall of Rogue Gerrard.*

Laurens's continuing novels featuring the Cynster family are widely regarded as classics of the historical romance genre. Other series include the *Bastion Club Novels*, the *Black Cobra Quartet*, and the *Casebook of Barnaby Adair Novels*. *The Curious Case of Lady Latimer's Shoes* is her fifty-sixth published work. All of her previous works remain available in print and all e-book formats.

For information on all published novels, and on upcoming releases and updates on novels yet to come, visit Stephanie's website: www.stephanielaurens.com

To sign up for Stephanie's Email Newsletter (a private list) for heads-up alerts as new books are released, exclusive sneak peeks into upcoming books, and exclusive sweepstakes contests, follow the prompts at Stephanie's Email Newsletter Sign-up Page

Stephanie lives with her husband and two cats in the hills outside Melbourne, Australia. When she isn't writing, she's reading, and if she isn't reading, she'll be tending her garden.

CPSIA information can be obtained at www.ICGtesting.com
Printed in the USA
LVOW01s2143160915

454530LV00013B/200/P